# THE SAMURAI-KNIGHTESS

# ORIGIN CHRONICLES

# DEAD ADRENALINE

# III

WRITTEN BY CLINTON J. KURTYKA

The Samurai-Knightess Origin Chronicles, Dead Adrenaline III is the third installment in the Dead Adrenaline series. Dead Adrenaline: One Man's Journey to Survive Beaver County, Pennsylvania is the first book, and Time Break Expedition the Return, Dead Adrenaline II is the second in the series.

The following is a work of fiction, names, characters, places, businesses, events, and incidents are either the product of the author's imagination or used in an entirely fictitious manner. Any resemblance to actual persons, living, dead or semi dead with a Dead Adrenaline virus is entirely coincidental.



Publisher: Clinton J. Kurtyka / Yosai Publishing

ISBN: 979-8-9904588-2-6 (Paperback)

ISBN: 979-8-9904588-3-3 (Digital)

**Two unyielding forces about to meet by fate and destiny!**

**The Dragon Realm is untouched by human breath!**

## CONTENT

## DEDICATION

"This book is dedicated to all of the kind and good earthlings on planet earth"

# ACKNOWLEDGEMENT

TO MY WONDERFUL WIFE, THANK YOU FOR STANDING BESIDE ME THROUGH THE TOUGH TIMES AND FANTASTIC TIMES IN LIFE, I LOVE YOU.

TO MY DAUGHTER, AND SON, YOU BOTH ARE AMAZING, AND WILL DO REMARKABLE THINGS IN LIFE.

TO MY FAMILY AND FRIENDS NEAR AND FAR, THANKS FOR THE SUPPORT, AS I CONTINUE THIS JOURNEY OF WRITING.

SPECIAL THANKS TO GRANT, FOR YOUR FEED BACK ON STORYTELLING.

CJ THANKS FOR THE THOUGHT ON THE BOOK COVER, PLACING THE SWORD ON FRONT COVER AND NOT ON THE BACK WAS AN EXCELLENT IDEA.

# PROLOGUE

THE BATTLE FOR PLANET EARTH AND HUMAN EXISTENCE RAGES ON IN THE YEAR 2026 IN BEAVER COUNTY, PENNSYLVANIA.THE MAN CALLED CLINT, IRISH WARRIOR, ALONG WITH THE BURENDO SHOTOKAN WARRIORS, COOL BLUE 2026, AND 2086 ARE AT THE THEATER OF OPERATIONS. THEY ARE ABOUT TO CLASH WITH THE EMPEROR VLAD, WHO IS THE LEADER OF THE DEAD ADRENALINE SOLDIERS. THIS WILL BE THE FINAL SHOWDOWN IN DEAD ADRENALINE TOWN, AND ONLY ONE WILL BE THE VICTOR.

THE SAMURAI-KNIGHTESS HAS ARRIVED IN THE YEAR 2026, TO HELP HER DAD, THE MAN CALLED CLINT, IN THIS END OF DAYS CONFLICT. HOWEVER, A DEEP QUESTION AND UNDERSTANDING ON HOW THE SAMURAI-KNIGHTESS CAME TO BE, AND WHY IT IS CHLOE, CLINT'S DAUGHTER. ONLY TIME WILL TELL THE TALE IF THE SAMURAI-KNIGHTESS IS THE KEY TO CONQUERING THE ALIEN DEAD ADRENALINES FROM OUTER SPACE. **THIS IS THAT STORY, THE ORIGIN CHRONICLES OF THE SAMURAI-KNIGHTESS, SO LET THE QUEST BEGIN AND MAY HER DESTINY UNFOLD, THE PROPHECY AWAITS.**

# THE REALM OF THE DRAGONS

## 10TH CENTURY

*They have existed long before humans ever walked the earth upright, and command respect from all species. Fear and respect intertwine and must never separate, the time of the dragon as reigned superior for thousands and thousands of centuries, but a change is coming, a colossal fracture in the future that will affect the present and the past. A Dragon must know the order of its strength and power, if it does not, the code of the Dragon shatters. Only one Dragon can be the King, and all other Dragons in the realm must obey this leader and respect and honor this undeniable doctrine.*

*Another dawn has arrived, and life has awakened to another day of blood and battle. The Dragon realm is untouched by human breath; this is part of the ancient doctrine; no human must ever enter the Dragon realm or set eyes on a dragon. Just as no dragon must never enter the human realm, this has always been the way, long before these dragons and humans even knew of each other's existence. A human realm and a dragon realm, both species understood this and followed this ancient agreement. Even with this accordance, ancient agreements sometimes break with unexpected consequences, as foretold long ago at the beginning of the 10th century, a man did battle with a dragon, you see it was by mistake, both the dragon and the human decided to leave their realm and crossed paths by accident. It is unknown if the human set foot into the dragon realm first or the dragon wonder into the human realm first, but on that day they both found each other, and locked eyes, which has never happened in this world or any other. This meeting of the man and a dragon started the first ever battle between a dragon and a human.*

*This man's name was King Fortis Caliburnus, and his kingdom was devastated by invading forces, and none of his people survived the attack. During that battle, King Caliburnus fought along side his people, until the very last cut of his blade. King Caliburnus was a young King, but unlike most kings of his age he was wise, and righteous. It was known throughout the lands that King Caliburnus represented strength, goodness, kindness, nobleness, and above all his family was his kingdom of people. On this day, the bloodshed was insurmountable, you see this was the cruelty and violence of this medieval bloodshed, as quickly as this carnage began, it ended without warning. None of his men, women or children survived, the battle had ended, but the King survived, the invading forces left him alive to wallow in grief, pain, and suffering. They did not battle for the land or his kingdom, only to cause him living pain that he would have to carry for the rest of his remaining days on this earth. As he stood in his crumbled blood-soaked kingdom of death, vengeance and hate began to erupt into his soul.*

*At that moment, he made a choice to annihilate the invaders that had taken his life but left him alive. King Caliburnus packed up some supplies and embarked on a quest to find the Dragons Realm, he thought if he could capture a dragon and break it to his will. He could battle the savage enemies with the raging dragon's help, insane as this thought was, King Caliburnus had no sanity left to stop him from this treacherous journey. He traveled towards the dragon realm, based on ancestor knowledge that foretells a location of this realm. This Dragon realm slumber's somewhere in the Airgid Silabh Casaide (Silver Mountain Cascade) region. Yes, Dragon's love water and rocky terrain, but this place has a mystical gift, the water and the rocky terrain have an abundance of silver contained within. Stories from the past tell the tale about how dragons love silver and have silver coursing through their veins. Also, the water turns to liquid silver when dragons' breath heats the water up. Even though this is a chemical element of high value, no man, women nor beast ever tried to find and enter the Realm of the Dragons, death would be the outcome.*

*As King Caliburnus was making his way to the Dragon realm, a particular dragon was deciding to question the order of his strength and power. On that day, the Dragon leader knew this, and made a choice to let this dragon live, but this dragon had to stay on the outskirts of the dragon realm, until a final verdict on the matter unfolded. Either this dragon would return to the center dragon realm or put to death. This dragon's name was Invictus (Invincible), and the Dragon King knew that the only verdict would have to be death for Dragon Invictus, because if not now, one day this dragon would challenge the dragon doctrine again and take the King Dragon position of power.*

*Two unyielding forces about to meet by fate and destiny. Dragon Invictus waited and knew the verdict would be death, and was preparing to battle the entire dragon realm, then a thought came to mind. This thought was to leave the Dragon realm completely, and find a new home or place to survive, so at that very moment Dragon Invictus started to head towards the crossover between the dragon realm and human realm. This is when the meeting happened, King Caliburnus had just pulled himself up on a rock ledge, which led to a large cave opening on the mountain side. This was it, the entrance into the Dragon realm, which no human had ever tried to enter, based on fear and breaking the oath set fourth by human leader ancestors. The oath foretold that if a human enters the realm of the dragons, death and destruction will follow. King Caliburnus had no retreat left in him; he continued and started to walk into the dragon realm. At that very moment, Dragon Invictus was moving towards the human realm, about 10 ft down off the cave opening. Both were halfway into each realm when their eyes met, and the altercation had begun, one human, one dragon, and one cause, DEATH! Both King Caliburnus and Dragon Invictus faced each other and began to engage in a vicious battle, but just as they were ready to clash, they both stopped at the exact same time. No one knows the reason for this, but on this day, man, and dragon both had an understanding or should I dare say a compassionate agreement not to fight each other.*

*It could have been that the pain and suffering Dragon Invictus saw in King Caliburnus eyes, or emptiness King Caliburnus felt coming from Dragon Invictus. Either way in those passing moments, they both knew that they could be allies.*

*King Caliburnus would help Dragon Invictus in the land of the humans, and Dragon Invictus would help King Caliburnus take out his revenge to honor his dead kingdom of people. Unfortunately, for them this was not to be, a different story unfolded at that very moment. The Dragon King had arrived with his winged dragon legion of death. They were here to destroy Dragon Invictus, and no man would stand between this ancient way of the dragon. As this was unraveling the enemy invaders had returned, because they decided they did want to kill King Caliburnus. This medieval army had scaled the rock mountain side face and were standing on the outside of the cave entrance. Arrows were getting ready to release into the cave, at the same moment the Dragon King ordered one of his dragons to let loose its dragons' tail, whipping, and clipping King Caliburnus down to the ground, knocking him onto his back. King Caliburnus sword had been in his hand as he collapsed, and as he fell back his sword blade flew out of his hand and struck Dragon Invictus under the lower right rib cage area, you see, all dragons have a weak spot, no humans know this, but all dragons do.*

*This weak spot if targeted can be a fatal blow, and Dragon Invictus knew this at the very moment King Caliburnus blade found the kill spot.*

*As a last hope reaction, Dragon Invictus launched quickly over to King Caliburnus fading body and covered over him gently, in hopes to save his live from the arrows that were getting ready to be set forth into the cave, but it was not to be. King Caliburnus was already dead from the dragon tail hit to his body. While cradling King Caliburnus, Dragon Invictus took the last breath of dragon air and passed into silence. The enemy invaders never let their arrows fly on that day only because they heard dragons inside the cave, and believed King Caliburnus had met his fate, even though they only heard sounds of death from within the cave. The enemy invaders fled the area out of fear, never to return, and felt that the dragons had killed King Caliburnus, which just so happen to be the ancient truth.*

*The King Dragon looked at his dragon legion and summoned them to all leave and go back to center of the dragon realm. The bodies of Dragon Invictus and King Caliburnus remained where each had fallen, as reminder that humans and dragons cannot and will not exist together as told within the dragon doctrine. As their bodies lied on the stone floor of the cave, a silence filled the air, a mystical powerful thing began to happen. Both the dragon and the human body began to glow with a pure light, which was coming from the embedded sword inside the body of the dragon. An unexplainable phenomenon was occurring, and Great Dragon Power and Divine Kingship were becoming one within the sword. The sword of King Caliburnus and Power of Dragon Invictus.*

*On this day in time, the sword* **Excalibur** *was born, and as quickly as the pure light began, it stopped, and went into a deep sleep, still embedded in Dragon Invictus' carcass. Dragon*

*Invictus and King Caliburnus remained in the cave entrance halfway into the human realm, and halfway in the dragon realm. Their untouched bodies, along with the Excalibur sword lay silent for over 200 years.*

***King Fortis Caliburnus and Dragon* Invictus**

# PLACEMENT OF THE SWORD

## 12th CENTURY

*It had been over 200 years since both Dragon Invictus and King Caliburnus had met and perished at the inside cave entrance to the dragon realm, which is the Silver Mountain Cascade. Both slowly were deteriorating with the passage of time; time waits for no human or mythical beast; it will take control of your conclusion and make the decisions til nothing exists. Except time did bring a man to complete the final stage of the Excalibur sword. A mysterious figure of man appears dressed in emerald colored cloak, this unique man reaches his hand into the powdered dust of bones and flesh with unflinching movement, removes Excalibur from its worthy tomb. With Excalibur in hand, this unknown person did not walk the direction of the human realm but continued into the cave towards the dragon realm.*

*You see, this was an extraordinary man, and not just a mere mortal human being, he could see visions into the past, present and future events. This man was a powerful collector of magic that he could wield without a blade, this magic was both pure and dark but balanced on supernatural level. One would ask themselves, why would a man even with magic enter the dragons' realm, knowing only death and destruction awaits. The answer is of mystical nature, this is not just a man, but a Sorcerer.*

*The Sorcerer called **Merlin**, he is known through the ages and is both feared and respected just like the dragons. Merlin does not fear the Dragons, but does respect their kind, just as the Dragons do not fear Merlin, but they respect him. Merlin not only is an unexplained magic maker but has the power to control Dragon-lord magic. Yes, with this magic, Merlin can speak dragon and cast magical incantations. This conversation and magic must take place because what is about to happen has never occurred into the dragon realm. To bring an object or in this case a sword into the dragon realm completely is dangerous and unpredictable at best because the code of the dragon will not allow such treachery. Nothing from the human realm can enter the dragon realm, including humans and their weapons, but this was Merlin and Excalibur. Time will tell the tale of this conclusion, death, or life.*

*Merlin finally completes the walk from the human realm into the heart of the dragon realm. The center of everything, this is where the Dragon Leader will be, along with other dragons. This is the place where decisions are created, on covered rock-stone ground and silver water. It is the judgement place and only dragons know the true power within. Merlin knew this and brought the sword, Excalibur, to this place to fulfill the prophecy. The water that covers the ground is unified with the purist Silver to ever exist, which is endless and has power beyond a Dragon's or even Merlin's abilities.*

*Merlin is now in the arena of the dragon, he must choose wisely, and only speak to the Leader of the dragons, if he speaks to the wrong dragon, a battle to the death will begin, which would be a catastrophe for humans and the dragons. The dragons are surrounding Merlin, but he does not surrender to this winged force of power and strength. He waits focused with unshakable fortitude, knowing to follow the dragon doctrine within the dragon realm.*

**Merlin Stands in the Arena of Dragons**

*You see, the Dragon Leader, wants to speak with Merlin and does want him to chose wisely. Merlin must make this choice, because he has entered the dragon realm, and not the other way around, where a dragon has entered the human realm. Ironically, Merlin lives and survives in many realms, so he is prepared to choose without hesitation. You see, it is not always the most imposing dragon or the one that hides in the cave shadows waiting for its next meal. No, this Dragon Leader is in the presence and has the patience's to win the day no matter the sacrifice. Merlin does not look for this dragon leader, he senses it, and only sets his eyes on the the red dragon, the Dragon Leader! This dragon's presence does not come from its size or confidence, also the patient intentions this dragon shows is not because of kindness or goodness, but for uses of controlling outcomes. The choice has been made, and Dragonlord magic has begun, so now Merlin will speak with the Dragon King, and the tale of the Excalibur sword will cut sharply and true, so there will be no doubt this is the one and only chance to intertwine humans and Dragons for the prophecy to be fulfilled.*

*Merlin stands before the Dragon King, who waits for him to speak, This Dragon King knows Merlin's voice must be truth, no trickery, or perfidious words, for this is the dragon way. If Merlin speaks false, faithless words, death and destruction will follow. That is the way of the dragon, which is the only way in the dragon realm, no matter the outcome. Merlin stands like a Yosai (Fortress), and out of respect places his cloak hood back over his head, as a sign that he does not come to this place seeking glory or victory, but only truth. If the Dragon King decides not to speak on this day, the bloodshed of battle will begin. Both Merlin and The Dragon King look at each other for a moment, and then Merlin begins to speak.*

**Merlin Ambrosius Meets with the Dragon King**

"I stand before you Dragon King, not as a Sorcerer's, or a man, but as messenger of a prophecy that will happen and must crystallize to keep the balance between pure light and pure darkness. A never before event is coming, destiny has provoked this, and the sequence of this outcome is unknown, but this force is coming either way. I am here on this day to help prepare a foretold placement of a sword. This sword is Excalibur, forged on the border of the human realm and the dragon realm. As you know already Dragon King, both King Caliburnus and your Dragon Invictus perished, while befriending and becoming allies with each other moments before their death.

One human killed by a Dragon; one dragon killed by a human. One accidental and one intentional, this is not a judgment on the Dragon Realm, but the words of truth. You see, the Dragon Realm intertwines in this prophecy, and on that day of death, one of your dragon's made the choice to cut down King Caliburnus by your order, which caused the death of this noble king, along with the death of one of your own. Dragon Invictus suffered an accidental fatal cut from King Caliburnus sword, when the sword released from King Caliburnus hand. The prophecy confesses this and will not retreat from the destiny that is upon us.

Now as I stand before you Dragon King, I respectfully demand that this sword, which is now of magical power and unmatched strength fulfill its rightful place in the dragon realm. By placement of this sword in the center rock-stone ground, and silver laced water, the sword will be a protected, until the day a warrior claims the sword that is worthy of *Great Dragon power* and the *Divine Kingship*. Excalibur is this sword, and only a warrior of true Pendragon power can wield, which would mean this warrior would be the head of the dragons in medieval times, but also must be able to lead in the ways of King Caliburnus or Uther Pendragon, or shall I say King Uther, the father of King Arthur of Camelot. The sword Excalibur will know if this warrior is worthy to fulfill the prophecy. I have spoken the words of truth; you Dragon King must now speak your words and decide the path."

*The sound of silence imprisoned the decisive moment, but this silence stopped once the Dragon King begins to speak. A slow rumbling voice with pronounced words, begins delivering a mighty warning, with an impactful decision that would decide the fate of Excalibur.*

"YOU, Merlin Ambrosius of the Caledonian Forest have entered the Dragon Realm under the assumption that I, the Dragon King would even entertain this prophecy. I have been the Dragon King for many, many centuries, and the dragon doctrine has always been accepted, no matter the cost, but you Merlin have arrived with something more, something powerful, something not just of the human realm and not just of the dragon realm, but a of both. This is beyond our imagination and power; this sword cannot be wielded by a dragon nor a human, but the Dragon Realm can protect Excalibur and keep it frozen in time."

*The Dragon King paused for a second, as if he was thinking through this with a clever mind of possibilities, then he spoke.*

"I will empower the Placement of the Sword; and **EXCALIBUR** will have a final resting place in the heart of the dragon realm. You will place Excalibur into the rock-stone ground, which is infused with silver waterpower, I the Dragon King and my dragons will heat the silver water with our dragon breath, until the rock-stone is soften enough for you Merlin Ambrosius to place EXCALIBUR into ground for all time. Once fulfillment of this ancient action is complete, the rock-stone, along with the silver water will hold Excalibur in its permanent outside tomb, but this will not be the only power of protection for Excalibur.

You see, the silver water will cool faster than it took to heat up. I will let you know a little secret Merlin, as a gesture of good faith, my dragons and I not only can destroy with the firestorm of death, but our species can also freeze with our breath. Yes, our species of dragons are unique, we breath fire and ice, which is different from other dragons throughout the centuries. How this came to be, I will not tell you, for this the dragon way, but the silver water around Excalibur will be chilled, and protected for all time. This is the path; you must take if the Placement of the Sword is to be here in the dragon realm. Make your choice, choose wisely because this will be for all time, no matter the cost."

*The Dragon King finished speaking and waited with cruel curiosity for the response from Merlin*

"I have made my choice, Excalibur will secured in the Center of the Dragon realm, but this will not be the final resting place of this magnificent sword. No this will be just a fortress of protection for the sword to wait, when not in use."

*At that moment, the dragons began to heat the Rock-Stone ground, causing the silver water to boil, and with this action, Merlin without hesitation threw Excalibur into the air, and by some unknown power slowly guided the sword downward blade point first into the soften rock-stone and silver water. Excalibur pierce the rock-stone 12 inches into the ground, and the dragons quickly began to cool the rock-stone and silver water with the power of dragon breathe. Within seconds the ground was a solid piece of shiny silver with Excalibur in the center, secured in a rough edge roundish shaped rock-stone.*

*A sinister grin comes over the Dragon King's face, as if to say the deed is over and nothing can undo this truth. In that moment, Merlin returns the grin and begins to speak.*

"Yes, great Great Dragon King, the deed is over, but the prophecy foretells of a warrior that will be coming to claim Excalibur as her own. This warrior will know your true name Dragon King, and she will wield great Dragon Power and Divine Kingship that is undeniable in the human realm or the dragon realm. Be ready for this storm of pure light that is coming and nothing can stop this."

*The Dragon King looks at Merlin one last time and says these words.*

"We have our Dragon ways, and if, and when this so-called warrior reaches the dragon realm, she will be put to the test, this will decide her fate. But, know this, no human or other beast on this earth knows my true name, so even if she survives this unstoppable dragon test. This warrior will never be able to say my name in the ancient dragon way, so her destiny is for nothing."

*And with these last words the Dragon King grins and saunters away.*

*Merlin stays silent and leaves the dragon realm, knowing the prophecy is coming and her destiny will unfold, and nothing can stop this story from happening.*

**(EXCALIBUR IS PLACED IN THE SILVER WATER AND ROCK-STONE OF THE DRAGON REALM)**

# THE DAUGHTER

## YEAR 2026

*A young girl 17 years of age is practicing with complete precision various Kata(s), making sure to extract the Bunkai (fighting technique application) from the powerful and fluent movements. The sequence of patterns has such purpose that only a Burendo Shotokan practitioner would embrace and understand. Not the misinformed person, who takes the position that Kata(s) have no value when training for full combat. This person usual knows not of what he or she speaks, for they have little or no knowledge of kata(s) and have not practiced them on a high Burendo Shotokan level. Finally, the last crushing technique within the Kata is over, and this young warrior ends the training session. Then a conversation begins, and a mom yells out to her daughter.*

"Chlo, are you done with your karate practice because I just got lunch ready for us. It is just a couple of sandwiches I picked up from the store, but we can go outside to eat and talk about your dad, and I can give you an update of what is occurring in Beaver County."

"Ok Mom (Kim), be there in a minute."

"See you outside Chloe by the picnic table, right by the sliding doors that enter the living room area. I have to say this Bed and Breakfast is working out for now. I got a clear view of my son

Luke sleeping on the couch through the glass sliding doors. The trip back from Florida must have tired him out, because he is taking a little midday nap. This is a good thing, because now we will have some time to talk about the terrible events occurring in Beaver County, involving your dad or should I say, "The Man Called Clint."

"Yea Mom, it is unbelievable what has happened, but I need to go help dad somehow and make it into Beaver County."

"Chloe, I know honey, but that is impossible on so many levels. Listen to me Chloe, I know this is bullshit, and explainable to say the least, but we must stay focused and strong. My husband Clint, your dad, will return, somehow, someway."

"I know mom, but about 2 hours ago, we all heard the announcement on the Beaver County Radio station, which reported the war is raging inside Beaver County, PA, and my dad, "The Man Called Clint"is in the heart of the battle to save humanity and planet earth. Something needs to happen because the Government will not help. They are still trying to claim that the radio broadcast was fake and just a hoax, made up to confuse and trick the people of planet earth."

"Chloe, this is so incredibly sad and difficult to deal with and understand, but we must stay the course. We all have a destiny to fulfill, and the outcome will be the outcome. Remember my words and know I feel this with every fiber of my being. I will see your dad again in this life or the next, and I will be waiting for his return. This is what I must do to survive mentally and physically. You, my daughter Chloe, have your fathers fight in your blood, action is the only outcome for you, but waiting might fulfill your destiny. When the time is right, you will know what to do. Now as far as your brother Luke goes, his path is different and with me, but you have destiny further than here and now."

"Wow Mom! I must say, the wisdom coming from you right now is giving me peace and focus to prepare for the future, if that makes sense."

"It does make sense Chloe, somehow, I just feel and know that waiting this devastating nightmare out will show the way forward. Some how I believe that your dad, my husband is telling us to stay the course, which is not easy to capture fortitude and patiences in life when the outcome is fading into a painful direction."

"Yep Mom, I will continue with my training and capture the fortitude and patience's dad is asking us, as the battle rages on in Beaver County, PA. Time will tell the outcome of this tale, and I will wait for a sign."

# THE SIGN

## YEAR 2086

*Time did unravel the direction of the future, but time can be cruel and unyielding, you see, time passed, and no one knew what was going on in the Terminal Realm of Beaver County. Chloe and her mom (Kim), along with Luke waited for a sign from the Man Called Clint, but nothing happened. The Government still was claiming it was hoax, and that no alien invasion had happened, eventually silence fell upon Beaver County, Pennsylvania, and no one every really knew what had occurred in the year 2026. Other people or family members of humans trapped in the terminal realm protested and, in some cases, fought back to find out the truth. The Government leaders and United States Controlled Military, made sure to silence these people, which did not end well for them. The entire State of Pennsylvania remained on the terminal realm list, no humans were allowed in, and no humans or any other creatures were allowed out.*

*Hope was the only friend they had to survive the pain surrounding them. Chloe continued her training in Burendo Shotokan way and captured fortitude and the patience's to wait for a direction or sign to materialize. Overtime age became an undeniable enemy that was systematically chipping away the hope in both Chloe and her mom's physical and mental stability. Kim who was still waiting for her Clint to return was now the age of 114, Chloe was 78 years old, and Luke was 73 years old. The future brought many great medical advancements that helped people live well over a hundred years old comfortably healthy. Unfortunately, time does not stop and wait for the outcome a person wants but moves forward like an enemy in battle.*

*Even-though time, and age was holding with a tight grip, Chloe, and her mom, and Luke still held on with a small piece of hope. Somehow, they knew something was coming, and they were prepared for the outcome either way. Then hope arrived, both Chloe and her mom and Luke were hearing reports of a man that was from the past year of 2026 arriving in the present time of 2086. At that moment they knew it had to be him, and this was the sign they were waiting for.*

*The Hall of Knowledge was putting out information that this man, they called, "The Man Called Clint" had battled in terminal realm, but had survived in a cationic state of animation, which prevented him from aging physically or mentally and was113 years old. His body that was in state of animation was in the terminal realm of a Karate school called One Strike Karate, which was in the town of Monaca, PA. This school taught a unique style of Burendo Shotokan, which Chloe was all too familiar with the teachings, due to her dad, The Man Called Clint and Master G's training methods taught at this dojo.*

*Bits and pieces of information from the Government Officials showed that they were assembling a team of warriors, led by this Man called Clint to go back to the year 2026. As unbelievably as it sounded, time travel was involved and this team of warriors were going back to the year 2026 to stop the infection of humanity in Beaver County, PA. This time travel action would create a new timeline in the past and change the future; however, this, would not alter the Man Called Clint from arriving in the future, only to be sent back to the past to create a new timeline, because that past journey was a different timeline of events. The mission became definite for many reasons, due to all of these years passing and the government coverup about the terminal realm was slowly coming to light, based on the violent and bizarre events happening in the Land of the Five Governments, which were broke down and created in the year 2036, due to political and governmental*

*disagreements. You lived in the state or sectors in the United States that best suited your belief system.*

*The entire Land of the Five Governments had one military, which was the USCM (United States Controlled Military), but a deadly echo of treacherous events was becoming more violent in nature. Human's eating humans, transformation of human beings into raging cannibalistic animals of death were surfacing here and around the world. This was why the team of warriors needed sent back to the year 2026 and stop the past from unfolding in the same days of direction, so the future can set up a new timeline of events.*

*With these current events reported and information that this team, led by the Man called Clint, launched back to year 2026, just recently. Hope was a possibility again, Chloe, her mom and brother Luke knew this and wondered what would happen next.*

*At this time, they were both in safe location, far from the carnage surfacing around the world. The Government for sector 5 had contacted them and they moved to an unannounced location that was secure somewhere in the Mountains of West Virginia, a guy by the name of Austin Maximilian requested this invite. Both Chloe and her mom liked this promising idea, and somehow knew destiny was knocking on the door. Then about a week, after this occurred a man showed up at their door with an unbelievable request.*

“Hello, my name is Sullivan, and it is a complete pleasure to meet both of you, along with Luke. You see Kim, I know your husband, Clint or should I say Sensei Clint. The world now knows him as THE MAN CALLED CLINT, but he trained me in the Burendo Shotokan ways of battle, so he will be forever my Sensei. Kim, your husband is still alive and is battling these Dead Adrenaline Zombie-Aliens as we speak, back in the year 2026.”

“Wait a minute, so you are one of the Burendo Shotokan Warriors sent back to the year 2026 just recently to stop this invasion and possibly change the timeline of events, and save humanity from future pain and suffering, such as what is starting to occur here in 2086.”

“Yes Kim, your exactly correct in your deduction of these unfortunate circumstances.”

*Chloe was listening intently to the conversation between Sullivan, and her mom, and could not stay silent.*

“Okay wait a second, then why are you here and not back in the year 2026, fighting these Dead Adrenaline savages, I bet my dad gave these evil creatures the Dead Adrenaline name. Mmm? Did you leave and abandoned my dad in the terminal realm. Answering me now!!!”

“I get it Chloe, you need answers, and I have to say, you are, definitely your dad’s daughter and yes, he did give the Dead Adrenaline name or DA for a shorten way to say it. I did come back, but your dad sent me back, with Dragon's Slayer blood in my system, which happens to be somewhat of a cure against these cannibalistic Dead Adrenaline savages. Also, I brought back pure Dragon's Slayers blood, which came directly from your dad. In an unusual turn of events when the Dead Adrenaline Hive Queen, tried to take your dad as a host but failed, his blood became a powerful weapon against the Dead Adrenalines. A cure of sorts or at least a chance to stop this infection.

I know this is a lot of information mixed in with tons of out of this world stuff, but I need you to come with me back to the laboratory in an undisclosed location. Austin Maximillian and Gordon Scott are waiting with other scientists and experts. You see Chloe, you are the only hope for humanity, you need to further your training and go back to the year 2026 and help your dad and his warriors battle these alien-zombies to the end, save planet earth and humanity. If you come with me, all will be explained in great detail, but I must warn you, what you are about to embark on is not for the weak and unfocused person, you will be asked to complete a journey that as never been done before by any human being."

"Listen Sullivan, I will go with you, but understand I'am 78 years of age, and have kept up with my training, but time has taken more of my life away, and I have less time to live than I have been alive. On a side note, what good would 78-year-old women be in the future to help the past."

"Chloe, let me just say this, what you think is possible is just a mirage in your mind, you see, the key to our salvation is within you. You are of pure blood, the daughter of Kim and Clint. Your dad has the cure in his blood, which prevents him from changing into a Dead Adrenaline, but he is the source. This source, which is Dragon Slayer blood helps people, and sometimes it brings them back from the savagery of the Alien-Zombie virus, if they are not too far-gone.

We need to inject you with the pure Dragon Slayer blood directly from your dad. The mixture of his blood and your pure blood will maximize the strength of this blood. Once this happens, distributing this blood mixture throughout the world to help stop the dead adrenaline infection would be the planned. Unfortunately, this will help cure people but not stop these Dead Adrenaline shits from killing humans. These alien A-holes can adapt and know not to bite humans to avoid any blood transfer into there system. Meaning they will find ways to hurt and kill humans but not consume if necessary.

Obviously, the scientists and government are trying to figure out a way to just inject these DA(s), but it is on a more complicated level. You see these Dead Adrenaline(s) only get the cure if they bite someone in pure fear mode. Meaning that an individual thinks he going to die and knows this is it, so figuring out the emotional part with blood transfer is still a mystery. Now this is only part of why we need you to help us, the second part is on a most unbelievable level, which involves time travel, training, and selflessness. You will get more of the details when you get to the lab, which is at a secure location within the sector as of now."

"Ok Sullivan, I will go with you, just let me say my goodbyes to my mom and brother."

"Absolutely, I will be waiting outside for you when your ready to go, just let me know. Thank you, Chloe, you are our only chance of surviving this evil force of mayhem that has arrived in the future. Kim and Luke, as I said before, it was a complete pleasure or as the Man Called Clint (Aka Sensei) would say, my coolness Goblet is overflowing."

"Mom, I will pack up a small bag of supplies, of needed items and clothing, but I think these guys and gals will have everything I need at this lab place, I guess."

"Chloe, I Love you and know in my heart this is your destiny, you will find dad, and you will triumph over evil. I will wait with Luke, who has his own destiny to fulfill. Also make sure you tell my husband your dad that I will be waiting for his return, no matter what happens. And Chloe, I know if time travel is involved, he may never return in this timeline again, but I will see him in heaven."

"I will mom, and he will know that you have never gave up on his return."

"Luke, my brother you are the most amazing person in my world, and I love you. As dad says, you are one cool dude, just so you know, I will help dad and save humanity."

"I know this to be true Chloe, I love you sister and say hi to dad. As mom says, my destiny is of a different path, even-though I want to go with you and fight this fight. Deep in my soul, I must stay back with mom for reasons, I do not fully understand, but this journey will unfold, just like pages turning in your mind. Be ready, be prepared and know that mom and I, love you, no matter what happens."

"I love you both, but know the time as come to embark on my destiny."

"Ok Sullivan, I am ready for this quest. So, lets get moving because it is time to "Clean the Fucking Dojo!!"

"Yeah! You are your father's daughter; he would be proud."

# DESTINY AWAITS

## YEAR 2086

*So, this 78-year-old women named Chloe, the daughter of The Man Called Clint travels to an undisclosed location somewhere on the border of Sector 5, which still has not been infested by DA(s), even though most of sector 5 is starting to get infested, this secret location is hidden and untouched. This sub-lab / launch location was set up because seconds after the launch of the Burendo Warriors back to the year 2026, a battle within the launch room went down, but some well-intentioned people of the future managed to contain the problem and fight back the Dead Adrenaline attack.*

*Both Gordon Scott and Austin Maximillian did survive, but the Dead Adrenaline virus infected them, based upon this cruel fact they were both captured and placed in a controlled holding tank that was transportable. The President Samuel Ely of Sector 5 placed an order to have these two brilliant men, along with other scientists and government people transported to this hidden location that was secure from the Dead Adrenaline mayhem. The hope was to find a cure for the Dead Adrenaline disease and bring Austin Maximillian and Gordon Scott back to the land of the living. This gamble paid off when Sullivan returned from the year 2026 with a cure of sorts, Dragon Slayer blood. It helped Austin and Gordon, but the cure was given in a barbaric way, they placed Sullivan in the holding tank, with Austin and Gordon under a controlled environment, which did not matter because the fear of death was real. Sullivan stayed focused but did register a high heart rate and anxiety that was enough to give the blood transfer ability to work when both Austin and Gordon bit him. The fear of death or changing into one of those DA beasts must be present when the blood transfer takes place. If this does not occur, nothing will happen other than you will become a Dead Adrenaline's extra delicious next meal.*

"Sorry for the rough ride Chloe, but we need to make good time to the secret lab location."

"No worries, I understand the sense of urgency, and I am ready to begin Sullivan. I do have a question, why did they only send you to find me and not more help."

"Well, I do have Dragon' Slayer blood pumping through my veins, and have been trained by the Man Called Clint, so the odds are pretty good I would find you and bring you back safely to the Sub-Lab. Plus, they did not want to draw attention to me with the Hive Queen lurking around in this year 2086. You see this bitch has showed up in our time and took over a lovely women named Liz Granite. Liz was the women, who help convince the Leaders and government officials at the Hall of Knowledge in Sector Five to send back the Seven Burendo Warriors. She read from the Journal your dad wrote that unfolded the true story in detail, this helped the cause. Also, when your dad showed up, people paid attention and waited for answers. As you know when The Man Called Clint enters a room the only choice is to Read, Listen, Learn, Survive, Remember, and Never Forget if you understand what I am saying."

"I do Sullivan, my dad is a Master teacher and definitely knows how to deliver the message."

"Chloe, not to change the subject, but are seeing what I am seeing. It looks like, a wandering Dead Adrenaline Zombie standing on the roadway waiting for something and it looks like it has not eaten for a while. Also, a car or something must have struck it because it has a mangled ass body."

"It sure does Sullivan, and it does not look like it wants us to pass, nothing worst then a Dead Adrenaline roadblock."

"Yep, it is not moving, and we still have some distance to travel, so we cannot damage our ride."

**ROADBLOCK DA**

“Stop the car Sullivan, it is time for some practice, if I remember correctly, you mentioned that each Dead Adrenaline Zombie has a weak spot or kill shot. It can be anywhere on its body. Going to try my luck, if I cannot end just one Dead Adrenaline-Zombie asshole, then why am I even here.”

“Ok, but do not tell anyone I let you do this, even though, I do not believe anyone is going to tell or stop the daughter of The Man Called Clint from doing what she wants to do. Plus, like Sensei Clint always says, no better time then the present to test out your Burendo Shotokan skills, even though Sensei Clint has tested these skills out in the past, present, and future.”

“See Sullivan, you have no choice, be back in a minute.”

*Without hesitation and fear, Chloe approaches the roadblock Dead Adrenaline and wants to end the pain and suffering with one strike (Ichigeki), which happen to be a Hammer fist (Tettsui). A quick survey of the Dead Adrenaline’s mangled body, it was obvious that more then likely the kill shot was waiting in DA’s head area, so Chloe moves in close, avoiding the hungry savagery awaiting with one bite from this DA. With one swift and exact blow, Chloe destroys the Dead Adrenaline’s dark-light and ends the pain and suffering.*

## Chloe Ending the Roadblock DA

“Wow! Chloe that was a solid kill shot technique, only one strike and that was it.”

“I feel sad Sullivan that a human life is gone, along with the Dead Adrenaline, but this is the world we live in, the Dead Adrenaline apocalypse. I have to say, this DA looked to be rotting on the outside and inside, in fact has I reached up by his left shoulder, his arm just peeled off as I hit him with a hammer fist.”

“Sounds like something your dad would say, and just so you know that Dead Adrenaline hunger machine was too far gone, and not even dragon slayer blood would have saved it. I bet this Roadblock Dead Adrenaline separated from the hoard and was wandering for quite awhile. The animal life kept it fed, but it was waiting for a human meal, even in itself destructing state. You see sometimes over time, the human body starts to reject the alien-entity organism and starts to sweat blood, and deteriorate, terrible to see, but makes it easier to kill in some cases. Although some host bodies hold up and become a long-term home for the entity, which the Dead Adrenalines love. Anyways, here is a sanitation kit, to clean up with and some new clothes.”

“I figured that was the case when you never mentioned trying to change this Dead Adrenaline back. And, who knows, this could be why, I was able to take that DA out very quickly Sullivan, it must have started to reject its Dead Adrenaline takeover.”

"No Chloe, that had everything to do with a Burendo Shotokan skill set. Well, that is that, now it is time to get back on track to the sub-lab location, as you can see, there is not much out here. This is why we picked such a secluded place, less chance of large groups of the Dead Adrenaline walkers."

"Ok Chloe we are about to enter the gateway to the safe location in Sector 5, it only took 50 minutes to get here, even though the trip from your location in West Virginia was actually 7 hrs away, got to love these new age vehicles of the year 2086. These rides cut travel time down by a ton, just a quick pulse, time jump by way of cold fusion, which reacts with this nickel-plated vehicle we are in. Not sure of all the technology behind this, but this future vehicle runs off deuterium-tritium fuel, which is isotopes of hydrogen.

Lucky for us this element is abundant on earth, but the only draw back is you and I just lost 6 hrs of our life to the past. The one good thing about these vehicles, as of now the Alien Zombie Dead Adrenalines have not figured out how to shut these types of cold fusion vehicles off, but that is only a matter of time. Brace yourself Chloe, because we are about to go through that solid mountain side wall covered with dead trees."

"Not sure about this, either you are going to smash us to the next life, or we will magically appear on the other side, just like the 2001 Harry Potter and the Sorcerer's Stone, where they entered Diagonal Alley by tapping a brick. No time for brick tapping, looks like you are just going to crash through, oh shit!!"

**Mountain side gateway to the Sub-Lab Sector 5**

"We made it Chloe, welcome to Sector Five Sub-lab, and by the way the movie reference reminded me of your dad again. I will have to check out the 2001 Harry Potter movie, which is only 85 years old I believe. Ha, ha!"

"As my dad would say, it keeps me going."

"Ok Chloe, you will get information about the mission in about 40 minutes, so I will take you to your temporary quarters to get a moments peace, along with some food and shower. As you can see, there is not a welcoming party here in this entrance location. It is better to avoid large groups or gatherings in one location, helps keep the DA(s) from focusing in on us. For some reason, these Alien-Zombie DA(s) are attracted to areas that have crowds of people, like a form of sonar that gets them excited and ready for a large human meal.

So, to avoid this, we have only a group of 20 people that are only in certain areas of the Sub-Lab at a time, meaning we only have groups of 5 working together at one time. Three Security protectors, one Astro-Physicist expert and one Medical Doctor that are in the lab at one time. They are working shifts and the rest of the time; each person is in their quarters separated from each other. Meaning we have total of 12 Security Protectors, 4 Astro-Physicist experts, and 4 Doctors. Although Professor Austin Maximillian and Lead Astro-Physicist Gordon Scott are additional people that over see the complicated details of this mission you will be involving yourself in.

Now Chloe, just so you know Austin Maximillian was involved from the beginning and was the one that brought your dad back from the terminal realm in Beaver County. Austin will be briefing you about your dad, you see he was the last person to speak with your dad before the sudden launch occurred."

"This is nice to hear about Austin speaking with my dad, it will be good to speak with him."

"In reference to Gordon Scott, you will discover that he is the brains behind the time travel knowledge, and believe me when I say this Chloe, Gordon knows exactly what he is doing. In a truly brief time, Gordon discovered how to time break to the past, even beyond what your dad and the Burendo Shotokan Warriors have done. It is on a level that is incredible to say the least, Gordon will get you up to speed with the latest time travel abilities, and few other things that will change the game for humanity."

"Ok Sullivan, sounds good, I'm definitely ready to get on with this voyage of mayhem."

*Chloe's patience's were starting to wear away, it has been over 60 years since she had last seen her dad, so the time for waiting patiently was over, but her fortitude was strong and the time for action was now. Chloe was ready to embrace the unknown with an open mind and focus. Her mind was ready, but how could her 78-year-old body survive, the path to victory would be a difficult journey that would take every part of her Chi or life force to carry out and destroy the enemy DA(s) invading earth. Even though Chloe knew that her age would slow her down, she was still willing to travel into the abyss.*

# THE CONVERSATION

## YEAR 2086

"Hi Austin, how are you feeling, no setbacks from your most recent return to the land of the living."

"Hello Sullivan, nice to see you on this extraordinary evening. Nope, I feel better than Bourbon syrup hitting the top of a pancake, might not be healthy, but taste so good! I will say that alien transformation into a DA, felt like an empty picnic basket, I just felt hungry all the time. Thank goodness, I changed back, before I got a bite too eat, if you know what I mean."

"I do Austin, becoming a cannibalistic Alien- Zombie Is no picnic. Plus, I see you have not stop wearing signature yellow suit."

"There you go Sullivan; a little bite of humor does your mind and body good, and yes, yellow is my favorite color. My whole wardrobe consists of yellow suits other than my sleep attire that is yellow style of pajamas."

"Well Austin, I see you have not lost your sense of humor that Sensei Clint talked about."

"How is the Man Called Clint holding up in the terminal realm."

“Well Austin, the last time I saw Sensei Clint, he was giving out nicknames and ass kicking the alien invaders.”

“Fantastic, geez that Clint fellow never gives up”

“Where is Gordon Scott, because Chloe will be here any minute.”

“Oh yes siree, there is Gordon now, he was just making a few adjustments to the Time travel gizmo, kinda like me eating, just never quite done to his liking.”

“Hello Gordon, Chloe should be here anytime now.”

“Great, because this journey needs to start, and there is no time to squander, time travel is a touchy thing, that we must respect. The time travel doors open and close like a person blinking their eyes on a given day, so let us get focused and set the wheels in time travel motion.”

“You oversee this entire process, so we are ready when you are. Ok, here comes Chloe now.”

“Chloe this is Professor Austin Maximillian and Head Scientist Gordon Scott; both were the main men involved from the beginning of the time travel shitfest. Austin is the man, who got your dad safely out of the terminal realm, and to the doctors and scientists that revived him from his state of animation. Gordon is an expert in Astrophysics and speared headed the entire time travel mission from the technology behind it, to the actual ability to make it happen.”

**Professor Austin Maximillian**

**Head Scientist Gordon Scott**

"Thanks for the synopsis about these two men Sullivan, so Austin and Gordon what is the plan for me. I have to say again, look at me, I am 78 years old and not getting any younger. Even though, I am the daughter of the Man Called Clint, how does that change my age, even if I get some of the pure Dragon Slayer blood that my dad sent back to us. You are the top Scientist Gordon, so enlighten me on how we get past this fact."

"Chloe, you remind me of your dad, straight forward, honest, and focused. Your dad is a unique unforgettable individual; he was in a definite wrong place at the right time in history. You see if THE MAN CALLED CLINT had not been in Beaver County, PA in the year 2026, none of us would exist right now. Just by him being present in the past, twice our future timeline has changed. This is a fantastic outcome to say the least. Meaning your dad's actions in the past, present and future have brought you to us, on this day in the year 2086.

Chloe what you are about to embark on has never happened before on such a level of time travel, you will be tested mentally and physically. And extreme battle training will be part of this; you will transport back to various time periods that will improve everything about you. At first your physical body will only be able to stay in that particular year for short periods of time, but over time, upon leaving and returning to that same year, you will physically adjust and be able to stay as long as you wish. In the simplest terms, you will launch from our Sub-Lab to a period in the past, adapt for a few than return here, just to do it all over again. We have selected a few places in time for you to go to assimilate your mind and body to permanently be able to time travel anywhere at any time, even into the future beyond the year 2086, once the process is completed.

When you reach this point in your time travel power, and ultimate fighting skills, you will be ready to transport back to the year 2026 and help your dad. However, on your first trip to the year 2026 in Beaver County, Pennsylvania, you will only be able to stay for brief periods, but than return and stay as long as needed. I know, you must be wondering why you could not just arrive and stay the first time, because your body would be already adapted to time traveling without any issues. Well, there is strange reason for this time travel issue that has to do with the Dead Adrenaline invasion.

Let me go over some of our findings, when Sullivan traveled back with the Burendo Shotokan Warriors to the year 2026, his body started to change in a destructive and bizarre way, he was getting younger by the minute, but his mind was aging forward. Some of the other Burendo Warriors just started to get younger, but their mind stayed the same age. This reverse age thing occurred in many ways, but the outcome would be the same, death. Originally, he thought, along with the Man Called Clint that it was some time travel issue because he had never existed in the year 2026, and Clint did exist in the year 2026 already and was not infected by the reverse age illness. A cure for Sullivan was discovered, after Clint's blood was administered to him, under violent circumstances involving a Dead Adrenaline biting Sullivan. Sullivan reverse age illness stopped, and he returned to his original age, mind, and body.

Also, no Dead Adrenaline blood disease happened because he had Dragon Slayer blood, curiosity of Clint.

With this knowledge, I ran tests on Sullivan's blood to try pin down why your dad (Clint) did not have any issues with the reverse age stuff. However, based on further experimentation with Sullivan's blood, a discovery of unknown pathogen, it was a stealth pathogen found in his blood; this unusual mutation was different than the Dragon Slayer blood in his system."

"It was of a different origin, a type of airborne illness brought from another planet or place. It was not related to the Dead Adrenaline infection, this unknown pathogen originated from another planet the Dead Adrenalines invaded, meaning they used it as a weapon against other species, knowing it would really mess things up. They discovered this stealth pathogen on one of the past planets they took over and collected it to use as an added defense. You see, the Hive Queen showed up in the year 2086 and told the Man Called Clint, she would be waiting for him in the year 2026. The Hive Queen thought Clint would just become a young child, which would be an easy kill when he returned.

I do not know if any of this makes sense to you Chloe, but I guess what I'am trying to say is, we have harnessed the ability to control the age reverse illness. We can now, alter this stealth pathogen, give it to a person, and reverse their age to a certain number, and stop the process of reverse aging, once carried out, the person's age stops at a particular number, and they will age forward from that point at normal pace. They will also keep the knowledge and training they had before this process happens. Think about it, If I knew all the things I learned through the years, but now I could be in a younger stronger healthier body with that wisdom. This would be a gift like the fountain of youth.

Also, the reverse age illness with not be a problem, due to the stealth pathogen in your body that has already changed your age, but your first trip to 2026 must be brief. You will stay and hopefully help than return to us in the year 2086. The reason for this is just to make sure things are working as designed. You see, we believe that the Hive Queen, only attacks people that arrive from the future or past with this reverse age illness. This is why none of the present-day humans or other species get the reverse age illness. Hive Queen rules the game of life or death.

One other valid point of understanding, you will be the only person on earth with your abilities when your training has reached its destination. Also, no other human being will be able to have their age reversed and keep all their accumulated knowledge. This is because you are a direct blood line to your father, which is why the stealth pathogen was taken from Sullivan's blood and mixed with the pure Dragon Slayer Blood from your father. So, it will be your blood, your father's blood, and the stealth pathogen mixed and bingo you will change. The only other person that this process would work on would be your brother Luke, but I understand he is on a different path as we speak."

“Wow, Gordon this is the fountain of youth, most definitely. Now I get what your saying, a reset of sorts, so I can begin this quest at younger stronger age, but with the life knowledge far beyond my age. I am ready when you are Gordon, sign me up, times a ticking and I am not getting any younger, although it sounds like that is about to change. In reference to my brother Luke, if for some reason things take a turn down shit sandwich road, I know for sure, he will decide his destiny.”

“You are one spirited women Chloe, I will get things prepared for your quest, this will only take me, exactly 20 minutes, no more, no less. Your life is about to change forever Chloe, but I can see, you are ready with a steady compass of direction. While you wait, Professor Austin, would love to speak with you.”

“Hello there Chloe Westwood, it is most delightful to finally talk with you, unfortunately it had to be under stressful and dire circumstances. Kinda feels like when I met your father, great to meet him, but I knew he was preparing to go on a journey that no one else could grasp.”

“Hi Austin, so you were one of the last people to speak with my dad, before the launch abruptly took place.”

“Yes ‘ma’am,’ yes indeed it was me, your dad is a great man, a unique force that was born on this earth to save humanity. Timing was everything, had he not been in Beaver County, PA when this hurricane from hell started to swirl, we would all be Texas Gator bait. I believe, GOD chose The Man Called Clint to be the human species savior, just has your destiny has brought you here to continue the fight."

"How was my dad, did he ask about us."

"Oh yes indeed, your father and I did talk about you, your mom, and Luke. We discuss how in the year 2086, life expectancy has been incredible, due to medical improvements over the past 60 years. You see, your dad wanted to see his family again but knew if he did, he might have not wanted to leave for the mission. So, his choice was clear, stay on mission, no distractions, no matter the cost, no matter the pain. Your father, The Man Called Clint also knew with all his heart and soul, if he completed and destroyed the enemy aliens forever. He would be able to leave the terminal realm in the year 2026, and find his family, knowing the threat was over. Kinda like me eating a Cherry pie, until nothings left, never to return, if you buy what this good old Texas boy is serving."

"I do, and my dad likes to say, what you brew today, you will have to drink tomorrow, so you better like the taste. In this case, no one would like the taste, because alien-zombie take over is not anyone's cup of coffee. My dad made the right decision, because any change would have changed this moment as we speak."

"Yes, more certain than a Texas Tornado's uncontrollable destruction. Well Chloe, here comes Gordon and the team, looks like you are about to begin this voyage."

"I see that is about to happen, well ok than, it was genuinely nice to meet and speak with you Austin."

"Absolutely, most definitely, this was an honor and an unforgettable moment in time."

"Ok Chloe are you ready because time is ticking."

"Yep Gordon, let's get this fury ride on the road."

"So, Chloe before we get into the journey you will be taking into the past, I would like to give you the mixture of the Dragon Slayer Blood from your father, along with the stealth pathogen extracted from Sullivan's blood. This can be, simply injected into your blood stream, and a blending will occur with your pure blood. This is the easy part; the unknown treacherous part is, if for some unforeseen reason this experimental theory does not go has planned."

"Meaning I might die Gordon, I understand the risk, but if I do not do this, I have no chance of survival if I do not get my body back to the best physical age that a human being could be. Like Sullivan has said, no human has ever attempted what I will be trying in the realm of time traveling. I must be the best physically and mentally, lets do this thing because the past is waiting."

"Ok than, you have decided, Chloe step into this secure holding tank area, my team will get you prepared, and I will administer the Dragon Slayer blood and stealth pathogen. Once I inject you, we will exit the holding tank, and lock you in as a safety precaution, until we know it worked or not.

Your body will be life scanned to collect data of the event, if everything goes as believed, you will decrease in age. We have decided, based on tests, checks, and balances that the prime age you should be is age 23. This is genetically the best age for you, ok Chloe, the injection has happened, now we must wait."

Darkness comes destroys the light

Suffer now then with the fright.

Fearsome fiends of the blackest night

Tear our souls to their delight.

Terror triumphs overall.

We hide away until the call.

Will it ever come?

Even if for only some.

# AGE IS NOT A NUMBER

## YEAR 2086

*The process begins, and Chloe this 78-year-old woman physically reverses in age, back to the age of 23. Like traveling back to a past time, Chloe's body transforms back to her prefect age of 23, but with all her wisdom accumulated up to the age of 78. This process is complete and was a phenomenal success.*

***Past Chloe at age 78***

**Present Chloe at age 23**

“How do you feel Chloe, is there any pain or confusion?”

“Nope Gordon, I feel fantastic both physically and mentally, as if my mind and body are working together without hesitation, if that makes any kind of Medical or Scientific sense. Also, I did not feel a thing when it was occurring.”

“This is great to hear because if my testing on this was correct, you should not have felt a single thing, until the age reverse process was complete. This is fantastic Chloe; the response you have given me is exactly how I hoped you would feel.”

"Well Gordon, you were spot on with this reverse age process, because I feel like a brand new me, but with a lot more amenities to say the least."

"Thanks Chloe, now your mind and body are ready to start the complex part of this whole thing, the journey you must take back in time, to acquire even more knowledge and fighting ability."

"Let us begin this quest, because times passing and your only young once, or in my case twice, if you get my humor at a time like this."

"You sound exactly like your dad, always finding humor in the most difficult of times Chloe. On the other side of the Moon-pie, you are one lovely young lady standing before us."

"Thanks, Austin, for the compliment, if I am going to be the heroine in this saga, I better look like a leading lady, as they say in Hollywood."

"Chloe the transformation of you changing from age 78, back to the age of 23, went seamlessly without any complications or rejective responses from your body and mind. Not only are you younger, but your lifetime knowledge as remained in untouched. This is remarkable in nature, and you are first person on this living earth that has experienced this. Now for more good news, your body and mind have received Dragon slayer blood that is a direct source from your dad, or should I say the Man

Called Clint, meaning in the best way of explaining this phenomenon, you Chloe have inherited unknown superpowers. This is a positive side effect to getting your fathers dragon slayer blood, which by accident got placed into his bloodstream by an unknown alien way,_when the Hive Queen battled him the first time, in the year 2026. Sullivan can explain this further, based on his knowledge fighting along side your Clint."

"No problem, Gordon, I will give the low down on what I heard and did see during my time in 2026."

"Yes, please enlighten Chloe further about her dad, Sullivan."

"Yea Chloe, your dad is a tough guy and has martial art abilities that go far beyond his training. He told me, along with Olivia and Sandra who are the last two members of the Burendo Shotokan warriors still fighting along side the *Man Called Clint* that his strength, stamina, and overall abilities have increased, not only in how he fights, but how he thinks. Also, he discovered that he could breathe underwater without drowning, which Olivia had seen, who verified this information. Sensei Clint told us that he believes there are many more gifts to unmask once he figures out how to tap into these powers. Now, I got Dragon Slayer Blood, but it was to stop me from reverse aging and reset my body back to my normal age. Along with Olivia, and Sandra, which did bless us with better overall martial skills, also, we cannot be infected by a

Dead Adrenaline bite by way of blood poisoning. If one of these Dead Adrenaline's bite us, it will change them back to a human, unless they are too far gone, which will just kill the human, along with Dead Adrenaline alien virus. It is believed that a Dead Adrenaline cannot turn us into an alien host, because our blood is protected from Dragon Slayer blood. Yet, no such superpowers beyond that have occurred with me. Now I do not know if Olivia and Sandra have improved further with any superpowers like Clint."

"Got it Sullivan, I understand it will be a matter of me unlocking superpower abilities that remain to be seen, I will not know until the moment unfolds like a violent unexpected Dead Adrenaline book."

"Ok Chloe, Gordon will bring you up to speed on the crazy ass journey you will be going on."

"Thanks for the info, Sullivan, and thank you for everything you have done up to this point."

"Well, I m ready to get this Dead Adrenaline party started Gordon."

"So here is the simplest way to present what will be occurring Chloe, you will be sent back to the year 2025, this will happen three times. The first time, you will only stay for 10 seconds, then return to us, only to be sent back a second time, which will last 15 minutes, if the plotting of these two-time travel locations is correct, you will meet Master G. both times, and you must convince him you are the daughter of Sensei Clint or should I say the *Man Called Clint.* If you are successful in convincing him, when you return the third time, your training will begin if that makes any kind of time travel sense. Assimilation of your mind and body in the past year of 2025, must take place, and this is the reason for the 10 second and 15 minutes. You see, when the first 10 seconds happens, you will automatically return to our year 2086, and the same thing will happen the second time when the 15 minutes passes. Kinda like a time travel interference that rebounds you back to us like a boomerang. Do not bother yourself with why this is, but understand my calculations are true and sound. After your training is complete with Master G, you will be contacted, via transmitter, which will be placed in your skin behind your left ear.

This will give you information directly to your brain that the time as arrived for your next part of the journey. You will be training for exactly one year with Master G and than leave for your next location of training. Now the Dead Adrenaline invasion in Beaver County, Pennsylvania has not happened yet but will occur in September of the year 2026. Now you may be asking yourself how you will leave after being there for one year. A time travel pod will be used, which is like the one Sullivan used to return to the year 2086, but more advanced. You will return to us in the year 2086 and then launch to your next location, and just like before 10 seconds the first trip, 15 minutes the second trip, then you will boomerang back to us and sent back to stay for a period to train and obtained more knowledge.

I will not tell you where or who you will be getting your training from on your second level of this journey, Master G will reveal this, upon completing your training time with him. You see, once Master G realizes and embraces that time travel is for real, he will know exactly where to send you. Now Chloe there is one other incredibly unique benefit that was discovered, every time you return to this year of 2086, your age will reset 23 again. So, even if you would age from age 23 to 24 if you stayed one year, from year 2025 to the next, your age of 23 will reset when you return to us.

This age reset happens every time you return from your time traveling. Now if you stay in your real lifetime year of 2086, which is your actual existence year, you will age normally, unless you decide to time travel again, meaning you could age here normally, reach a certain age, time travel to the past or maybe the future, at which time your age will reset back to the age of 23 again, and start aging at a normal rate in that time period. And if you time travel back to the year 2086 or any year after, you will reset back to 23 years old again. This a truly remarkable power, meaning if you wanted to, you could never grow old. Think about it, this is the fountain of youth like you said Chloe. I know this is a lot to absorb in this moment, but on one end we have time, but on the other end we do not. Let me continue, the time break expedition you will be embarking on will test you, first you will go back to the year 2025 in June, stay a year, and leave in June of 2026. This is three months before the first signs of the dead adrenaline invasion. So, the mission is you will find and locate none other than Master G, as you know he is the one that brought Sensei Clint your dad further into his martial art journey. I understand Chloe, you have trained with Master G when you were a lot younger. Master G will be able to fine tune your skills for the rest of this journey, which will be clearer as you travel further down the path of knowledge both mentally and physically. So are your ready to continue with this treacherous quest into uncharted territory, which will prepare you Chloe for the uncertain outcome and battle with the Dead Adrenaline army in the year 2026."

"Yep, I am ready for this expedition, and know this, I will not fail, because I am the MAN CALLED CLINT's daughter, and this is my destiny."

*The time travel quest begins, and Chloe is still standing in the holding tank area, which is magnetically incased, the entire tank is air and water sealed tight, suddenly a liquid magnetic substance starts to rise upward from the floor and fills the entire area. Chloe is floating inside this magnetic pool of liquid, quickly she starts to inhale this liquid, and realizes she can still breath and see clearly as the process starts to take hold. Fortunately for Chloe, this improvement in time travel, does not cause any side effects when entering a past or future year, the consumed liquid substance will evaporate naturally when the time break travel is completed. Like a static electrical shock, Chloe dematerializes and vanishes from sight, and the launch begins. The opposite magnetic poles, one laced in the actual holding tank, and one in the magnetic liquid substance meet. Opposite do not attract, and the launch begins, her journey has begun into this unknown voyage of light and darkness, where only the strong survive.*

**Chloe's Time Traveling Journey Begins**

# THE FIRST LESSON

## YEAR 2025

*An unassuming man stands in a pronounced fighting stance in a large open field, holding a Katana blade, suddenly and without warning the blade cuts through the air in a diamond shaped movement, and these blade cuts are power-full and fast, with accuracy never seen before. Each blade cut is both intentional and unintentional, the reason for this is so your opponent is not handed the blueprint for your attack. The pattern or form of the blade cuts appear, to be a diamond shape movement, but appearances can be just a mask that is covering up what destructions awaits. This is the secret to defense and attack, the ever-changing movement of planned and unplanned movements. As the blade cuts increase in speed, it becomes extremely hard to follow the movements, like a hummingbird's wing movement, you know the wings are moving, but it becomes a blur, but flight continues. Suddenly the blade cuts stop, and this man looks to the sky, and senses something or someone coming. Then it happens, a silvery bright light arrives from the heavens, like water pouring from a pitcher onto the ground. A smokey mist rises from the field edge, and women appears dressed in silver clothing, standing in the distance yelling out something.*

“Master G, it is me Chloe the daughter of Sensei Clint, remember this moment, I will return soon to further our conversation.”

*Master G did not flinch from the mysterious appearance of this woman, and thought to himself, I will be waiting for her return, and if this is Chloe, the true daughter of Sensei Clint, her training will reveal knowledge of the Burendo Shotokan way.*

*Exactly, one day passed and no return of Chloe has happened, Master G knew that destiny is destiny and if you wait for destiny to begin, it will be like waiting to fall asleep, no matter how tired you get, sleep comes when you are not focused on resting.*

*A second day passes, and than it happened, a slight knock on the door of Master G's Dojo (Place of Training) where Master G, had set up a second One Strike Karate school in the hot, humid landscape of South Carolina, Charleston to be exact. This second Dojo location had been a proven established place of training, but in the last couple of years the school has been closed for renovation, and for Master G to further his own personal training, because the evolution of the Burendo Shotokan way never stops. As Master G heard the door knock, he opened the door and a blue-eyed, blond hair women walked into the Dojo, Master G did not speak a word and walked over to the training area, he bowed towards the Torii gate and crossed over into the sacred ground, which happen to be hardwood bamboo floors. Master G, turned towards this woman, who claimed to be Chloe the daughter of Sensei Clint, and motioned for her to enter the training area.*

*Chloe bowed and walked through the Torii gate onto the bamboo floors, and began to speak to Master G.*

**TORII GATE: Entrance to sacred training ground**

"Master G, I know I look older than 16 years of age, which is my actual age in the year 2025, and would be the age you know me to be in this year, but a most unbelievable thing has happened. You see Sir, I have come from the future year 2086, in that year I was 78 years old, but with the help of science, medical advancement, and Dragon Slayer blood, my age has been reversed back to the age of 23, but my knowledge has stayed the same. Master G, in the year 2026, Beaver County, Pennsylvania will be invaded by Alien-Zombie beings from another world, they will be cannibalistic savages that infiltrate a human body and mind. They want to imprison earth and annihilate the humankind as we know it. Ultimately, they want to take earth as their own and rule it.

On a positive note, your top student Sensei Clint, my dad has been involved in saving Beaver County, Pennsylvania, and humanity. As I speak in a different moment in time, my dad (Clint) is battling these evil enemies with the help of an elite fighting team, which are called the Burendo Shotokan Warriors. Some of your training given to my dad has been passed on to them, so this force of Burendo Warriors would have half a chance of surviving and fighting this alien invasion. Fortunately, my dad is surviving with some of the Burendo Shotokan Warriors that are left, but unfortunately, they are hanging on by only a couple cuts of the Katana blade. You see Master G; they need me to complete the circle and give them the edge to destroy these alien-zombie creatures. My dad needs me, planet earth needs me, along with our human species. I know this is hard to believe or understand, but if given the opportunity, I will make you believe."

"This is a most interesting cluster of information, you have given me, and I must say knowing your father, Clint, he would, step forward into battle if called upon. Now based on my knowledge and research of ancient readings, handed down through Japanese folklore, it is not surprising about the unhatched alien invasion in the year 2026. You see, some of these writings revealed that a reckoning would come to earth and pain and suffering would transform the human species. What form this evil would take was unknown in the writings, most scholars and historians just chalked these stories up to ancient Japanese folklore and thought nothing like this would ever happen. In fact, I am, one of few Americans that even know of these writings, because of my past studying and training in Japan for many, many years. Now Chloe, the question is still, not that if I believe that in the year 2026; an alien invasion will take place, but if you are without an unshakable doubt the daughter of Sensei Clint. Meaning, I will put you through a set Burendo Shotokan movements or techniques to see if in fact, your Burendo Shotokan training was from your father and I."

"I will be ready for that test Master G when I return, you see Sir, I can only stay in this year for exactly 15 minutes, but when I return, I can than stay as long as I need to. This time travel stuff takes a little getting used too, but I will prove to you Master G, that I am the daughter of Sensei Clint."

"Ok than Chloe when you return, I will test you on your Burendo Shotokan skills, if you pass, the real training begins.

**MASTER G**

# THE KATA

## YEAR 2025

*Just as Gordon Scott believed, Chloe returned to the year 2086 to recalibrate her mind and body, and than returned to the year 2025 to stay and train with Master G. Her return was swift and without hesitation, in fact she bounced back to the year 2086 for a moment arriving in the holding tank, she could see through the glass window, Gordon and Austin looking back at her. They both had a look of fear and confidence, Chloe thought for a second this is how she feels, fearful of the future, but confident she will overcome and win the day.*

*Chloe arrived back to the year 2025, this time she could stay for as long as needed, but now she had to pass the test. Chloe entered the Dojo, where Master G, was waiting to begin the test.*

"Ok Chloe, now I will find out if you are the daughter of Sensei Clint, you must understand, it is not you trying to convince me that Alien- Zombies will try to take over Beaver County, PA, in the year 2026, or even proofing that Sensei is involved in killing them. I believe this will happen or is happening based on all the time travel mayhem. You see, none of those things need proven, but what does matter is you, Chloe, you must prove you are his daughter, and not just some young women from the future claiming this.

The Burendo Shotokan way must and will be handed down to only a person of true moral character. No lies, no anger, no weakness, but a person of true pure character. Plus, if you are his daughter, Clint and I have trained you before in the style of Burendo Shotokan. If you are Chloe, the daughter of Clint, you have already achieved a blackbelt rank. As you would know, a blackbelt is only the beginning of your Martial Art Journey, also if you have maintained and improved on your training throughout the years, it should be a benefit. Now are you ready for this test!"

"Absolutely Master G, tell me what I need to do."

*Master G, slowly started to step back into the center of the bamboo wood floor of the dojo.*

*Suddenly and without warning, he begins to complete a never-before-seen ancient style kata, it covered ever area of attack: defense, blocks, strikes, kicks, throws, grabbling, locks, standing movements of avoidance, ground techniques that placed a person in a position to recapture a standing position. This was everything wrapped up in an unorthodox formula of total power, speed, accuracy, and focus. Nothing as ever been, refined in such a pattern and non-pattern way. Master G, breathing was precise with every circular or linear movement, he complemented the technique with oxygenated power. The entire Burendo Shotokan Kata lasted only 10 seconds, but seemed like an eternity to the onlooker, which happened to be Chloe. The fantastic movement of defense and attack ended, and Master G stopped and walked up to Chloe; his breathing was normal as if he had just taken a casual stroll down the street. No signs of fatigue or struggle was obvious, as if he had just continued to speak to her and had never completed such astonishing undertaking.*

*Chloe stood in unexplainable amazement; in fact, she had no words to say to Master G.*

"Chloe, you see, this kata as never been shown to anyone before, the only other person to see this ancient kata is your father, Sensei Clint. This same test was given to him, which he completed with total perfection, now it is your turn to complete such a challenge. You must complete this kata, within a week, master its movements and than show me the exact precise kata, and if mastery occurs, and you grasp understand the Bunkai (Fighting techniques) within the ancient flow of battle tested techniques, then I will begin your training. One week, no more, no less. If you fail, you leave, because you are not your fathers' daughter. Do you understand what I am asking of you Chloe."

"I do Master G, and I will not fail my father, you, or humanity."

"Ok than, your practice to master this kata, begins to tomorrow morning, get rest, be ready, and show no fear or concern, there is no place for those emotions in training. Lastly, the name of this kata is *Tatakai,* which means *Battle* in Japanese, and speaking of Japanese, you will also further your knowledge of the Japanese language, which will be of the upmost important in your future. As you already may know, I am fluent in the Japanese language and have study this language in Japan for many many years. Enough said about this, I will see you tomorrow."

"Most definitely, I will see you tomorrow morning Sir."

# THE BURENDO WAY

## YEAR 2025

*Dawn arrived and Chloe began the start of her practice to capture the power, speed, and accuracy of the* ***TATAKAI*** *kata, which is the one kata that if master, will be unstoppable when applied to attack and defense. In the back of Chloe's mind, she wonders if any of her unique superpowers would show up to help her with the training. As of yet, nothing has manifested even though Chloe does have Dragons Slayer Blood.*

"Good morning, Chloe, I hope you enjoyed your breakfast because you are going to need the energy from it to push through this morning of learning."

"Good morning, Master G."

"Ok, Chloe, I will go through the first three set of movements, which have attack and defense strengths. Once you master these techniques, we will move onto the next set of three. Watch and learn how I breath with every motion of attack and defense. Focus must be accompanied by breathing, which is life in everything we do. Complete these three sets of movements, until you can complete without hesitation or confusion, but only with pure power, speed, and accuracy.

Know the Bunkai (Fighting techniques) within this kata, become friends with the techniques, because a loyal friend will protect you."

*Three days had passed, and Chloe was already fifty Bunkai techniques into the the kata, her precise attack and defense were getting sharper with every movement and blend of Bunkai (Technique). Master G told Chloe that there are Seventy techniques within the Tatakai kata. Seventy ways to kill or live, for each attack technique, the same movement can be a defense.*

"Good evening, Chloe, how is your practice going, are you starting to understand the kata techniques you know up to this point"

"Yes, Master G, I'am up to fifty techniques within the kata of seventy. Do you want to see the first fifty movements of defense and attack that I have been working on."

"No, I do not Chloe, you will show me the completed seventy of the kata when you are ready. Now let me go over the last 20 movements, and than you will have all the moves to practice. Your past training has aided you in understanding the techniques and remembering what they are, but it is not only a matter of remembering. You must remember and instinctively react with every technique, this is the Burendo (Blended) way."

"I understand Sir, I'am ready to learn the rest of the kata"

*Master G, continued with the last 20 movements of the Tatakai kata, and explained to Chloe the last twenty movements of technique will be the hardest, so she must react to each technique as if they are the first fifty movements. The teaching was complete, now it was up to Chloe to master the Tatakai kata and prove that she is the daughter of the Man Called Clint.*

*Finally, after practice and rigorous focus to make the Tatakai Kata her own, Chloe was ready to show Master G, the requested kata and prove she is worthy to continue further in the Burendo Way.*

"Good morning, Chloe it is good to see you, even though this may be your last day of training. That is question you must ask yourself, if you stay or if you go, you must now complete Tatakai, without mistakes, hesitation, or fear of failure. This kata at its best can be completed in exactly 10 seconds, which you must do, only two people in this world have every done such an incredible undertaking. Sensei Clint and I are those two people, so now it is your chance to prove your ability to go further with the Burendo Way. As you have said Chloe, the survival of the humankind is at stack, so now it is up to you."

"The time has arrived for me to show you Master G, that the daughter of Sensei Clint or as the world knows him, *The Man Called Clint* is here and ready to continue the Burendo Shotokan Way."

*Master G smiles and nods his head as to say begin the kata, but what happen next was unexpected and dangerous on a level that Chloe did not foresee coming. The sky broke open, and suddenly Red eyed Dead Adrenalines appear and started to enter the dojo, the number totaled 70 cannibalistic savages, which was the exact number of movements in the Tatakai kata. Master G did see the invading DA(s) passing through the Torii gate onto the Bamboo dojo floor, but he did not stop or block their entry, as if he knew the true test of the Tatakai kata was about to take place. Chloe who was standing near Master G, looked at him for a moment, and than realized this was her true test, not only would she have to complete the Tatakai Kata in 10 seconds with total perfection, but be able to utilize the bunkai (techniques) on real subjects that are both dead and alive, aka Dead Adrenaline(s). Master G, steps back from Chloe, and starts to speak.*

"I will explain to you how this came to be if you survive your battle, remember you are the daughter of Sensei Clint. Now it is up to you Chloe to end the nightmare walking through the dojo door."

## Torii Gate Dead Adrenaline(s)

"I see Master G, this is a fight to the death, now I am in a controlled state of pissed off, here it goes, *Its Time to Clean the Fucking Dojo!"*

*Chloe stepped back into the center of the Dojo floor and prepared her position for the onslaught of death moving her direction. At that moment something happened, and Chloe's mind slowed down to a focused and balanced way, she was in the moment, and no tunnel vision was around. Then the dance of death started, and Chloe methodically maneuvered around the dojo floor, without hesitation, and placed kill shots to each individual Dead Adrenaline- Alien- Zombified- human. Somehow, she new, just where the kill shot would be on each of the Dead Adrenaline's, and each attack only took a second. The design of the Tatakai kata was being revealed with each Bunkai (technique) destroying each Dead Adrenaline Zombie. Hand strikes and kicks, blocking and countering, throws, grabbling, recovering from the ground movements with complete control when needed were on full display. One strike, one kill and the last Dead Adrenaline collapsed too the dojo floor, and blood covered the bamboo floor like a horrific painting of pain and suffering. If* ***Hell*** *had legs and could walk, it was just cut down on the sacred ground, in this place of training. As the last Dead Adrenaline fell, Chloe walked calmly with no signs of fatigue or breathing issues over too Master G, who was standing back from the battle carnage and said these words.*

"I am the daughter of Sensei Clint; he is known to the world as the Man called Clint, he is trained in the Burendo Shotokan way, you Master G have put me to the test, which I have just completed, as you have said, the kata must be completed in 10 seconds, which I have not done. The entire battle took 70 seconds, one second a kill shot for each of the seventy Dead Adrenaline Zombies. 70 movements extracting the bunkai techniques to end the threat. Tell me Master G, in a non-battle condition the Tatakai kata should be completed in 10 seconds, but in real battle conditions, depending on the size and number of the threat, it takes as long as it takes. Is this the truth of the Burendo way or have I failed the test. I can complete the Tatakai kata in 10 seconds if you need to see it."

"No Chloe, there is no need for that, you are so very correct in your deduction of the fighting arts displayed today. This is the Burendo way, and you are your father's daughter, Chloe the daughter of Sensei Clint. You have past the test, now let us begin the real training, but first let us clean this mess up, and get rid of these poor souls' bodies lying on the dojo floor."

*The entire Dojo was cleaned and sanitized, and no signs of the Dead Adrenaline battle was left, it was a distance memory. The training with Master G had begun, and Chloe was told by Master G that he had been visited by a man named Sullivan from the future year of 2086, Sullivan told him that a Gordon Scott would be sending some Dead Adrenaline Zombies from the future to help with the training. Master G, told Chloe, he put an order in for 70 Dead Adrenaline Zombies and the request was honored.*

*Chloe understood the reason for this severe training method and knew it had to happen. The training with Master G, continued, and as the months passed during that time, Chloe revealed that she had the ability to see or sense where a kill shot was at on the body of Dead Adrenaline Zombie, which was the first of her superpowers to come to life from the Dragon Slayer blood coursing through her veins. In that year many more Dead Adrenaline Zombies arrived, Chloe and Master G, battled the* ***ZOMBIES*** *together, using many methods of the Burendo Shotokan way, Chloe was mastering the techniques taught by Master G, without the use of any type of hand weapon, because her hands, legs, knees, and elbows were her weapons.*

***Master G, & Chloe battling the Dead Adrenaline Field Zombies.***

***The Evolution of Chloe's training had begun; all fear was leaving her body and mind!***

*As the year went on, fewer and fewer Dead Adrenaline Zombies showed up, until no more would arrive, which meant that the future could have changed in a disastrous direction, and Gordon Scott, could no longer send them. Chloe's* training was ending with Master G, *now that the year was up, and Chloe knew she needed to leave and travel to her next destination, but where would that be. All these thoughts became more definite when the transmitter embed beneath her skin, behind her left ear was sending signals her time was over. The year was 2026 in June, three months before the first signs of the Dead Adrenaline invasion in Beaver County, PA.*

***One thing was certain; Chloe was ready for the next level of training!***

**Chloe was undeniably ready for the Journey to continue!**

"Ok Chloe, the training as ended with me, and you have earned an unquestionable high rank in Burendo Shotokan style of fighting. Meaning you are now the second highest ranked in the Burendo way of fighting. Your dad (Sensei Clint) is the only higher ranked student, but only because he has been with me longer training, and he is your father. I have taught you everything I know that is of value in fighting, which encompasses both mental and physical aspects that make you a more complete warrior. Also, your knowledge of the Japanese language is solid, which you will need soon. Now it has only been a year of training, but what you have done equals a training regiment of 3 years. I have only focused on empty hand defense and attacks, no hand weapons of any kind were introduced, so you could be totally committed to none weapon fighting, even though your hands and feet are a weapon. Also, the non-hand weapon movements can be the same as with a weapon, such has a sword. I could have taught you many ways of fighting with weapons, especially the sword, but you need to go to the source, meaning you must be trained by none other than Kensei Miyamoto Musashi, who is the greatest swordsman in Japanese history, and was given the title of Kensei, because of his 61 undefeated duels, also he was ronin or a masterless Samurai, which occurred because when the Warring period ended, and the peace of the Edo period began.

This meant no wars, meaning no battles or fighting, so Miyamoto continued studying the sword and devoted his life to becoming the ultimate swordsmen. Chloe you must meet and train with Kensei Miyamoto Musashi and learn the secrets, and skill set of his unorthodox sword fighting techniques. Miyamoto specialized in both the long and close-range use of a Katana, and a shorter sword called Wakizashi sword. It will be up to you to survive his training, and it will be up to Kensei Miyamoto if he wants to train you. Now Sensei Chloe, you have a time travel pod that Gordon Scott gave you on your trip here. I know this to be true, because Sullivan informed me of this when I spoke with him about Zombie DA(s) showing up and fighting with you and me. During that time, I told him where you needed to go next, which is the year 1634, and who you needed to find and train with. Gordon Scott sent the coordinates to that time travel pod, so you are set up when you leave to continue your journey."

"Master G, I can not put into words how much I appreciate and embrace the honor of getting to train and learn with you. The martial art training taught by you, will never be forgotten, or misused. This unbelievable fighting skill set will only be used to battle evil wherever it may hide, and the greater good will be the victor. Thank you for everything Master G."

"No worries, only positive thoughts and thank you daughter of Sensei Clint, now it is time to get a delicious meal, and rest for tomorrow's journey to the year 1634. Maybe if you are lucky, you will get the chance to train with the Sword Saint, Miyamoto Musashi in Japan and learn the Katana and Wakizashi swords. Now, the Sword Saint will be 50 years of age, eleven years before his death, which happens in the year 1645, so based on my knowledge of this man, his skill level in swordsmanship has reached pure precision and perfection.

You will have an opportunity of a lifetime to train with the best swordsman in the world, but I must warn you, Miyamoto Musashi will be a man of few words, but his actions speak volumes. Miyamoto Musashi will be the perfect blend of skill and knowledge to take you to the next level of your training. Also, Miyamoto was one of the Japanese Swordsman that believed in the Ancient Japanese folklore of the reckoning of evil coming to planet earth, and taking over humanity, so this Master Swordsman will understand what is at stake.

Chloe here is some authentic clothing from 1634 Japan, believe it, or not, Gordon Scott sent me this clothing via time travel mail. I'am not sure how he got these garments, but this will help you blend a little, even though your blond hair, blue eyes and white complexion might stand out, either way, here you go."

"Thanks Master G, pretty-cool garments, I might not blend in, but at least from a distance my clothing will not stand out. Ok I will see you in the morning, and then the next stage of my training begins."

*The night lasted long, and did not want to leave, almost has if an unknown force was holding onto this day, but finally night turned into morning and the day had arrived for Chloe to take the next leap towards her destiny, no matter the cost, no matter the challenge or sacrifice that would need to be made. After all, the human species is on the menu, and Chloe is the backup the world needs, so she was ready to move forward with her training, to save Beaver County, PA.*

# MASTER G'S CHALLENGE

## YEAR 2026

*Morning arrived with an uncertain grin and Chloe had just time traveled away to her next point of training, which happens to be the year 1634 the Edo period in Japan, a time of peace and prosperity. Master G knew this to be true and hoped for the best for Chloe. Master G believed if Japan's Warring period had ended, and the Edo period had begun, this would be the best time for Chloe to study and learn with the Sword Saint Miyamoto Musashi. As Master G pondered these thoughts, a bright bloody red-light beam shot down from the sky, as if the sky were bleeding blood from above. Then it appeared, a woman with vicious purple eyes, who looked to be calculating her attack on her prey, but this was no ordinary food item on the menu. It was Master G, and he was not happy about her arrival, and at that moment, Master G, knew he was about to battle with the Hive Queen, which could only mean one thing, it was* ***Time to Clean the Fucking Dojo!***

**The Sky is Bleeding from Above.**

**Hive Queen 2086 has come from the sky.**

**Hive Queen 2086(AKA Liz Granite)**

"Hello, let me guess, your name is Master G, and you are the fighting instructor for *The Man Called Clint,* so genuinely nice to meet you. I heard a lot about you, through my travels by way of mind sucking knowledge from the weak sad humans that had knowledge of you and your whereabouts. Let me see, oh yes, Chloe the daughter of Clint is not here now, but once had been, I can sense her presence from the past. Darn, that would have been fun, I would get to kill both Chlo, and you at the same time. Pity, oh well, I guess it will be just you on this day. If you have not figured it out, I am the Hive Queen, a name your student Clint gave me when we first met. Although, humans would say, I am the second version of the Hive Queen, because I traveled from the year 2026 to 2086, and took over a quiet warrior named Liz Granite, so if you want, you can call me Hive Queen 2086 or Liz. Now Liz Granite has served me well, as a host human, but it is time for another upgrade. I believe, it is time to take over a Master of fighting, and it just so happens there is one on the menu, which happens to be you Master G."

"Your time travel timing is not welcome, and as far as killing me you better have packed more than your empty emotional threats, because you are in my world and from the sounds of it, you have not even been able to destroy the Man Called Clint and his followers. Looks like you are the sad, pathetic Alien-Zombie Dead Adrenaline leader that just can not get things completed to be victorious. Now you come here telling me you are going to kill me, lets do this, because you have forgot the first defense in a fight, do not judge a book by its cover. No Dragon slayer blood coursing through my veins, no special powers, just my fighting skill set from many, many years of training."

*At that moment in time, Master G, decided with unflinching action, locked himself into fighting stance and was prepared to end this unearthly violence standing before him. The Hive Queen knew that Master G would be a worthy opponent, so she decided to have a secondary plan to start the hunt for Chloe and had brought one of her dead adrenaline alien entity's along with her. This abomination was in raw form, just a light sphere condensed down to the size of a marble. Hive Queen knew that Master G was strong, so a backup plan to hunt for Chloe had to be created, if for some reason Master G killed her. With this knowledge, she called out in an unusual language that sounded remarkably like a deer. Suddenly an enormous buck appeared from the wood line, and the marble light sphere was casted out towards the buck, like an evil spell, cursed upon this animal. The Buck transformed with a twisted contortion of its body and became a Dead Adrenaline Zombie Buck. Master G. did see this violent transformation taking place but never broke from his fighting stance and was waiting for the onslaught. As he watched on, the Hive Queen looked at him with total joy and told him something very disturbing.*

"Master G, this Buck Beast will hunt and find Chloe and destroy her. You see I can smell Chloe's life force and know she has just left in a time travel way. As you just saw, I have a total ability to time travel, which really is extremely easy for me and my Dead Adrenaline followers when we chose to. Now it may take moments, days, months or even years to find Chloe, but make no mistake, she will be found and annihilated. Just as you will meet your fate, by my hands, and so you know, this Buck beast is a meat eater now."

*As those final words were spoken by the Hive Queen, the Zombie Buck left out a hideous cry, which sounded like pain and suffering, but in the background the sound of joy was coming from the Hive Queen. As this was occurring the Zombie Buck began to glow and a bloody beam of light shot upward into the sky, and with this bizarre spectacle the Zombie Buck was gone. The Hive Queen began to laugh and turned to look at Master G with a sinister smile on her violent face and started to speak.*

"Now Master G, you have seen just a shred of my power, but the time has come to end your pathetic life. Let us battle, let us bleed, so we can find out who will be the victor. Enough talk, now you will see and feel the full wrath of our species."

*"With those menacing words, the Hive Queen's presence transformed into even a more vicious, crazed eyed savage, and the battle unfolded.*

***Master G Fights Hive Queen 2086***

***The Battle Raged On!***

***This battle will end with only one victor,*** *Master G must avoid a bite from Hive Queen, along with not becoming a meal, but that is not what Hive Queen 2086 wants. She wants to take over Master G's mind and body as a host to her evil entity. You see, she believes the only person that could beat the Man Called Clint is the one who trained him, but Master G is not an easy take, and the bloody battle rages on. The outcome will be the outcome, but even if Hive Queen 2086 wins or Master G wins, sacrifices will occur on this day. Soon nightfall is upon them, and the violence of their clash becomes as silent as death, and no sounds or sight remain.*

# THE SWORD SAINT

## YEAR 1634 JAPAN

*As the mist travels upward off the mountain tops, lush vegetation surrounding a village nestled silently in a forest of green appears. The name of this village is Mimasaka, which is an early village town found in the Aida district, Okayama Prefecture Japan. All places in Japan in this period have banned any foreigners into the country for political and safety reasons, so the EDO time of peace and prosperity will survive without any interference. All of this is about to change on a dynamic level of unique quality and strength because Chloe is about to arrive in the year 1634 and must meet and convince the Sword Saint Miyamoto Musashi that she is the chosen one from the future to save the human species. This must happen, so the human existence continues to thrive, until only* ***God*** *decides when judgement day happens, not a Dead Adrenaline apocalypse.*

*This man Miyamoto is a solitary man that decided after Warring period, which was the bloodiest era in Japanese history, to avoid conflict and continue embarking on further mastering of the sword, so he traveled deep into the woods away from Mimasaka village. This is where Miyamoto found his peace and continues his existence with this undeniable focus, which sword mastery requires. Miyamoto's peaceful existence is about to be interrupted by Chloe, who for the first time in her journey knows this will be a perplexing task to convince not only a man that is a deadly swordsman, but from an era with truly little technology to help explain her arrival is real.*

*The sky parts with biblical similarities, but it is not a* ***God,*** *or one of his many angels from the heavens, only a "Women Called Chloe," and she has arrived to in 1634 Japan, to continue her mission to save humanity. Chloe believes in her quest with total commitment but does have a fading believe her training up to this point is enough. Chloe will soon discover that believing and knowing are two remarkably different thought processes. As Chloe completes the time travel to 1634 Japan, her body feels different, this time no signs of slow-paced accumulation are present, she feels transformed already and adapted to the 1634 year, she is standing and living in. Meaning she will not have to leave this time-period twice to accumulate her body and mind. This result was not a predictable outcome, but it is occurring, Gordon Scott would be fascinated by this time turn of events. Chloe realized at that moment, she only needed to accumulate in one time travel period, and her body would remember, so now she can time break travel, and not have to adapt when she arrives. Chloe thought, this is just another tool in her toolbox of skills, but now she is standing on 1634 Japanese soil, and she must find Master Miyamoto Masashi and try to communicate with him in Japanese. Luckily, for Chloe, her ability to speak Japanese was good, because her dad (The Man Called Clint) had taught her a little bit of the*

*Japanese language that he learned from Master G. This was useful language knowledge, but her ability to speak Japanese only climbed to a higher level, after learning the Japanese language directly from Master G, who had lived and study the language, culture, and Martial Arts that Japan had to offer. Master G. had lived in Japan for over three years, so this was a second language to him in many ways. All of Master G's training made sense to Chloe now, including learning the Japanese language.*

*Miyamoto was known to live deep in the forest away from all other people, historically documents given by Master G, showed that the location of Miyamoto's home, which was 30 miles north of Mimasaka village. With this knowledge, Chloe starts to walk into the forest and embarks on the journey to find Miyamoto.*

"Geez Dad, I am talking aloud, just like you used to do when I was a kid. If you could here me now Dad, or should I say, "The Man Called Clint," you would be getting a real karate kick out of this. Oh well, I will just think what I am saying instead of speaking it. Let me see, it looks like I am about 15 miles into this hike, which means 15 miles more, so hopefully I will find Master Miyamoto. Something is not right; I feel or sense an unwelcome presence coming my way, time to peek behind me, oh shit, looks like movement coming from the forest trees directly behind me. Might be a sneak attack, well, the movement is for real, because here they come a group of desperate looking forest bandits with violence in their eyes.

Too bad for them because they pick the wrong women, and wrong time to show up to derail my mission. This means only one thing, **"It's Time to Clean the Fucking Dojo Forest!"** And it starts with these forest bandits looking to stop me."

***The Woman Called Chloe is Ready to Battles Forest Bandits.***

"Time to test out some of my Burendo Shotokan skills, looks like these Forest creeps are ready to cut me down with some katana style swords. I guess, they fight to win and take every advantage possible to make sure that happens, I have a count of at least seven or eight of these forest rats. They must kill their prey and take what ever valuables the victim has on them, which could be a terrible way to go. Unfortunately for these non-seven Samurai(s), I am no victim, and as my dad would say, they are not Seven Samurai, like in the 1954 Seven Samurai movie. Either way, I must fight them or die trying, because those are my choices. This will be an extremely dangerous fight, out numbered and they have hand weapons. Here goes everything, time to find an opening in the pack of forest bandits running my way, looks like a lead runner coming forward. I am going to take him out forever and get his sword, than I have half a chance to survive. I do have some sword time training logged over the years, thanks to my dad teaching me. According to my dad (AKA: The Man Called Clint or Sensei Clint), he learned most of his sword skills from Master G, although my dad always says, in the world we live in presently, the bulk of your training should be focused on empty hand defense and attack, but weapon knowledge is always a plus. I bet he might think a little different now, based on the crazy ass sword assassin coming my way. Although who plans for a trip back to 1634 Japan, let me think, what should I have packed, a sword maybe? Ok now I'am cracking myself up, time to make my move."

*At a fast-paced run, Chloe makes her way to the lead attacker. His blade slices towards, and tries to cut her stomach, but misses. Chloe moves in a circular motion and gains a position behind him, quickly grabs his wrists and hands that were holding the sword, and redirects the blade towards his mid section. The blade cuts, and he falls to the ground without warning. Chloe disarms him and takes control of the Katana sword. At that moment, Chloe realizes the Forest Bandits have surrounded her and knows this may be her last stand. Suddenly one of the Forest Bandit's screams out a word, "**Kensei**!!!" Without hesitation the Forest Bandits run off like scared children, leaving the injured man that Chloe cut down on the forest ground. Chloe looks on in amazement, wondering for a second what just happened, as they run off deep into the woods.*

***Frightened Forest Bandits***

*As the last Forest Bandit disappears, from sight, the word Kensei, bounces back into Chloe's thoughts, no shit she thinks, it means Sword Saint! This means he is here, in the Forest, and just the sight of him, blade cuts fear into the souls of men and women. With that thought, Chloe gets her mind and body balance back in working order and calls out to the Sword Saint.*

**Kensei Miyamoto Masashi! Kensei Miyamoto Masashi!!!**

*Suddenly a man appears from a remarkably close distance, which shocked Chloe, who did not sense his presence. Then the full appearance of this man was in clear view, and it could only be Kensei Miyamoto Masashi.*

***The Sword Saint***

*Chloe had found him, or was it the other way around, Miyamoto had found her. For a moment, Miyamoto looked at Chloe, as if he were sizing her up as a possible worthy opponent, it was obvious that Miyamoto never judged any book by its cover. As Chloe watch Miyamoto, he walked over to the barley alive Forest Bandit, and with the drawing of his sword from its scabbard, a quick and efficient movement took place, Miyamoto ended the dying Bandit lying on the Forest floor with slight flick of his katana sword, to the side of the neck, putting the suffering bandit out of his misery. With completion of this action, Miyamoto looked back at Chloe and then started to walk away from her, leaving the deceased body of the Forest Bandit, for carnivores' forest animals to consume, after* nightfall.

*As Chloe was watching Miyamoto walking-away, she realized this was her only chance to convince this Sword Master that he must train her in the Art of the sword, so Chloe began to speak to Miyamoto in Japanese.*

"Watashi o kunren shite kudasai (Train me), Kana jaaku suisan-suisoku motte iru kuru ni tsuchi (A evil reckoning has come to earth)."

*Miyamoto suddenly stops his movement, and turns around to glance at Chloe, nodded his head as if to say yes, then turned back around and started walking deeper into the forest. Chloe looked around for a split second and began to follow.*

# PERFECT BALANCE

## 1634 JAPAN

"Well, I made it to Miyamoto's home, and he did not kill me, so that is start. Unfortunately, he is giving me really upset bitter looks and I bet he is wondering why I'am talking to myself out-loud, especially in this strange English language. I guess, it will be up to him what happens next, but this is nerve racking, and time a ticking. Oh shit, he just went into his cottage and closed the front door."

*Nightfall silently closes in, and the cottage door opens, and Miyamoto finally decides to speak with Chloe, who was waiting outside of his small sized cottage.*

"You know my name, so you know my ability to survive, you ask me to train you because the evil reckoning has arrived on earth. You are a foreigner with blond hair and blue eyes, and you are not from this time I live in, because no Man, Women or child would ever set foot into my domain asking me to train them. I know that I'am a living legend to the people of Japan, and respected by most, but feared by all. Yet you do not fear me, and you stand here asking, and in someways demanding that I train you in the art of the sword. I do not want to know fully the reason you must have me train you, but it is your destiny. And let me tell you, I believe in destiny, because my destiny brought us to this chapter in both our lives. Go into the cottage, food and water is inside and a place to rest is set up for you. I will see you in the morning, and we will begin without hesitation to continue these paths of destiny."

"Ok, Kensei Miyamoto Masashi, but are you sure you want me to stay in your home for the night."

*Kensei Miyamoto smiled in a profoundly powerful way.* "This is not my home, the forest is my home, and I sleep wherever I want to, I have many places of comfort within these woods." *And with that, Miyamoto walked off.*

*The entire conversation took Chloe off guard, she did not expect such dialogue between them, based on her information from Master G, that Miyamoto was a man of few words. Also, she was very appreciative that Master G, had taught her Japanese, because as Miyamoto spoke and she spoke back to him, it sounded and felt like they were speaking English. As if the Japanese language had become her first language for this part of her journey. Chloe smiled and thought this language situation was like the 1999 movie The 13th Warrior, staring Antonio Banderas, where the Viking language became natural and understandable, just by him hearing the Vikings speak. Although Chloe knew it was a little different because she already knew how to speak Japanese, but what the Hell she thought, nothing is better than movie comparisons, which she could thank her dad for. Martial Arts, Movies, and books were always something her dad made sure Chloe had available to her, for the learning value, but also just for the fun of it. With that last thought, Chloe went inside the cottage for the night in hopes to get some rest.*

*Morning arrived like an uncontrollable rabid dog; and the sound of this violence was about to erupt. Chloe had been up for about 1 hour in the early morning hours and began to hear loud voices outside of the cottage.*

"Why do I hear loud arguing going on outside. Shit! It looks like the Forest bandits have returned. I wonder how they knew to come here, I guess it does not matter now because the Japanese language I'am hearing coming from this rough group of violent men is not friendly. They know someone is inside this cottage, and they want blood."

*It was showtime, and the movie playing was going to be a very graphic, bloody battle to the death. Live or die, Chloe had no choice but to fight, at least she had the Katana sword taken from the slain Bandit from yesterday and her remarkable Burendo Shotokan skills. One of the bandits, tried to open the cottage door, and Chloe met him with a sharp katana blade thrust to the solar plexus, (area just below the center of the rib cage) dropping him like a math test memory that you will never need again. This left, what looked to be five more bandits, who had separated into a large half moon circle around the outside front of the cottage.*

"Ok, time to end the rest of them, I better find out who the alpha bandit is in this group of renegades."

*Chloe surveyed the group and focused in on the one that did not have his sword drawn, this man was just standing there looking directly at her, with absolutely no emotion on his face. Chloe thought, this had to be the leader, so she decided to call him out.*

"Anata wa ridadenakereba narimasen! (You must be the leader)"

*With a look of total hate, this man yelled out at Chloe, these words.*

"Anita wa watashi no Otto o koroshimashita! (You killed my brother)."

*Once Chloe heard those words from this deranged forest bandit, she knew the time for talking had left the building, just like ELVIS would do at the end of his concerts. Even though she most definitely started the death of this man's brother, but Miyamoto ended the pain and suffering quickly for him. Chloe understood that blood was still on her hands, no matter how justifiable this killing turned out to be, but from the Leader of the forest bandit's perspective, she was the enemy.*

"Ok than, time to end this here and now, I have had about enough of these guys showing up and interrupting my destiny. My sword fighting ability might not be up for this challenge, but if I blend in some Burendo Shotokan, I will have a chance."

*The blades were slicing through the air, attacks, and counter attacks were occurring faster and faster. Chloe managed to cut down two of the* ***Forest Bandits*** *with four slices of her katana blade, two blade cut movements for each, causing them to collapse, and bleed out onto the Forest carpet. Three Forest bandits were still standing, which included the leader brother of the bandit that Miyamoto took pity on and ended his pain and suffering. The other two forest bandits* *were different, each of them seemed to be more present in the moment, they were waiting for Chloe to advance and make the first move. Almost has if they knew she would not survive this day, Chloe thought, the other Forest bandits were amateurs that had fought her before. This got Chloe thinking that these two were not just Forest bandit scavengers looking for their next meal randomly, but Samurais that have went* ***Ronin****, and now they were a sword for hire. Hired by the so-called leader of the other bandits, who just wants revenge for the death of his brother. Now a Samurai warrior becomes Ronin for many reasons, some honorable, and some not. Chloe knew that if in fact these are Samurai's that went ronin standing before her, the chances for her to survive have drop to dangerous levels. As Chloe stood there knowing death was a blade cut away, a shadowy figure appeared next to her, it was Miyamoto, and with a powerful and direct voice he spoke to Chloe.*

"Step back, I will finish this!"

*And just like before the words sounded like English to her, due to the solid grasp of the Japanese language. Miyamoto began to speak to the three-man remaining men. One a forest bandit and the other two, swords for hire.*

"You know who I am and what I believe to be true and righteous, so leave these woods now, or your final breath will be at the edge of my sword blade. One of you is just a simple, misguided Forest bandit that wants revenge for the death of a brother that chose his path and knew the consequences. Now, you other two think you are Masterless Samurais like me, but you are unshakably mistaken. You see, wisdom is not something you can steal or buy with wealth, either you have it, or you do not. You both have lost your way, and your master is *shiharai (payment)*. Wisdom will never find you, only the cold blade of greed"

*Chloe began to think outlook.* "Shit, this just got real, and Kensei Miyamoto Masashi is not fucking around. This is going to be something to see, two evil Samurais against one True and just Samurai. **Dishonorable's vs Honorable,** a tale as ancient as time."

*No matter what Chloe expected to see, nothing could have prepared her for the skilled violence that Miyamoto was about to unleash on this day. No ancient Japanese historical records could capture this pure precise sword cutting.*

*Both dishonorable Samurais decided to move to the front and back of Miyamoto, thinking that he could only focus on one attacker at a time, they were both wrong, because he was focusing on neither, but his blades were focusing on both unworthy Samurais. Miyamoto with the speed of a lighting flash, and power of an earthquake, revealed a second sword, the WAKIZASHI (Shorter companion sword), along with the Katana (Longer primary sword). You see, Miyamoto would be using a two-sword style technique called Niten Ichi Ryu (two heavens as one), using both swords at the same time. At the very moment, the second sword appeared, the dishonorable Samurais knew they must react quickly, so with a prepared movement, both Samurais began to attack Miyamoto and tried to cut him down like an old tree in the forest. One blade cut was high to low downward slice too Miyamoto's back shoulder blade area, which would damage the lung area, and the other blade cut was a straight thrust movement, which was heading towards the front left side heart area of Miyamoto. Both sword cuts would be a fatal attack if effectively used, Miyamoto sensed the in coming blades and decided to give them both back their deadly gift.*

*Miyamoto understood that his movements must be without mistakes because he only had one chance to return the gift, based on this, he moved closer to the disgraced samurai standing behind him, and with his body bladed he could see the hands, holding the sword by just a slight movement of his head and eyes. Miyamoto now had a perfect vantage point of both of his attackers and now his mind, body, sharpen eyes, long-sword, and short-sword were ready to taste blood.*

*Then the onslaught began, both evil Samurais used their swords at the same time, believing that Miyamoto would not be able to defend against both attacks at the same time. They will soon find out in deadly fashion that Miyamoto has the mastery to use both swords simultaneously in completely different directs of defense and attack. And with this, Miyamoto uses his WAKIZASHI sword to High (Jodan) block and parry the Dishonorable Samurai's Katana blade, and with this movement the enemy Samurai flipped around with his back exposed. Miyamoto ends the counterattack with a-single handed downward blade cut slicing through to the lung area of this misguided fool. At the same time, this fantastically fatal blade defense and attack occurred, Miyamoto was also parrying the other Enemy Samurai 's Katana blade with just the very tip of his Katana blade, catching the enemy sword, than sliding along the top of the blade and puncturing into the left chest heart area, causing a fatal wound. Miyamoto paused for only one second and reflected on his kill, he glanced at the disgraced Samurais has they fell to the forest floor covered in their own pathetic blood, grasping for the breath of life. As the last breath of air exited the dying dishonorable Samurais, Miyamoto stood over them and said a most unexpected thing.*

"Now you have grasped completely as death as arrived, if you live by the blade, you die by its edge. Real Warriors must never live by the blade, but live with it, make it a part or a way of life, respect the blade, honor the blade, use the blade for a righteous cause, protect the weak and never use the blade for evil, but only to release a person from his or her evil misguided ways. A true Samurai finds a **Perfect Balance** between **Sword** and **Warrior**, you two dishonorable Samurais never found that perfect balance and never will."

***The Sword Saint Miyamoto Masashi finds Perfect Balance***

*And with these powerful and true words, Miyamoto the Sword Saint, walks away from the two disgraced Samurais,*

*over to Chloe and begins to speak to her, as this was occurring the vengeful brother looked at Miyamoto and ran away into the forest.*

"You now have a place to stay Chloe, out of the elements, our training has already started, you have managed to survive with just a small amount of sword training. I can work with you and get your sword skills up to a level that no man, women, or beast would ever be a challenge. I will be back in an hour, and we will continue your training. Also, do not worry about the vengeful brother that has run off, he will return with others and try to kill you again. This will be good for your training that is why I let him live."

*Chloe thought for a confused moment and began speaking.*

"Yes Sir, sounds good, I have to say, how did they know to come to this cottage so far out in the woods."

"Well Chloe, this was the cottage of the brother that you started to kill yesterday, and I finished off out of pity for him."

"So, I was fishing bait for the fish to show up basically Kensei Miyamoto?"

*Miyamoto smiled slightly, as if it were amusing to him.*

"Exactly, like I said your training has already started, see you in an hour."

*As Chloe pondered this morning's events, she understood this was not a controlled environment. Obviously, the blood-stained forest ground caused by the two dead unworthy Samurais is a definite reminder that this is real, and death is death. This is not a movie, not video game, not a sport competition, but deadly combat with only one survivor. For the first time in her training, Chloe realized that no one is a winner in this type of environment, but only a survivor.*

## *MAKE FEAR YOUR FRIEND*

### 1634 JAPAN

*The hour had passed, and Miyamoto returned as he said he would, and the training of a Samurai continued. Chloe would have to focus totally on the teachings of Miyamoto, because training had a very brutal edge to it. No controlled environment, no time to say, I will figure it out next time, only survival or death were the choices. Although if Chloe survives, she can stop and think about what she did that almost got her killed. A lesson of living is always a good lesson.*

"Time to learn why the sword is not only a weapon, but also part of you. Wherever you go the sword or swords go with, if you die, the honorable thing to do is bury you with your sword. I promise you three things Chloe, first, if you survive my training, you will become the first *American Female Samurai,* second, you will respect the sword beyond its ability to kill, and third, if you die here in 1634 Japan, I will bury you with your sword, unless I die before you. Now let us begin your quest for knowledge."

"Geez, Kensei Miyamoto you really know how to make a person feel welcome."

*Miyamoto looked at Chloe and smiled.*

"Chloe your lucky I get your humor, which I enjoy, hopefully you can keep this sense of humor about you, because this sword training you are about to embark on will take a solid mind set."

*Miyamoto wasted no time in his training methods, within the first hour, Chloe was learning that the hands that hold the sword are a prized target of the attached weapon. Miyamoto explained that if you hurt the hands that hold the weapon with devastating cut, how ever so slight, you have gained the advantage. Miyamoto explained in detail that even if an attacker does not have a sword or other type of weapon in his hand, cut them anyway. Also, the feet or legs of an attacker are targets, to prevent a kick attack or even a knee technique. Plus, if you take out his or her foundation, your advantage improves. Miyamoto went onto say that limb attacks can be fatal for your opponent, if you cut an artery or certain veins, but still treat these blade cuts as a starting point of your defense and attack. Meaning that any attack to the limbs of your opponent is only a distraction to blade cut a vital kill area, something that will put the attacker down and end the battle. Miyamoto explained what blade cuts to make and how to redirect the blade after a limb cut happens.*

*Chloe was amazed with the knowledge and speed at which Miyamoto taught her and knew that she must absorb what he was teaching with the same intentions.*

**The Training Begins**

***Miyamoto was an extremely focused teacher, and the sword training was a blend of techniques and pressure testing the blade cuts.***

*The weather was growing colder, but still extremely comfortable for training. Even though the sword training was physically and mentally taxing, Chloe was grasping each movement or technique and practiced even harder when she was not understanding certain sword concepts Miyamoto was teaching. Like a flick of a blade, 6 months passed, and Chloe had been training in the way of the sword with full commitment. Chloe determined her arrival to 1634 Japan was at the end of April, and now it was the end of September, which was the same month that the Dead Adrenaline apocalypse started in 2026 Beaver County, Pennsylvania. During this time, Chloe explained to Miyamoto about Dragon Slayer blood, and how it has improved her fighting ability, along with undiscovered powers that may show up somewhere along the line. Also, Chloe talked about about how the Dead Adrenaline started and her dad, "The Man Called Clint" who has been battling to stop the destruction and take over by this alien force of evil. Miyamoto was surprisingly interested in the origin of the Dead Adrenaline apocalypse, and told Chloe, he always believed a reckoning was coming, and this was why he trained without interruption in the way of the sword, so he would be ready if this wrath on humanity ever showed up. With that Miyamoto told Chloe, with his training and her ability, she would become one of the best swordswomen in the entire world.*

*The training continued with Miyamoto, and Chloe was becoming an extraordinary swordswoman.*

"Chloe you are a fast learner, whatever system of fighting you have trained in before is serving you well. Even some of your sword cuts were decent at the very start of our training.

"Well Kensei Miyamoto, my training is in Burendo Shotokan, and within this system, knowledge of weapons is part of this training, the sword being one of them."

"Interesting, whoever taught you the sword movements, respected this weapon."

"This would be Master G, and my dad, Master G was his instructor."

"This Master G, and your father must have understood *to make fear your friend.*"

"OK Kensei, I am trying to grasp exactly what that means, *make fear your friend.*"

"You will discover what this means as our training moves along, but now it is time to stop and get some food to eat. I hope you like deer venison because that is what I will be hunting. You see Chloe, I only kill for two reasons, one to survive and two for food. I kill only when I have too, and when I am of need of subsistence. Those who kill or take more than they need too, show complete dishonor to the way of the sword. I will be back shortly with our food, so get a fire started, so after I get the deer prepared, we can cook some of the meat. The rest of the meat will put in the ground, deep enough to keep it cold and protected from other animals looking for a meal.

This deer, depending on size usually last me 100-160 days, if I eat a half pound a day, but with you here it will go faster. Also, with our training regiment, we will need more food to eat. Deer is not my only food source, but I stock up on it, so when the weather is too treacherous to hunt, I will still have the food I need. Currently, we still have enough deer meat for now, but we are going to need more, because it is no longer me eating."

"Ok Kensei Miyamoto, I will get the fire started and await your return."

*Miyamoto went deep into the forest and only brought his swords with him; he could have brought a bow and arrow but always sought the opportunity to test his sword skills. You see, Miyamoto would be hunting this deer with just his swords. The Katana in his right hand and the Wakizashi in his left, a pair of swords called Daisho, which means "big-little." The hunt begins, and Miyamoto knows the landscape, almost better than the creatures that live in this forest. Then it appears, an enormous size Buck standing on the edge of a forest cliff, looks to be alone, but does not look right, some blood is seeping from its fur, and when Miyamoto gets a good look at the eyes of this animal, they looked to have been dipped in blood.*

*Just as this was unraveling, the grotesque Buck starts to slam its hoof onto the ground and lets out a loud hideous sound, which sounded like pain and suffering, with a hint of happiness. Miyamoto prepares for battle and tries to get the high ground on the cliffs edge. He knows this must be the Dead Adrenaline showing up to find Chloe, so the time to kill has arrived again. The Dead Adrenaline Zombie Buck is enormous and looks like nothing ever seen in this forest.*

*Miyamoto has never seen the likes of this creature but knows it must end here and now. Then with a shocking advancement of rage the DA Zombie Buck leaps towards Miyamoto. Miyamoto reacts without mercy, knowing he must be precise with his blade cuts.*

**ZOMBIE BUCK ATTACKS**

*Miyamoto unleashes a fury of precise blade cuts, cutting through the blood coated fur of the Zombie Buck. By skill and luck of the blade, the kill shot has landed, Miyamoto had no*

*knowledge of a weak spot on this Zombie Buck, but always knew to blade cut, until your opponent falls. Miyamoto looks on as this beast starts to fade on the cliff side, and knows this kill had to happen, but wished it would have been for purposes of gathering meat.*

**A DYING ZOMBIE BUCK**

*The last signs of life leave the Zombie Buck's carcass, so Miyamoto leaves silently from the cliff side and decides to hunt smaller game for tonights dinner. He returns shortly to the cottage with some rabbits and squirrels and does not tell*

*Chloe about the Zombie Buck attack. As cruel and unpredictable as this might be, Miyamoto considers this more training, so not knowing what might be coming next only makes you a better fighter.*

"Chloe I am back, let us get these small animals prepared and cook them up."

"Ok, Kensei Miyamoto, but just so you know, I will not eat rabbit, because as a child I used to have a couple as pets, which must have left a soft spot for these little creatures."

*Kensei Miyamoto looks at a Chloe with a smile, and thinks to himself, even though the rabbits are dead, Chloe still respects these little creatures and will not waiver from her position. With another smile Miyamoto starts to laugh aloud and is glad Chloe did not have a pet deer as a child. Then he speaks to Chloe with another smile and bit of seriousness.*

"Well Chloe, it is good to know there is a line you will not cross, luckily for you I have brought some squirrels to eat, along with the rabbits, so I guess you did not have squirrels as pets, so enjoy."

*As night began to fall like a silent enemy, Miyamoto gets up, leaves, and walks away deep into the forest. This is what he had did every night for the past 6 months, Chloe had no idea where he went or where he slept but knew he would return with the morning light to continue her training.*

*As the sun light bursted through the tree line of the forest, and into the cabin, Chloe realized that Miyamoto had not shown up this morning for some unknown reason, so she got prepared for the days training and waited.*

"Well, no sign of Kensei Miyamoto, I wonder what happened, I guess I will continue working my single and double hand sword cuts, as I talk out-loud to the forest."

*Hours into Chloe's blade cuts, she begins to here sounds from the forest, suddenly five men reveal themselves from the forest clearing. One of the men looked familiar, Chloe realizes at that moment, it was the vengeful brother of the forest bandit killed 6 months ago. This vengeful brother has returned, but this time he brought four men with him that looked to be former Samurais with payment on their mind. Chloe thought, if they kill her, this vengeful brother will pay them, and that was not going to happen.*

"Enough of this bullshit, it is **Time to Clean the Fucking Forest!** Ok, let us do this, you scavengers of the forest, all you do is take and never give, now it is time, for me to show you the way of a true warrior."

*Chloe dropped back into unique sword stance, holding the Katana sword with both hands, she would only test the use of one sword on this day, not "Niten Ichi Ryu," which is using two swords simultaneously. Miyamoto had taught her this sword fighting method but told her to only use this style when absolutely needed. Miyamoto told Chloe the meaning of this, is "two heavens as one", which essentially means using two swords as one weapon.*

*Chloe begins another fight for her life, five against one, four dishonorable Samurais, and one vengeful brother. Blades cuts begin to happen, and Chloe manages to avoid any injuries or fatal blows. Finally, after 30 minutes of battling, Chloe lands a fatal blade cut to one of the dishonorable Samurais and uses this dishonorable Samurais body as a shield before he falls, and sword thrust throw his body into another dishonorable Samurai. Dropping two for the price of one sword cut. The two remaining dishonorable Samurais look onward at Chloe; they realize with her savage like sword cuts that Kensei Miyamoto has trained her. Knowing this, they both understand they must kill her, so there is no chance of her telling Miyamoto about their arrival on this day. The disgraced Samurais begin to circle Chloe, knowing she will have a demanding time focusing on two moving targets, and without telegraphing their blade techniques, they both blade cut at exactly at the same time. Within those fleeing seconds, Chloe removes her Wakisashi sword from its scabbard, now with the Katana and Wakizashi sword in each of her hands, the odds have just evened up.*

**Chloe prepares to end this attack**

*Chloe movements are precise, she slightly steps off the center line, and blades her body in a position, so her eyes can scan quickly at both opponents' attack. Like an artist placing paint on a canvas, Chloe begins to paint, simultaneously blade cutting both of dishonorable Samurais hands, causing massive blood loss, and grip strength to weaken. These cuts in their raw form cause the attackers sword cuts to fall off the centerline of their attack, which is just where Chloe will be. Chloe follows each attacker's arms upward towards there head with each of her blades, and with this motion, both disgraced dishonorable scavenger Samurais are decapitated. Both heads roll away from their bodies and land next to each other. As the lifelessness lays on the forest floor, a late September chill is in the air, steam comes off the dead disgraced Samurais and blood begins to pour like a dark red blanket around their decapitated heads. Chloe realizes she just made fear her friend, just as Miyamoto told her she would discover what this means. Meaning if you befriend the battle, you will never fear it.*

**Dishonorable Samurais Exist No More**

*With this thought Chloe looks up and see the vengeful brother, who had just seen the violent battle, as she looks at him, he runs off, knowing if he returns, more dishonorable Samurais would be on his pay roll to have her exterminated. Chloe does not care and makes friends with the fear of more returning.*

**Vengeful Brother Runs Off**

# UNNATURAL CREATURE

## 1634 JAPAN

*Silence surrounds the carcass of the Dead Adrenaline infected Buck lying lifeless on the cliff side where Miyamoto left his kill for nature to absorb. Death comes in many forms, but always has the same outcome on earth, a final ending. The buck is dead, but the evil entity is clinging onto its Dead Adrenaline evil life force. Miyamoto had injured the Buck severely and had caused enough blade destruction to drop the deer to a near fatal end, but the Dead Adrenaline entity is surviving and waiting for a new host to infect. Then it happens, an enormous size Ussuri or Ezo Brown Bear that Japanese call Kumui (God of the Mountain) comes slumbering along the cliffs edge and spots the blood-soaked deer. This species of bear has darker fur than typical brown bear and is far more aggressive by nature. This bear senses something is wrong and pauses in its tracks and does not go near the Buck, as if it knows the violence that awaits is even deadlier in power than the God of the Mountain. Only seconds passed and than like a well-placed throwing star, the Dead Adrenaline light sphere captures the bear's mind and body. No struggle or resistance occurred, because this unexpected takeover caught the bear completely off guard, but this* **God of the Mountain** *embraces the violence with total partnership. You see a Ussuri bear diet is mostly vegetarian, but it is able kill any prey that enters its* *habitat, and usually this species finds burrows at a lower elevation, such as a hillside, unlike the Ussuri black bear species that prefers higher elevations such as a cliffs edge. But, on this day, destiny stepped in and for some compelling reason this Ussuri Brown bear decided to go to higher elevations in search of food and a den for the upcoming winter. This chance meeting between Bear and Dead Adrenaline entity has turned this Ussuri Brown Bear into a meat eater. The hunt has begun, and the hunger will guide this violent beast to its prey. This unnatural creature, Kumui!* ***The GOD of the MOUNTAIN*** *has no equal, and the true test for life or death is coming.*

**KUMUI, THE GOD OF THE MOUNTAIN IS COMING!**

*Several more hours pass, and Miyamoto has not returned, so Chloe decides to venture into the forest in hopes to find him somewhere in the near by area.*

*Twenty minutes later Miyamoto returns only to discover Chloe is gone, he looks down on the forest floor and sees the decapitated heads of the dishonorable Samurais. Miyamoto smiles and nods his head with approval, knowing Chloe is becoming the first ever American female Samurai in Japanese history.*

"*Kensei*! Are you near, can you hear me, I am just wondering what is going on with today's training! Well, I guess all the creatures in the forest, must think I am a crazy American women talking to myself. Mmm, this must be part of my training today, fighting off dishonorable Samurais, and doing it all by myself. It will be interesting to see what the rest of the day has in-store for me."

*Chloe may live or die to regret what she just said aloud, because what is only seconds away from showing up, will not stop, it is hungry, violent, alien, and wild on a level beyond a human's comprehension.*

"Well, I better go back to the cottage, to see if Miyamoto returned and is waiting for me. Hello! Creatures of the forest it is me again giving you my thoughts in surround sound, sometimes I just crack myself up."

*Chloe's moment of humor is shattered like glass striking steel, and now she knows for certain the true test of her sword skill will be pushed, beyond the boundaries that no one could have visualized. A rumbling and breaking of trees are echoing through the forest wind, something was moments away from her location, it sounded vicious with the huffing, jaw-popping and loud growls of hate. Then it appears into view, Kumui!* ***The God of the Mountain*** *was galloping towards Chloe at an extremely fast violent pace, and this was not a bluff charge. Nothing was going to stop this abomination, it was here for one reason, and one reason only, to end Chloe. This unthinkable clash was about to happen without warning, without time to think, and without any help. Just Chloe, and her two swords, this will be a battle that makes a legend, a leader, and warrior that can face anything. It was time to put Kensei Miyamoto, Master G's, and her father, the Man Called Clint's teachings into full use, because on this day in time, she either lives or dies a Samurai!!!*

**Chloe faces Kumui, The God of The Mountain.**

"Oh shit! This crazy ass bear has the Dead Adrenaline disease, not sure how this happened. No time to think about this, I only have time to kill this prehistoric bear before I become a Samurai shit sandwich."

*Chloe uses the NITEN ICHI RYU sword technique, which is two swords used simultaneously with fury, purpose, and a deadly outcome. Chloe moves to the left side of Kumui and simultaneously cuts the front paw and rear paw, slicing inward from the outside in, causing a continuous motion of both blades, which intentionally has the sword blades cross, and Kumui is cut a second time in the same area by the Niten Ichi*

*Ryu technique. During this fantastic movement, Kumui does inflict damage back on Chloe, and injures her right shoulder by biting Chloe, which causes Chloe to drop her Katana sword from her right hand. Blood begins to gush from the bear bite; this outcome prevents Chloe from slicing upward towards Kumui's neck and head area. The injury is severe, but Chloe's manages to get behind Kumui and starts to slice the entire back and spine area of the Kumui. The Wakizashi sword is a shorter sword, so Chloe keeps her body in close with every slice of the blade and advances the blade to base of Kumui head. The Wakizashi sword thrust upward and forward into the back of the head and neck area. As this violent attack is going down, Kumui starts to fall forward onto its right side, breaking the fall with the right front and rear paws. Chloe starts to roll away from Kumui as the beast collapses onto forest floor, but the left side whips upward, impacting Chloe. With this uncontrolled earthquake movement, Chloe is flung through the air and cracks off a large Japanese Oak tree.*

*Her body falls to the forest floor, and no movement or any signs of life are present. Kumui is still alive but injured from Chloe's blade cuts. Also, the Wakizashi sword is firmly stuck in the base of Kumui skull, but Kumui is not stopping, this bear is hungry and slowly moves towards Chloe's lifeless body. Just as this is unfolding, Miyamoto shows up and is standing next to Chloe 's damage body, he quickly kneels beside her and checks for life. Miyamoto realizes at that very moment Chloe did not survive; he thinks of all the time spent with Chloe and training her, just for it to end in this horrific way.*

***MIYAMOTO REALIZES CHLOE DID NOT SURVIVE***

*A complete sadness falls into his mind, then anger, then control, Miyamoto removes his Katana sword from his scabbard, and is ready to battle Kumui,* ***The God of the Mountain!*** *Kumui starts to move in for another kill, but than something extraordinary happens.*

"It's okay Kensei Miyamoto, I got this."

*Miyamoto feels a hand on his shoulder, and he hears Chloe's voice, Miyamoto turns and see Chloe standing beside him.*

“Yep, Kensei it is me, back from the dead, no more fatal injuries, all healed up. My Dragon Slayer superpower kicked in, crazy, I can not be killed, at least not this way. Might be some type of injury or way to take me out, but a bite from an infected Dead Adrenaline Bear, and waffled off a huge tree, is not one of them. Now if you do not mind, I liked to finish off this prehistoric Dead Adrenaline Bear, finally.”

*Miyamoto smiles, steps back from Chloe, and nods his head of approval. The battle is back on* ***Chloe*** *vs* ***Kumui the God of The Mountain!***

“Ok you unnatural beast, time to end your suffering, I have no sword yet, but I do not need one to finish you.”

*Chloe works her way to the weak side of Kumui the Bear and lands a powerful full jumping side kick to the rear hip joint of Kumui. Kumui thrashes his head about trying to bite Chloe. Chloe manages to bounce off the rear hip area upward towards the Wakizashi blade stuck in the base of Kumui skull. With one last leap upward, Chloe grabs the handle of the sword, and twist the blade to the right and left, and with total speed and power, Chloe pulls downward on the sword blade and slices Kumui completely in half, minus a few inches from completely cutting Kumui totally in two.* ***Kumui, The God of The Mountain,*** *spills open like red wine covering the dinner table. No more vicious sounds of huffing, jaw-popping and loud growls of hate, Kumui has become another failed attempt to stop Chloe.*

*Chloe takes a moment, and thinks about this Dead Adrenaline entity sent to destroy her, and how it has only made her stronger. As this thought quickly travels through Chloe's conscious, something unpredictable happens. Kumui the bear is dead, but the Dead Adrenaline entity remains and is injured but not annihilated. Suddenly a small marble size light sphere emerges from the right temple area of Kumui, and with great intent this Dead Adrenaline entity speed towards Kensei Miyamoto, but Miyamoto skill is strong, and he will never be a victim.*

*As the evil Dead Adrenaline light sphere is within seconds of striking Miyamoto, a silence comes over the forest, and a loud ringing sound begins to echo through the forest air. Kensei Miyamoto reacts with one exact blade cut, slicing the evil light sphere in half, causing both halves to fall to the ground. A blade cut that only the Sword Saint could have made. While on the forest ground, a blue and red light spark off both halves of the sphere. Then both halves go completely dark and leave off a smell of death.*

*Chloe looks at Kensei Miyamoto and yells these words.*

"This is why you are the Sword Saint and will always be the Master of the sword!"

*Miyamoto responds back to Chloe.*

“After what I have seen today, you are more than just a skilled swordswoman. You have crossed the threshold between the boundaries of earthly fighting skills obtained and Cho Taikoku (Superpowers). Ok, time to go back to the cottage, rest, and you will find out what is in store for you tomorrow.”

“Yes Sir, I guess today, I found out that I can not be killed like everyone else, what a cool ass superpower. This gives me an advantage on an elevated level, but I’am sure my body and mind can die if the right attack occurs, so I better fight as if my life depends on it. See you tomorrow, Kensei.”

*Miyamoto nods with approval and disappears into the forest.*

# *BEYOND SAMURAI*

## 1634 JAPAN

*The morning arrives and a white carpet of snow has fallen throughout the forest, which is very unusual for late September in Japan. Miyamoto shows up and believes the snow fall is a sign that a change as come over the forest. A beautiful silence travels through the air, as if the forest creatures large and small are awaiting something fantastic to occur. Chloe comes outside and meets Miyamoto, who is standing in front of the cottage, holding a bow and arrow, and just as their eyes meet, Miyamoto spins around and launches the arrow directly into the forest woods. The arrow vanishes high up into a treetop, then a man dressed in village clothes plummets into view from the treetop. Chloe realizes this man is the vengeful brother coming back for another try at her assassination. The silence in the forest is only broken for a brief moment as this vengeful brother smacks off the snow-covered ground at high speed. Miyamoto spins back around facing Chloe and says these words.*

"Training is over!"

*Just as Miyamoto looks at Chloe and says those words, twelve dishonorable Samurais appear in the distance, standing by the crumbled body of the dead vengeful brother. Miyamoto does not turn around, but Chloe knows that Miyamoto is aware of their presence and Miyamoto tells Chloe this.*

"No complete payment will happen now with a dead vengeful brother, so these dishonorable Samurais will take the money they have made for just showing up and forget about the money they might have made if they were successful in ending you. Obviously, they would have lost that fight, and these weak dishonorable Samurais know this."

"I see Kensei, they are leaving one by one, and the last pathetic Samurai has just slipped away into the forest."

"This is a good thing, now I can complete the last step you must take to fulfill your training."

"Absolutely Kensei Miyamoto, I am ready for what ever battle you throw my way."

"Chloe, you see, I know this to be true, and that is why your training is over, you have mastered my teachings I have revealed to you. As with any art of fighting, be it with a weapon or not, there is always more to improve on and learn. This is exceedingly rare occasion, where I do not believe this to be the case with you. You are a unique warrior that has a special gift or gifts still to come, so I must make sure your knowledge of sword fighting does not just belong only to my way of training. You must still have room for your Burendo Shotokan way, and other ways of battle, you have yet to train in. I hope this all makes sense, if it does not, it will in the extremely near future."

"For some unknown reason Kensei, I do get what you are saying, and I know my training is ending with you, and there will be a new training regime on the horizon, and all will be revealed."

"This is an uncontrollable fact, your next level of training is coming, but before you continue your journey. I have a small but especially important ceremony planned for you."

*The silence returned to the forest, and like a scene from a cool Samurai movie, Chloe is standing in the snow-covered forest with a backdrop of trees as a small sized fox, which signifies luck begin's to watch this historical moment unfold like a chapter from a Dead Adrenaline book. Miyamoto stands before Chloe and tells her what she has carried out.*

"Chloe, you have completed all the training, both practice and for real. You have made the sword a part of you, your strength, wisdom, and emotion run through the steel of any sword you use for justice, peace, and prosperity. You are now and forever be swordswomen, and with that you are the first American women to become a Samurai. But, talking about all these words said on this historical day, are not enough. You must understand you are not just a Samurai sister, but you are **Beyond Samurai,** Cho Taikoku (Superpower) and Kenjutsu (Sword Skill) meshed in an unstoppable way. I release you from my training, and here is a set of swords from my personal collection. One is a Katana sword, and one is a Wakizashi short sword, a high caliber set of swords, forged with Tamahagane steel or "Jewel steel" as we call it.

The best of the best! You may never use these swords in battle, but either way, this is a gift to honor you and your unduplicated accomplishments, remember this, you are **Beyond Samurai!"**

**Kensei Bestows Chloe with The Jewel Steel Swords.**

*Chloe is very thankful and knows her training with Kensei Miyamoto Musashi is once in a lifetime and realizes she would not have experienced this phenomenal sword training, had she not had her age reversed from 78 years old, back to 23 again. In life most things or opportunities pass by like distance memories, but time travel changes everything, and even periods in time you never lived in are possible.*

*Another morning arrives in the forest, and it is time for Chloe to be time traveled to her next location of training, but where could that be and with who would her training continue with.*

"Good morning, Kensei, I hope all is well with you."

"Yes Chloe, all is well on this crisp forest morning. Do you have your things prepared for your next journey."

"I do Kensei, and I just want to thank you again for everything you have taught me, it will definitely give me an advantage for the battles to come, especially the one in 2026 Beaver County, Pennsylvania."

"Ok then, I know you have some sort of time travel pod with you Chloe, which would bring you to your next location."

"How do you know this Kensei, I really never told you in detail how I got to 1634 Japan from the future."

"You see, I know this Chloe because I met and spoke with a man by the name of Gordon Scott from the future, he showed up one night and found me in the forest. I would have cut him down, but he started to talk about you, and I knew this had to be a man from the future. Gordon told me that they are surviving barely and are constantly on the move to avoid capture, death, or turning into one of those Dead Adrenaline soldiers. He wanted me to tell you to continue your quest for training and knowledge, and to never give up, because the worlds salvation is counting on you."

"Wow! Gordon Scott is a very brilliant man, and if it weren't for him, I would not be here right now."

"I understand Chloe, and based on my impression of Gordon, he sounded knowledgeable and believed in everything he said. Gordon gave me what he called time travel pod destination, which will take you to your next location in time. I did not understand how this would happen, but he said you would."

"Yep, these coordinates will be my next place I will go for my training, I guess Gordon did not tell you where or with who I would be training with."

"The only thing Gordon said was the location and scale of training would be on a Medieval level, which will be unbelievable in nature. Sounds like a shit sandwich to me Chloe."

"Why Kensei, you made a joke, I guess there is a first time for everything."

"No Chloe, I have been making jokes this whole time, you just do not get my blade cutting jokes."

"Ha! Okay Kensei you win."

"Well, it is time Chloe to continue your quest for knowledge, skill and peace."

"Ok Kensei, I got my gear, and I am ready to time travel out of here."

*Chloe walks over to Kensei Miyamoto and bows and tells him he is a one-of-a-kind person, and it was incredible honor to meet and train under his guidance. Miyamoto smiles and tells Chloe; it was his honor. Chloe slowly walks away from Miyamoto over to a clearing in the forest, the Time Travel pod is prepared, and the process begins.*

*As this is occurring Chloe sees ten or more dishonorable Samurais appear and surround Miyamoto. Some family members of the two dead brothers must have paid for their return. There is nothing she can do because the time travel process as started. Miyamoto smiles from a distance and bows to Chloe, he is ready for battle.*

*Just as she starts to time travel away from the year of 1634, Miyamoto slices down the closest dishonorable Samurai near him, the blade cut is violent, but controlled, causing the disgraced Samurai to crumble beneath Miyamoto's feet.*

*The head of this defeated foe rolls away from the body on too the snow-covered ground. As this happens, Miyamoto discovers the eyes of this dead dishonorable Samurai are blood red. Miyamoto looks at the enemies surrounding him and realizes the dead adrenaline disease has infected them.*

***Kensei Miyamoto Faces Dead Adrenaline Samurais***

*This could only mean one thing, Hive Queen has sent more dead Adrenaline soldiers, and they have taken over these pathetic Samurais, who have returned to kill Chloe and him. Miyamoto takes a split-second glance at Chloe, then looks back at his attackers and a vicious unhinged battle takes control of the snow-covered forest floor. The white snow quickly becomes covered with blood like cherry snow cone liquid on ice.*

*Chloe's last image she sees is the red eyed dishonorable Samurai's and Kensei Miyamoto fighting for his life, and there is nothing Chloe can do, because she is time podding away from 1634 Japan, and is on a deliberate course to her next timeline in her quest. Chloe hopes and prays, the Sword Saint has **GOD** on his side and is victorious or the timeline for 1634 Japan and the world could change forever. Chloe puts these emotional* *thoughts away, and focuses on her next location of training, wherever or whatever this will be.*

*Miyamoto is in the fight of his lifetime, battling not only trained Samurais that are dead adrenaline infected with the taste for human flesh, but they also want to kill and feast on the Sword Saint. During this feeding frenzy, Miyamoto cuts down two more of these abominations, and realizes that they have a kill shot or blade cut that will take them out of the game of life. Knowing this is one thing, but finding the weak spot is another, so he must blade cut until no life is pulsing in these Samurai Alien creatures. Then it happens, Miyamoto slices open the front chest of one of the dishonorable alien Samurai's, the body of the Samurai drops and has no signs of life, but a blood red sphere of light pops out of the chest cavity and whizzes by Miyamoto's head.*

*The evil light sphere point of contact was not Miyamoto and travels up into the sky, and with unexplainable speed launches into space, and attaches to Chloe's time travel pod that she is encapsulate in like a parasite attaching to its victim. This dead adrenaline hitchhiker wants to go with Chloe to her next location of training, and than kill her or take over her mind and body. Miyamoto knows it will be up to Chloe to discard the Dead Adrenaline parasite, and with that thought, Miyamoto continues his onslaught against the Dead Adrenaline enemies and let his blades be the deciders of life or death.*

*Within a blink of an eye, the time travel pod is circling a wormhole in space, which will transport Chloe to her next location in the past. As this process starts to ramp up, the time travel pod starts to spin counterclockwise on the outer rim of the wormhole and anything on the outside of the pod shell, cannot handle the great force of the time travel acceleration, so the dead adrenaline sphere is peeled off the time travel pod. This causes the dead adrenaline sphere to spin clockwise, which sends this infection to the future. A separation of good and evil, evilness to the future, goodness to the past, which is even further in the past than1634 Japan.*

*Chloe still does not know what past place she will be meeting but knows the location is predetermined, and she must continue her quest. Now time travel can have treacherous consequences especially when a dead adrenaline sphere entity loses its compass to an unknown location in the future. Time will tell the story of this rogue Dead Adrenaline alien entity and how or who it will possess and turn into a walking Dead Adrenaline Zombie.*

*Time travel is a very fast and unpredictable thing, but Chloe is ready for her next adventure and embraces the last step in her training, and then it will be time to meet up with her dad,* **The Man Called Clint, a***nd battle the Dead Adrenaline invasion, and save humanity.*

## ROGUE IN THE CITY OF PITTSBURGH

### SOMETIME IN THE YEAR 2010

*A slight breeze is blowing over the city, which is lit up and ready to display all the glory of a stationary light show. The City of Pittsburgh, know for the Steelers football team, Great restaurants, Broadway shows, and Concerts. There is always a certain flavor of excitement to unlock especially for the city dwellers near and far but like with any city, crime can arrive like an unwelcome guest on your doorstep, even if it is from another planet. The breeze over the* ***Three Rivers*** *begins to increase where the Allegheny and Monongahela rivers meet at Point State Park to form the Ohio River, death is arriving with a hungry belly of hate. A large bright glowing light appears in the sky, and it is falling into the heart of the city. The speed quickly decreases, until just a small size light sphere materializes, and floats in an alley called Garrison Place, which is found between Liberty and Penn.*

*This Dead Adrenaline entity light sphere does not care about the name of the alley or its location, but quickly realizes the light display contained within this alley is the perfect hiding place, until a decision will happen to reclaim the trail of Chloe and destroy her. Fantastic purples, whites, and florescent blues light up the alley in a most unique way. This peaceful calming atmosphere unknowingly changed, now a rogue alien contamination has arrived in the City of Pittsburgh.*

## ROGUE DEAD ADRENALINE IN THE CITY OF PITTSBURGH

*The Dead Adrenaline alien entity is very clever one, different than your typical cannibalistic savage that are marching with the Hive Queen. This DA is at a higher level of consciousness, for which the Hive Queen especially crafted this front-line DA soldier to seek out Chloe and end her existence. This Dead Adrenaline goal was not to kill Kensei Miyamoto, but to leave this dishonorable Samurai host back in 1634 Japan and track down Chloe to stop her from fulfilling her destiny. This Dead Adrenaline must focus now, because the City of Pittsburgh is busy populated place, humans are everywhere and the urge to posses one is great. But choosing the correct and strong human host must happen, so this alien Dead Adrenaline entity can survive, thrive, and feed. If the conditions are perfect, then maybe this DA can figure out away not to get killed by humans and continue its evil mission to stop Chloe. Until then, assimilating in this environment and avoiding attention must take place for this lost DA.*

*As night leaves and enters early morning, the alley of Garrison Place slowly becomes a quiet ghost town, only traffic and voices from a distance are echoing. Sounds of laughter and anger resonates throughout the city, but only bits and pieces of conversation. The city is starting to wake up, and the land of the living will be back in full force, so the Dead Adrenaline entity must make a move before daylight takes hold. Then it happens, a man walking alone, down Garrison Place alley who is in a great hurry and decided to take a short cut. This male human wearing a business suit, in decent shape, a look of stress devouring his face. As the man walks past, the Dead Adrenaline decides to take possession of this unsuspecting human. Suddenly with the accuracy of sniper and the speed of cheetah, the Dead Adrenaline conquers its prey, like a well place punch the Dead Adrenaline entity latches on to the top of the spinal cord of his host victim. Now this man, stops and freezes up in cationic state, his eyes are wide open, and the eyes begin to roll back and forth in his head, as this erupts, they begin to change from red to blue in color. After three minutes, this process stops and this human host eyes are blood red. As morning dawns, a flood of people starts to walk through the alley. As the assimilation of human and alien are complete, standing in a crowd of human prey is a* ***Dead- Adrenaline-Zombie****, which will make it the first ever Zombie to walk the streets of the City of Pittsburgh. Or at least a zombie from outer space, even though this is true, the walking humans do not pay much attention to this DA-Zombie, because in life there are just some people that are living zombies struggling through life, due circumstances, mental illness, bad choices, and extreme amounts of drug use. In some cases, it is not their fault, but some people just abuse the free will* ***God*** *has given them.*

*As the crowd slowly disappears, no one gives second look at the man standing still, breathing heavy with red eyes. Lucky for these poor souls, this Dead Adrenaline Zombie has a unique control and ability to make a logical decision, so no Pittsburgh people will be on the menu today. The hunger to feed is agonizing, but this Dead Adrenaline Zombie knows that feeding in the city would be a mistake, and bring major attention, and could cause the evil entity inside this human to be destroyed. The humans outnumber this Dead Adrenaline Zombie, so every move is decided with full intention to survive. The DA- Zombie must get out of the City of Pittsburgh, and get to a less populated place to feed, rethink, and avoid capture or annihilation. Also, this free-thinking DA-Zombie must control or slow down the physical changes, so it looks more human than Zombie. This will be a difficult undertaking, but this DA-Zombie knows and understands what it must do.*

***FREE THINKING DA-ZOMBIE***

*Full daylight has arrived, and the DA-Zombie makes it way through the busy city, blending into the crowd of people. During its travels, it sees a man in sunglasses with blankets covering him, the man is sitting on the ground asking for money. The DA-Zombie realizes that this homeless human is begging for its survival, but not willing to fight for it. With that thought, the DA-Zombie reaches its hand out, places its palm on the man's forehead, and squashes the homeless man's head off the brick wall directly behind where this man is sitting. The DA-Zombie quickly covers the dead homeless human up with the blankets surrounding the man. Then the DA-Zombie takes a tin can that has what humans call money inside, picks up the sunglasses that fell off the face of the homeless human, and puts them on. The busy bustling commotion of human traffic walking and running through the city is a perfect formula for such a graphic murder to go unnoticed.*

*The DA-Zombie continues to walk through the city with sunglasses on, and money in hand. You see when a DA-Zombie takes control of a human host and gains all the knowledge from the transformed human. Past, present, and future knowledge is obtained, which gives this DA-Zombie a quick synopsis of the human experience. The DA-Zombie suddenly realizes that the human host he took over has a money clip holding, cash, credit cards, and other identification material. With this realization, the DA-Zombie begins to smile and is happy with enjoyment, knowing that he did not need to kill the homeless human for money but got extreme excitement to make its first kill in this timeline on earth. Plus, now this DA-Zombie has a cool pair of sunglasses to cover his blood red eyes, which gives this alien intruder a better chance to mix in to the crowd. As the walking trip continues through the city, the DA-Zombie struggles to control its hunger to attack and feed. Then in a short distance a tour bus is in view, this bus is heading to Amish land, North of Pittsburgh, in Lawrence County, PA, which touches Beaver County Pennsylvania. The DA-Zombie quickly boards the bus and tries to pay the fee for the trip, but the driver tries to explain that this a pre-booked trip, and he only takes pre-bought tickets. With that response, the DA-Zombie pulls out a large bundle of cash and hands it to the bus driver and smiles. The bus driver smiles back takes the cash and the DA-Zombie finds a seat way in the back of the bus.*

*As the road trip gets underway, the DA-Zombie looks over the passengers sitting on the bus, which looks like a buffet of fresh meat to consume, but for now control is more important than food for survival reasons. The DA-Zombie needs to get to a less populated area, so the temptation to feed decreases. Several hours pass, and the DA-Zombie goes into a half sleep state to help control its hunger. During this time, the DA-Zombie decides to find out more about its human host, so recent memories are extracted from this human shell. It discovers that this human host worked in the City of Pittsburgh for a massive computer technology company. This human host was deeply knowledgeable and was an expert in his field; however he had too many bosses overseeing him, all of them were assholes, and they loved to have fucking meetings that were a total waste of time.*

*Over the years, this human host began to really hate his bosses, not only because he knew more than them but also because they were arrogant know it alls that would take credit for his work. Behind closed doors they would tell him that he was doing things incorrectly and these bosses were self absorbed assholes that used people and took advantage of anyone they considered useful or not.*

*The DA-Zombie discovers that this human host had been on his way to another meeting to meet with one of his asshole bosses and that is why he took the short cut through the alley, so he would get to work early to prepare for the bullshit. Now the DA-Zombie understood why this human host had a look of stressful agony on his face this morning, just before he was taken as a host. The DA-Zombie thought with great excitement that this hate and distain this human host harbors will be allies when feeding time begins.*

*The DA- Zombie wakes from its half sleep to see how much further before the bus arrives at a place called Amish Countryside, located in Lawrence County, PA. Suddenly a large deer runs out in front of the bus, and the driver attempts to avoid the deer, which was a mistake because he loses control of the bus and goes over a hillside and down into a tree covered wooded area. The bus rolls onto its side and is hanging and trapped up against several large trees. The impact was violent, and the passengers' bus of 50, plus one driver and the DA- Zombie are thrown around inside the buses metal shell. Half of the passengers are dead, and other passengers are injured from major to minor injuries. Blood is splattered everywhere and the DA- Zombie can feel and hear the pulsing and pumping of the hearts of the injured passengers. The smell of fear, blood and guts begins to make an appearance. The perfect opportunity for a cannibalistic hunger, which has reached uncontrollable levels. Nothing will stop what evil savagery is about to unfold like a* ***DEAD ADRENALINE novel.*** *The blood hunger for human flesh is too great, and the DA-Zombie has no choice but to feed, and humans are on the menu. Like a tornado of death of carnage, this DA-Zombie, unleashes pain and suffering that would make a battlefield look like amateur hour. The feeding is only on the living humans, which any Dead Adrenaline Zombie would prefer, you see the screams of agony adds extra flavor to the human flesh, blood, and bones. The blood fest happens quickly because this DA- Zombie is off the charts with bloodlust. The hate for humans is alive and surging within this Dead Adrenaline-Zombie.*

*The last human heart stops beating, except for the driver of the bus, pinned behind the steering wheel like a trapped rat waiting for the end. The bus driver begins to plead for his life, as the DA- Zombie approaches him, hoping that mercy is given today. The DA -Zombie walks up next to the bus driver, who has become very silent and reaches down with his blood covered hand and removes the bundle of cash from the driver's jacket.*

*With this action, the DA- Zombie smiles at the bus driver, and for a brief second the bus driver smiles back and quickly learns this is not a smile of happiness, but a smile of hate. The DA- Zombie, opens his mouth wide and begins to chew on the bus driver's face, and bites his throat and blood begins to gush. The taste of this suffering is so satisfying to this Dead Adrenaline- Zombie, and finally after devouring parts, pieces and blood of the human prey, this DA-Zombie can stop feeding for now. Like criminal fleeing from its crime, the DA-Zombie climbs out of the bus, bolts and runs crazily into the woods.*

***DA-ZOMBIE ON THE RUN***

*The DA-Zombie has been running for an hour, and finally decides to stop running in the woods, which happens to be Lawrence County Pennsylvania. Cautiously, the DA Zombie comes slightly out from the wood line, and peaks out to see what surroundings are present. A large wooden sign is visible in the distance and the words, Amish Countryside. Lawrence County, Pennsylvania one mile north. Also, several small buildings and one enormous size building with the name "All Sports Complex." The DA-Zombie can understand this because he can obtain information from his human host, which will be of use while on this planet. The evolution of this Dead Adrenaline Zombie will even give this alien entity the ability to speak while in the human host's body. Up to this point, only the Hive Queen would speak, but this Dead Adrenaline has found the ability to speak, to aid during this time on earth. The DA-Zombie decides to sit down in the woods and recalibrate the mind and body of the human host, and bring back a more human looking zombie, a defense mechanism to blend in again with humans.*

*A man, a short distance from the wood line where the DA-Zombie is near, comes out of a Sports complex building, where he had been competing in a jujitsu tournament. This man is carrying a gym bag, and looks pissed off, and begins yelling aloud.*

"This is bullshit! I got ripped off, no way I would tap out during that match. What bullshit, not fucking cool!"

*This upset man decides to walk into the wood line, so he can complain some more by himself, away from the crowd of people that are leaving the sports complex. As this agitated man walks into the woods a little deeper, the DA-Zombie focuses in on him, and decides to get an easy kill. As the DA-Zombie approaches this human, the human reacts by yelling tough guy comments.*

"You better back off man, I know Jujitsu, I have competed and everyone knows I train! Did you hear me, I have been training in Jujitsu for at least a year, so do not even think about attacking me, because I am deadly."

*The DA- Zombie looks at the pathetic human and smiles at him, which causes a further response from this easy kill human.*

"Why you are smiling, you think this is funny, ok you will find out when I choke you out!"

*This easy kill human starts to back up and, in a panic, trips over a log laying on the ground. The stumble causes this human to fall backwards onto the ground. Upon hitting the ground, this human decides to stay on the ground laying on his back in a defense ground fighting position. One thing this human did not know but soon will find out in a very painful bloody way.*

*Never battle a Dead Adrenaline Zombie on the ground, unless you have no other choice, because if you do, you will die!*

*It is always a bad idea to ground fight during the Dead Adrenaline apocalypse.*

*This unprepared, ignorant, overconfident man says three last words. "No! Stop! Please!!!"*

*As this easy kill human is begging for his life, the DA-Zombie methodically decides to bite off some of his fingers. Then like a rabid animal, the man's abdominal area is split open, and blood and guts spill as the DA-Zombie tears away at the insides. The lungs of the easy kill human are eaten, along with the heart, just a little snack to keep this DA satisfied, until the next kill. The DA- Zombie, realizes he must keep moving, and opens the gym bag the easy kill human had with him. Inside the gym bag are some extra clothes, so the DA- Zombie takes the cloths in the gym bag and runs silently into the woods, heading north to Amish Countryside, which is one mile north.*

**DEAD ADRENALINE-ZOMBIE GETTING A SNACK.**

*The Dead Adrenaline Zombie eyes are now red and blue in color, because its hunger has been satisfied from eating the bus people and the easy kill human. This state of a Dead Adrenaline makes this alien species less aggressive, but still extremely dangerous. Even though this DA-Zombie is extremely deadly, it is different than most and can control its violent emotions much better than majority of Dead Adrenaline soldiers, and this is why Hive Queen sent this one to seek out Chloe.*

*Twenty minutes has past, and the DA- Zombie finally makes its way to Amish Countryside in Lawerence County, PA. A place where the Amish community lives and thrives, also it is known for tourists to visit, and get a small taste of the world of the Amish. This will be a perfect place for the DA-Zombie to blend into the landscape and feed.*

*A near by lake is spotted in the area, so the DA-Zombie decides to take a dip in the water to get rid of the blood covering his face, and body. The clothing inside the gym bag is removed and put on, and now the DA-Zombie is wearing a blue colored sweatshirt and pants but keeps the dress shoes on from the host human. The DA- Zombie looks out over the Amish country landscape and sees Amish humans in the distance working the field, next to a farm. A barn looks to be getting built by Amish workers on the other side of the field. The DA-Zombie begins to smile and starts walking in that direction.*

*The outcome will be the outcome, this DA-Zombie is trapped for now in this time on planet earth, but has an uncanny drive to survive, if Chloe is successful and the Alien Dead Adrenaline(s) are destroyed in the year 2026. This outcome will change things in the past, however; time travel can have a cause and effect, which can cause a new timeline to be born, and the past, present, future can have many different timelines and outcomes. No one knows the outcome, until time reveals it.*

*(Coming soon from Author Grant A. Miller, the 3rd book in the Detective Shiokawa Mystery series,* ***Blood Harvest, Under the Amish Moon!*** *In this book you will find out the fate of this Rogue Dead Adrenaline Zombie from Dead Adrenaline III series)*

# THE NEW PROPHECY OF CAMELOT

## 13TH CENTURY

*One hundred years had passed since Merlin spoke with the Dragon King in the Dragon Realm in the 12th century, and placed Excalibur in the silver rock-stone, where the sword exists in the center of the dragon realm. At some point, the Dragon King lost interest in wondering when the so-called prophecy of a women showing up to claim Excalibur would ever happen. The Dragon King thought even if this hero showed up, she would perish on her quest and would never be able to say the real name given by the dragon ancestors from long ago. Humans and Dragons still exist together in the 13th, which happens to be the time of Camelot, and the Knights of the round table.*

*Both the Dragons and the humans honor the dragon doctrine, which declares, no human must ever enter the dragon realm, and no dragon must ever enter the human realm. This has been this way since the birth of the dragon and only was broken once in the 10th century when King Caliburnus and Dragon Invictus crossed path halfway in the dragon realm and halfway in the human realm. On that day they became allies and forged a power, and mystical energy that created the sword Excalibur. This sword has great Dragon Power and Divine Kingship blended, which gives it the strength of a Warrior King and the mystical power of the Dragon. Pure light of the righteous, with a blade cut of a leader. The Dragon King will soon discover that destiny does not stop, even if it is one hundred years later.*

*A bright blue glow starts to shine through the white clouds floating in the blue skies over the green landscape of Camelot. Suddenly the clouds break open, and a human size white glowing shape appears from the heavens, it is Chloe, she has arrived in the 13th century, and has time traveled to the Kingdom of Camelot. The last step in her quest of training has unleashed in the medieval land of kingdoms, unforgiving battles, mystical magic, and fantastic creatures. Chloe will find out what a large scale bloody medieval battlefield will be and must be prepared to push her ability beyond any training she has completed, because not only her life will depend on it, but the salvation of humanity.*

*The time travel pod lands and evaporates and Chloe is now standing in the amazing but treacherous land of Wizards, Witches, Kings, and Dragons.*

*Chloe pauses for a moment to take in this land and starts to speak aloud.*

"Wow! What beautiful scenery, lush green valleys and mountains covering the landscape like a blanket of magic. This is something too see, but I know this last evolution in my training will not be all beauty. I have no doubt that bloody, violences and barbarism waits for the edge of my blade, along with my foot and fist. Ok, enough said about that shit sandwich, where could I be and with whom will I train with."

*In the distance two castles appear nestled on the hillsides, one small and one larger. This makes Chloe start to realize that she is in a medieval place in time. With this thought she decides to get this quest underway and walks towards the castles in the distance.*

**Chloe has arrived In a Medieval Land**

*Chloe is close to the castles now, and decides to go to the lager castle first, which up close looks destroyed from past medieval battles. The walls are mostly crumbling stones, with no structural strength left in its bones. As Chloe starts to enter the damaged front gate, she catches a quick glance of a green cloak whipping behind a stone wall and disappearing. Chloe picks up her pace with her katana ready and tries to find the person wearing this emerald cloak. Just as she is rounding the stone wall, a man wearing an emerald cloak, with gray hair and beard, steps out in front of her. This man's eyes are incredible bright emerald in color and have a hypnotic quality to them. For a split-second Chloe thinks, shit is this another Dead Adrenaline Zombie solider sent by Hive Queen, but with green eyes. Then Chloe senses with an undeniable believe that this person means no harm but does have an unstoppable power to wield if needed. Chloe lowers her blade and waits for this unknown force to make the next move and starts to speak to him.*

**Merlin The Legendary Wizard.**

"Ok, Mr. Man in the medieval green cloak, let's talk."

*And just like the wind starting and stopping, this mysterious man's eyes stop reacting with the emerald glow, and he begins to speak.*

**Merlin Ambrosius**

"The cloak is the *hue*(color)of **Emerald,** and for this *ispeken (talk)* moment, my *neme (name) is* **MERLIN***!"*

"Holy shit sandwich! If I'am up on my medieval words, you are speaking some old English, and I can not believe I'am saying this. **Merlin!** If this is true, then I time traveled back to the medieval age."

"Oh yes, my lady, you are here to fulfill the prophecy, so keep the faith, for you are the chosen one Chloe."

"Take a breather Sir, and I will too, how do you know my name."

"Why Chloe, I am **Merlin the Wizard,** throughout these lands and beyond, I am all knowing, and all seeing. I have many powers of the mystical arts, and seeing the future is one of them, now seeing the past is a different thing, but I have a prediction that is about to change. So, you see, I knew you were coming Chloe, my abilities to see into the future told of an unknown outcome of a young women from the the future, time traveling to the past. This young woman is you Chloe, and as you know you are on a quest to master knowledge, power, and a fighting skill set that is unmatched on earth or any other planet.

Evil has arrived in the future, and you are the key to save humanity. Now you have showed up in the 13th Century, a time of great battles to unfold, a time of King Arthur and The Knights of the Round table, and the Kingdom of Camelot is thriving, which makes enemies of King Arthur very envies.

They want what he has and will stop at nothing to remove him from his kingdom. If the future outcome in this time, does not change, this might very well happen. You must understand Chloe, knowing the future can be a very painful and regrettable thing, but knowing the past can help change the future."

"Wise words Merlin, you are the first to have ever thought or said this. I am kinda getting the vibe you are my tour guide on this quest, and you are here to help me through the rough patches."

"Chloe, I will say this, I will teach you the way of mystical wizardry, as you know, you have unique powers that are of a supernatural nature, some have been revealed to you, but some are locked deep inside your mind and body. I will help you unlock these elements of power, which you call dragon slayer blood, interesting name given the place you have arrived. Also, I will introduce you to King Arthur and his Knights and Knightess's, you will train with them and learn the ways of Medieval battle, which will be more brutal than anything you have completed up to this point. Lastly, you shall travel to the **Dragon Realm** and meet the **Dragon King**, who will test you, what that will be is unknown, not even I can see the total future in the dragon realm, because the power of the dragon is a formidable advisory, and the Dragon King is very clever and unpredictable. If you survive all of this, you will have the opportunity to claim and wield the most powerful sword in the realm.

"Merlin, does this sword have a name."

"**Excalibur!"** Created with the intention to even up the medieval battlefield between good and evil, the master of this sword, must have no fear of death, and must always protect the weak."

"**Excalibur**! Now you got my attention, it is time to get this quest underway and see King Arthur's Castle and speak with the man himself, King Arthur the legendary King of Britain. I guess the folklore about Camelot is for real, and this place does exist in all its glory."

"Yes Chloe, you will be meeting King Arthur, but nightfall is upon us, so we will rest here tonight in the Castle Tintagel the actual place where King Arthur was born. I sometimes come here to reminisce about past times, as you can see past battles got the best of this once beautiful castle, along with the smaller castle a cross the way, where visiting kings would stay with their traveling medieval warriors. Unfortunately, a visiting Evil King and his medieval soldiers destroyed Castle Tintagel."

"Luckily, I can see the future, but I must not try to change it directly, so indirectly I find ways to help. So, as Castle Tintagel was under siege, I showed up and took a newborn baby Arthur from the arms of his dead mother, who just so happen to be Queen Igraine of Castle Tintagel. I returned baby Arthur back to the King of Tintagel, King Uther Pendragon when he returned from the crusades. King Uther did raise Arthur for a period, and did rebuild his kingdom, unfortunately, Uther needed justice for the death of his wife, but it turned into revenge, and Uther died in battle, and lost his kingdom forever. You see, it is quite easy to mix up justice with revenge, which never ends well. To protect Arthur, I left him with a family that were farmers far away from the battle ridden fields of blood in the Island of Britain."

"This family was expecting a newborn, and the mother was getting close to having the baby that would be the named Kay, it was to be a boy. Even though this family was going to have a son born, this couple welcomed young boy Arthur with love, kindness, and respect for life."

"Unfortunately, in tragic fashion baby Kay died in child brith, along with Arthur's foster mother, which left the foster father with only Arthur. It turned out that Arthur's foster father went by the name Sir Ector, and he was an expert swordsman and once was a full empowered knight from a far-off kingdom. This man left the Knighthood, after the kingdom would not except a common woman that was not wealthy or in high standing that he wanted to marry. So, this Knight left with her and the kingdom that he defended and chose love over violence, and traveled far, far away, and became a farmer in the lands outside of the violence."

"The journey for Arthur was unleashed by one simple act, the night I saved him from definite death, the rest is Arthurian legend, as you know from your future time, which is not totally accurate, but one powerful truth remains, King Arthur Pendragon became an outstanding swordsman from the training Sir Ector gifted him, and Arthur came back to reclaim his birth right to be King. He has been a King, for quite sometime now, and in this 13th century, the Kingdom of Camelot is unmatched with righteousness, prosperity, power, and battle tragedy, all because Arthur is the King of this land.

However, a brutal storm of battle is coming this way, I can feel its wrath getting closer. Invaders from the North Sea will soon place footsteps on this land, these invaders originated from Germanic tribes banding together to avenge the deaths of past warriors that showed up on the shores of Camelot hoping to conquer this kingdom. They will be coming in the hundreds, and they are more than just costal raiders, looking for an opportunity to pillage and plunder. They want to unseat King Arthur Pendragon from power and take over his kingdom and lands, so they can rule Camelot. If my powers of belief are exact, they are of both Saxon and Viking blood line, so hate for this world King Arthur and his followers have created is beyond vengeances."

"Wow! What an extraordinary retelling of King Arthur rise, but it just happens to be the truth, someone should write about this version of the Kingdom of Camelot. On a less extraordinary note, if both Saxons and Vikings are on the same team now, than one hell of a medieval battle is coming to Camelot town."

"Yes Chloe, it is an extraordinary true story, I should know because I was there for all of it, helping when I could, staying in the shadows even when I did not want to, but being a wizard takes a toll. Like I said before, I can indirectly help, but I can not directly interrupt or change what the future holds, and from what my visions are telling me, death is close to Camelot's shoreline."

"Ok Merlin, maybe this is a stupid question, but does King Arthur know of the invading enemies making their way here."

"Oh yes, Chloe, **Daughter of the Man Called Clint, and from the land of Beaver County, Pennsylvania,** Arthur is aware, but he has grown a little to confident over the years of triumph and believes that nothing can harm him or Camelot and its people. Arthur is always prepared, but this evil force, feels different to me than mere mortal men and women, something is uncanny, and I just can not place my mind on what this could be. An unknown force is stopping my visions and will not let me see what evil is traveling with the Saxons and Vikings. As the army of enemies gets closer to this land, I should be able to decipher what evil is with them."

"Ok, fascinating stuff Merlin, but if I were a betting woman, the evil traveling with them could be some Dead Adrenaline soldiers sent by the Hive Queen. Also, you can read minds Merlin, because that is the only way you would have know about the Man Called Clint, who happens to be my father, and as you say, the land of Beaver County, PA."

"Yes Chloe, *Daughter of the Man Called Clint,* it is just another one-of my supernatural gifts. Now, I must say, you do not give up the information easily, and I only can grab hold of certain details about you. Now this Hive Queen, I have seen visions of this abomination, many, many centuries ago, but the evil was on a dominating level, so I blocked her out, because it felt as if she wanted to control my mind. Hive Queen is not of this world, and no one to cross blades with.

I do know Chloe, you are here because of the invasion with the Dead Adrenaline army, so your purpose here must unfold, if there is any chance of humankind in the past, present, and future to survive.

Now here is some food, get some rest, Lady Chloe, and we will embark on the short, but uncertain journey to King Arthur's castle when morning dawns. I will keep watch for any dangers that might be looking for a tasty meal for the taking."

"Merlin, do you want me to share the night-watch with you, so you can get some rest before tomorrow's trip to King Arthur's castle."

"Chloe I truly do appreciate your kindness, and thoughtfulness to be concerned about my wizard health, but I have slept for centuries, which is wonderful way to recharge my wizard mind and body. But I have been awake in time, for the last two centuries, a time of **High Adventure, Dragons, Prophecies, King Arthur, and the Kingdom of Camelot.** You see, there is a reason I woke from my slumber, and have been awake for the 12th century and the beginning of the 13th century, to teach, guide indirectly, and help you fulfill your destiny."

"Oh! I get it, **High Adventure, Prophecies, Dragons, King Arthur, and the Kingdom of Camelot.** Ok, I will see you in the morning, good talk."

*As nightfalls in the land of Camelot, Chloe can hear the howling of a Wolves in the distance, followed by the sound of something dying. Chloe now realizes why Merlin wanted to wait til morning to make the trip to Castle Camelot. In this medieval land, anyone can become a meal when hunger and wrong choices are involved.*

**The Wolves of Nightfall.**

# THE WITCHES

## 13TH CENTURY

*The medieval morning arrives like a focused Mawashi Geri (Round kick) to the face, without warning screeching voices of violent conversation echoes outside Castle Tintagel crumbling walls. Chloe gathers herself and thoughts and looks outside and discovers Merlin is having a very contentious argument with what looks to be a medieval witch, dressed in a muddy colored gray, looking very distorted, and giving off an odor of muddy swamp water. Chloe realized at this moment that the medieval folklore about witches is true, and if memory serves her, a witch like this can be a very unforgiving creature. As Chloe watches on, this unholy Witch stops talking to Merlin and looks straight at Chloe, points and begins to yell out to her.*

"You will be ours, so just come with me and meet my sisters, we have foreseen the future and possibility of a sacrifice in the mud marsh, before night fall a decision shall take place! My dear Chloe, if you want to go without pain and suffering, then walk with me into the Shrieking Marsh, and I promise you, no harm will befall you if you come with me now. Chloe this must happen now to protect you from the violence of the marsh. You see Chloe, the High Witch of the Marsh will make a judgement, she will decide if you may pass through or will just be another sacrifice in the marsh."

## THE WITCH OF THE MARSH

"What a shit marsh sandwich this is, not much of a choice if I'am hearing you right. I will take my chances with Sorcerer Merlin, so really there is nothing else I need to say, other than it is kinda neat and creepy to see a real living *Witch* standing in front of me."

*And with those last said words from Chloe, the Witch withdrew back like a Cobra getting ready to bite its prey and said one last thing.*

"You will regret your decision, because no one ever survives the Shrieking Marsh, and even if they make it through, the scars of what they encounter will kill them slowly in life, so beware, misfortune is coming, and the *Mark of the Witch* can never be erased."

"Begone, Witch of the Marsh, and tell your High Witch that I Merlin Ambrosia the Wizard of this land and beyond, and I will be accompanying Chloe, of Beaver County, Pennsylvania through the Shrieking Marsh."

*The Marsh Witch did not like this outcome, and wanted to cast a curse spell on Chloe, but knew her powers are weaker outside the confines of the Marsh, also she knew that alone, Merlin is too powerful to battle with on this day. So, for now, she would return to the Marsh and wait with the other Witches for the opportunity to take Chloe.*

"Chloe, you see Camelot is a beautiful place, but evil and cruel intentions are always circling the kingdom. You have just met a Witch of the Marsh, these witches are very clever, cruel, powerful, and violent when they need to be. They speak in many directions and are prone to trickery and deceit if it helps their malevolent cause."

"So, Merlin do you think any of what this Marsh Witch said was true."

"I will say this, the part about no harm coming to you, if you would have left with this Witch and went into the marsh to meet the High Witch is partly true. You would have been safe, until the High Witch and her three low-level sister Witches met you. Then they would have tried to pluck your eyes out and eat them, just to see how they would taste. No understandable reason, just because they are Witches and that is what they do. These witches do have names, the yellowish eyed one you just met name is **Artifice**, she has three other sister witches."

"Let me think, ok Chloe here is the **Witch list** by eye color and name and meaning. The gold eyed witch is **Artifice** (trickery), emerald eyed is **Trahir** (betrayal), cerulean eyed is **Ruyn** (ruin), and last is the High witch, a scarlet eyed leader of the coven named **Yvel** (evil). Each of these witches are dangerous and unpredictable in their own way, but the High Witch is the alpha, so beware of the scarlet eyed witch."

## ARTIFICE THE WITCH(TRICKERY)

## TRAHIR THE WITCH(BETRAYAL)

## RUYN THE WITCH(RUIN)

**YVAL THE HIGH WITCH(EVIL)**

"Geez Merlin, good to know, sounds like I am going to be cutting some Witches heads off, because evil, ruin, betrayal, and trickery definitely need to be decapitated."

"Ok Chloe, going through the Shrieking Marsh is the quickest way to get to Castle Camelot, plus, there is a reason for everything we do in this medieval world, and you will soon find out why I would take you on such a dangerous trail to get to Camelots castle. Also, I do not want to use my teleport magical power because that would directly be helping you on your quest. Now indirectly, I am just your medieval tour guide, going the same direction and just so happen to be a badass Wizard."

“Ha! That is the spirit Merlin, as my dad, the Man Called Clint always says, humor keeps the mind clear and ready for the next steps in life. Good Stuff. I am ready for the next steps.”

“Hope you can keep your humor Chloe, because entering the Shrieking Marsh is no small endeavor, especially when the Witches of the Marsh have marked you because you hold the key to the fountain of youth. You see, these witches can see into the past, and before you had your brief conversation with that Marsh Witch Artifice, that uncanny spell castor was talking to me about how they know you have reversed in age, so they want to study you and tap into this fountain of youth magic.”

“Wow, those are some creepy Witches, I guess like you mentioned, they say one thing and do another. Sneaky little Witch bitches, but they are out of luck, because they do not have the correct genetic code, dragon slayers blood, and Gordon Scott’s scientific and medical technology. Plus, I am the daughter of the Man Called Clint.”

“Well Chloe, let us embark into the Shrieking Marsh, and find out what is waiting for us. You see Chloe, I have passed through the Shrieking Marsh many times throughout the ages, but each time is a dissimilar experience. We will find out very soon what witchery awaits.”

“Well Merlin, my blades are ready and willing, to cut down this Witchery.

# SHRIEKING MARSH

13th Century

*The sunlight is glowing down on the green landscape of this medieval land; the sound of wildlife is bouncing off the clouds and blue sky, like an orchestra of perfect music. But, like a nightmare showing up in your dreams, a change starts to happen, the sunlight collapses, black clouds and a mud grey sky arrive, no beautiful music of wildlife is playing in the background. The Shrieking Marsh is upon Chloe and Merlin, the entrance into the marsh only has one entrance and one exit, those who enter will find doom, and wickedness. Chloe and Merlin must go fourth without hesitation or fear.*

*The witches who live in the Shrieking Marsh are waiting and already know Chloe and Merlin have arrived, this brings a very desirable taste for knowledge for the witches. The Witches of this Marsh crave knowledge and are always seeking ways to bring them more power. With Chloe's arrival, she brings something they have hungered for their entire existence, the secret potion or magic to the fountain of youth. Chloe holds this chalice that each witch wants to drink from, but make no mistake a sacrifice will happen, and the witches will stop at nothing to capture this supernatural power of youth and vitality.*

“Ok Chloe, we are about to enter the Shrieking Marsh, you will begin to hear a faint but distinct sound of death, which is different for everyone, fortunately for me, I have sound magic to combat this sound, I would have been hearing. The sound of death, you will be hearing personally is enough to make a person go insane. Once we enter, you will have to keep your mind concentration in a positive place, or your eyes will begin to bleed and and you will leave the world of sanity. I will cast a sound blocking spell to silence or at least turn down the volume of the death sound. You see Chloe, everybody thinks death is silent, death is not, death waits and wants you to hear it, and you are about to hear its cry.”

“Holy shit sandwich Merlin, this is some creepy stuff, ok than let’s roll the dice of life and walk towards this witches brew.”

*As Chloe and Merlin entered the Shrieking Marsh, in the distance the Marsh Witches begin to cry with joy and happiness, they know the opportunity to seize the power of youthfulness is within the grasp of their crippled hands. As strangely as the cries began, they abruptly stop, and the witches evil anger starts to boil outwardly. The High Witch Yval looks at the three other witches and begins to cast a verbal spell to echo through the marsh. In the witch world their can only be one alpha witch, who rules and controls the chess pieces, and this is that witch. The High Witch begins to chant her evil death sound spell.*

"This is our domain, evil grows like a parasite in your brain, no power of resistance is possible, you will hear death's sound. It will break your mind, and your eyes will bleed with agony. I cast the death sound on Chloe, and she will pray for death, so the un-silent personal death sound stops. Merlin, you may stop the death sound from intruding your mind, but I have a special gift for you, the gift of forgetfulness. Let my words be final and the Shrieking Marsh except this evil air borne potion."

*And with those spell casting words; the High Witch lets out a shriek of hate and excitement that echoes through the marsh."*

*In the near distance Chloe and Merlin, here her hideous cry!*

"It is coming Chloe, be ready, I will try to stop the death sound from consuming your mind."

"Ok Merlin, let us get this witch festival underway!

"Chloe! I have sound blocked myself from the sound of death, but for some unknown witches' spell, I can not remember the correct sequence to help you block the death sound. The High Witch is a crafty creature of confusion, and she must have casted a forgetfulness spell. I will work on breaking its grasp on me, but you must battle this on your own for now."

"Oh no, I can start to feel and hear my own personal death sound, what a shrieking marsh shit sandwich this is going to be!"

*Chloe collapses to the mud marsh ground, and begins to struggle to keep her sanity, her body starts too awkwardly roll and flip around on the dead ground. Chloe's eyes close than open, and blood starts to fill the sockets of her eyes. Then her movement stops, Merlin walks over to her, believing that she has left the world of sanity, and tries to cast a spell to bring her back, but the forgetfulness spell is still nipping at his medieval sandals. Just as Merlin, almost has the sound block spell back in his mind to cast on Chloe, she awakes, which surprises Merlin. Chloe's eyes are not blood red anymore, and she begins to speak.*

"*Bad ass* Dragons Slayer blood is kicking these witches' asses, and their pathetic spells! I guess another one of my superpowers is folioing average spell casting."

"Yes Chloe, you most definitely abolished that death sound spell."

"Yep, sure did, but wow I heard the death sound, and it was a total complete nightmare, everything that person fears wrapped up in one big painful gift. What that nightmare was, I do not want to discuss, but I was a goner, my mind was ready to collapse into insanity when suddenly a woman that looked just like me arrived, she was dressed in a bright silver armor and reached her hand out to me and smiled. I took her hand and woke up to you Merlin."

"Chloe your destiny is marching forward, and you have just met yourself as the Samurai-Knightess! Time will unveil what and who you will become."

"Wow! I guess you would know this Merlin because you are a mystical wizard. Anyways, I am glad to be back in the land of the living, so let us keep my destiny moving forward. I must say, the Samurai-Knightess is a cool warrior name, kinda a *Medieval Warrior* with a Samurai Warrior all blended together with Chloe the daughter of the Man Called Clint wielding its power. Ok Merlin, let us move on through to the next stage of the Shrieking Marsh."

"Yes Chloe, let us continue through the labyrinths of the marsh."

*Yval the High Witch is not happy and becomes very enraged with the outcome of her death sound spell and decides to find and meet Chloe up close in the marsh. In her rage, this wicked abomination has a moment of complete clarity and realizes no simple spell casting magic is enough to control and take Chloe. Her blood is different, one of a kind, it holds power and magic that has never touched this medieval land. Also, with Merlin at Chloe's side the witchcraft must elevate beyond simple spells. So, the High Witch decides to unleash a brutal onslaught of marsh creatures. The creatures of the marsh are of a hideous nature and will break Chloe's mental and physical ability. In this weaken state, the Witches of the Marsh can take the secret of the fountain of youth from Chloe.*

"Okay Chloe, we are close to the exit of the marsh, which brings great concern, because other then the death sound spell, no other trickery, betrayal, ruin, or evil has showed up to create mayhem. This can mean only one thing Chloe, it is all coming at once, because the High Witch realizes your power and the fact you are with the greatest wizard of the ages. Be ready, the creatures of the marsh are coming, and these things embody everything the Witches of the Marsh have become. Evil, Ruin, Betrayal, and Trickery!"

"Got it Merlin! A big nasty shrieking marsh sandwich will soon be boiling out onto us."

"A *crippling chant begins to engulf the marsh; a calling is happening, Yval the High Witch is ordering the marsh creatures to appear from the wet marsh mud*, capture Chloe, and prevent Merlin from stopping the onslaught. The chant suddenly stops and two mud soaked abomination appear, the Marsh Creatures have arrived.

**THE MARSH CREATURES**

"Chloe! These are the Marsh Creatures, some magic works on them, but most does not because the *Marsh Creatures* souls have decayed to appoint of elimination. Meaning I must search for a powerful spell to shut these creatures down. For now, Chloe you can take the two sworded one, and I will take on the single sword one."

"Yep, no worries, Merlin I have set of swords that will fit the fight. My Katana (Long sword) and Wakizashi (Short sword) is ready to cut down one or both mud creatures."

"Let us begin the fight Chloe, remember these Marsh Creatures are hollow in thought and do not fear, so never let them get close enough to take your soul because they will and you will become another creature of the marsh."

*As the battle begins the High Witch and her low-level sister witches arrive and watch on in a quiet calmness. But inside the twisted minds of these Witches of the Marsh is great excitement and hunger for the secret of youth and vitality Chloe owns.*

"Chloe! As you can see, we have some visitors, *The Witches of the Marsh* have arrived, the one with no coned hat on is the leader, Yval the High Witch, she always wants to stand out and be different from her sister witches."

**RUYN, TRAHIR, YVAL, AND ARTIFICE HAVE ARRIVED.**

"Got it Merlin, Yval and her sisters will be next after I cut down these *Mud Pie Marsh Monster!*"

"Be incredibly careful Chloe because these creatures of the marsh are not an easy kill. They want you to take your shot with a kick or a hand strike, just to get stuck in their mud-soaked bodies. Then they will have you, once stuck you are like a bug stuck in a spider web."

"Nice piece of fighting information, but what about a sword, can it cut through their bodies."

"Yes Chloe, a sword will cut and slice them, but you must wield the blade with a continuous fluid motion, cutting completely through the body with no stopping motion, or retraction. How do I know this, well because I'am Merlin the Wizard, Ha! No Chloe, there used to be three of these *Marsh*

Creatures, but a man destroyed one, this man just happens to be our King, Arthur himself. He passed through the Marsh, just to test himself, met the witches briefly, but they looked at him as a simple man, and just had their Marsh Creatures attack him. No death sound spell, or other spell casting. The Witches missed their chance to kill the man that would be King of Camelot. If my memory serves me, Arthur told me he took his sword blade and cut each limb off the Marsh Creature. Upon doing this, his last blade cut was the head of the Marsh Creature, which turned into a liquified blob of mud as the head left the body. Arthur said that the Marsh Creature's headless, and limbless body then exploded and seeped back into the marsh.

Luckily for Arthur, the Witches called off the other two Marsh Creatures so no more blade cutting destruction from Arthur's blade would happen. Arthur escaped before anymore spell casting occurred. On this day, Arthur was so incredibly lucky, because had he stayed, the witches would have gotten him. Now with every action a consequence occurs, as you see now, these two Marsh Creatures wield swords to help battle any sword carrying opponents."

"Wow! I cannot wait to meet this Arthur guy, pretty badass, ok time to slice and dice."

# *SACRIFICES*

## 13TH CENTURY

*The Double sworded Marsh Creature moves towards Chloe at a fast pace, gliding through the mud marsh like a dolphin on water. Chloe avoids the soft mucky ground as best she can, if she steps on hollow wet mud, it will trap her feet. Chloe's double set of swords collide with the Marsh Creatures swords, and sparks begin to fly. The strength of the Marsh Creature is formidable, but for some unknown reason Chloe felt the sword blows would have more power. The Marsh Creature is very clever, seems to be holding back on Chloe, as if to give her a false ability that she can destroy the creature of the marsh.*

*Chloe senses this trickery and tries to prepare for the outcome. Finally, Chloe harvests the left arm of the Marsh Creature, causing the sword and arm to fall to the muddy marsh ground. Chloe is using the skill set that The Sword Saint taught her, go for the limb that is holding the weapon. As Chloe is trying to cut off the right arm of the Marsh Creature, a short distance away, she catches a glimpse of Merlin fighting the second single sword holding Marsh Creature. Merlin is a wizard, but does posses many fighting skills, suddenly a glowing staff appears in Merlin's hand, and he starts to spin and strike the Marsh Creature. Caving in the head and arms of this Mud Marsh Beast, causing pieces of the creature to splatter off and back into the muddy marsh. The Marsh*

*Creature responds with a quick flick of mud from its body, which latches onto the glowing staff. Merlin quickly releases the staff and sets a spin on the staff seconds before he releases it. As this is happening, the Marsh Creature, causes the poison muddy marsh water to blast towards Merlin knocking him backwards. Merlin uses his extraordinary power and places a large glowing shield directly in front of him to protect against the burst of the poisonous muddy water, knowing that the toxin in the muddy water can burn or in some cases kill a human being. Even though he is more than just a man and more than just wizard, Merlin knows that the toxins in the Shrieking Marsh are nothing to toil with, and finding a cure spell would be a great undertaking. As the muddy poisonous water forces Merlin backwards, Merlin redirects the attack and bounces the water onto a marsh tree and floats back down to the ground. Just as the Merlin lands in wizard style, his spinning glowing staff is heading directly towards the Marsh creature he was battling. And, with a sound like lighting striking a steel tree, the staff strikes the Marsh Creature and causes it to explode. The glowing staff had speared the Marsh Creature directly through one of its hollow eye sockets.*

*The intense battle between Chloe and the last standing Marsh Creature continues, at this point one arm is gone and one leg, but the creature still stands, as if is does not need two legs to stand. Chloe goes for the last sword arm, and the Katana blade and the creatures blade meet. As the swords spark off each other, Chloe's blade snaps in half. A piece of the broken blade shoots off and strikes Chloe in the chest, causing her to crumble back into the wet marsh mud. Chloe is bleeding out but manages to sit up in the mud. Chloe is still holding the Wakizashi short sword but is starting to lose consciousness. The Marsh Creature starts to move in for the kill, you see the witches of marsh do not care if Chloe dies or lives. Either way they just want the power and the secret to the fountain of youth that she wields. They want to extract it, and at this moment, believe it lives in her blood. Just has Chloe is ready to fade, she hears Merlin's voice.*

"Chloe, aim for the eye socket!"

*Chloe hears what Merlin is yelling and reacts with speed and aggressive, the Wakizashi sword is throw with speed and accuracy at the eye socket of the Marsh Creature. The witches look on with disbelief and start to laugh and cackle, thinking Chloe has no chance of victory. Suddenly, and like a sound of trumpets from* ***GOD*** *the sword hits its mark, and without warning the Marsh Creature explodes before everyone's eyes. And, from where the Marsh Creature came, the creature returns and mixes back into the marsh. As the Marsh Creature washes away the witches start to shriek and yell out in a rage like way. Chloe looks on for a second, but then her body gives out, and she passes away from her injury.*

"What is this, sisters! Look Chloe is dead; both the Marsh Creatures and Chloe are dead. Oh, how delightful, it may take centuries, but we can always create more Marsh Creatures. Now Chloe is exactly where we want her to be, dead like our black hearts. Haaaa! Heeee! Yesss! See Merlin, you lose, no destiny to save the world, no prophecy, just death and now my sisters and I will take and consume the vitality from Chloe. Soon we will be young and healthy again, once this happens our supernatural powers will stretch beyond the Shrieking Marsh, and nothing will stop our witchery!"

"Yval, you are so wrong, a prophecy is a prophecy, and nothing can stop it, not even death. You will soon find out that you are metaling in magic beyond your scope of twisted spell magic."

"Stop the babbling Merlin, sometimes evil wins, and on this day in the Shrieking Marsh, evil is the victor." (*The Witches begin to laugh and cackle like Hyena(s) getting ready to eat their prey).*

"Remember these words, foul Wiccans of the marsh, you are about to find out what the true light of goodness is. Chloe is no mortal lady, she is the daughter of the Man Called Clint and has trained under him, Master G, and The Sword Saint Miyamoto Masashi. Dragon Slayer blood courses through her veins, and her return will soon be your end!"

"Silence Merlin, your great words of nature worship are nothing more than fables in the mist, you have lost and so has Chloe."

"Sisters! The time of our evolution is at hand, we will soon become young again and rule beyond the marsh, and youth and power will be ours. All human entities will bow before us and beg for our forgiveness. Humans have shunned us for centuries, now they will feel the true pain and suffering of our curse."

"Not on this day! *Witches of the Marsh,* you will be the ones begging for forgiveness. Heed my message, stop and back way from your direction of demise, because you are about to travel down the path of trickery, betrayal, ruin, and evil!

Remember you were all once human women that lived a happy and prosperous life. The curse of the marsh has taken you, but if you have any sense left in your rickety, wrinkled twisted up minds and bodies. You will stand down and find a pure righteousness way to break the curse. This is the only way to your salvation"

"Do not listen to these false words from the Wizard Merlin, he is friends with the humans and despises our coven and everything we are in this human infested world."

"I am not sure Yval, possibly Merlin is right, maybe we need to find another away."

"Be silent Trahir, now in these ultimate moments, you want to betray me and your sisters!"

"It is okay Yval, let us wait on this, we can think about how we are going extract Chloe's essence and be more prepared. I will watch over Chloe lifeless body, and you, Ruyn and Trahir can meditate on it for a night in the marsh."

"So now you think you are in-charge Artifice, you will watch over Chloe's body, while we witchcraft mediate on it.

How dare you challenge my ruling; such trickery is seeping out of your mouth. Now I see sister Artifice that you want the power of youthfulness all to yourself."

"Yval! You are wrong about Artifice, because I want the essence, knowledge, and power of the fountain of youth to be mine entirely. I shall be the only witch today to own this magic from Chloe's passed on body and mind."

"Ruyn you always want to destroy everything for the purposes of your own pleasure, which is perfectly fine, unless it means turning against your sister witches. Stop this now! I am the High Witch of the Marsh, and you will obey!"

"Well, *Witches of the Marsh, the need for* Merlin magic in marsh is over, because all of you have began to feed on each other. Heed my warning, disembark on this foolish, treacherous magic. Death will meet you at the door if you start knocking."

"Goodbye forever *Witches of the Marsh,* I see nothing this wise wizard can say will change your minds."

"Merlin! So, you are leaving Chloe here and not even trying to stop us from our evil ways. Good, tell the humans the witches are coming!"

"Chloe will be explaining your dire mistake in a moment, witches of your nature, which is evil, ruin, betrayal, and trickery should never invite pure goodness and light into your marsh. Soon you will be nothing more then past witchery."

*And with those final words Merlin points to the sky and vanishes, leaving the Marsh with a little translocation magic.*

*At moment in the marsh, Yval the High Witch lets her evil take over and decides without remorse to keep the secret of the fountain of youth all for her wicked self. Yval cast a cruel reverse spell towards her sister witches, causes each sister witch to spell cast against themselves. The* ***Witch Ruyn*** *starts to believe that she is destroying herself and begins to shriek in agony, the* ***Witch Trahir*** *is confused and starts to believe she is betraying herself, and finally the* ***Witch Artifice*** *becomes distracted and lost in her own trickery. All three sister witches start to slide into insanity, which is even more cruel and wicked then their black hearts. Yval believes she is in control of this sinister outcome and turns away from her sister witches and begins her witchcraft on Chloe's silent body. As Yval is about to chant her first line of witchery, Chloe opens her eyes, begins breathing and returns to her feet. Chloe thinks to herself, how nice it is to have dragon slayer blood, which gives her the gift of immortality so far, under most circumstances.*

*Chloe's return to the land of the living shocks Yval at first, but her evil takes over, she begins to laugh and cleverly speaks to Chloe.*

"I see you are more than a mortal; you have the fountain of youth and magic to live forever. Chloe, join me, and we rule this land from ocean shore to ocean shore. You will be the sword, and I will be the guide, and humans will bow before us. I can teach you so many spells of witchcraft that you and I can have the kingdom of the world. You can have the pure-light half, and I will rule the dark-light half. Please child of *The Man Called Clint,* embrace this syndicate and we will be unstoppable. Just give me the secret of the fountain of youth, and I will become your allies, trust me, believe in me and I will open the chamber doors to supernatural powers you have not seized before."

Nope! I am good. Yval it is time to end this bullshit witch soup sandwich, I have had enough of the shrieking marsh salad, so it is time to end your evil existence!"

*Yval starts to walk closer to Chloe thinking she still could capture her essence and power with her "take spell" and reaches out. Big mistake, Chloe completes a spinning side kick, and hits Yval right in the witch face, knocking Yval back ten feet, slamming her crippled, wrinkled body up against a Black Willow tree. Yval's back crashes into the tree, causing her head and neck to flip back and get stuck in the fork like limbs of the tree. Chloe walks over to Yval and goes to the back of the tree and see Yval's head flipped backwards. Without a second thought, Chloe executes an outside inside Ax kick downward onto the face and head of Yval. The power of the kick and position of Yval's head, causes immediate removal of the head from the dethroned High Witch's torso.*

*As the head comes off, no blood or liquid comes gushing out. Only dust and dried up mud appears from the separation of the head. Witches really do have a black heart that does not beat and pulse blood through their body, and now Chloe knows this for certain. Yval's mud stone head falls next to the tree, and her lifeless eyes turn ash grey.*

**YVAL THE HIGH WITCH WILL REIGN NO MORE.**

*As this is occurring Chloe sees Ruyn, Trahir and Artifice standing a short distance away. They seemed disoriented and uncertain about what as just happened. Yval's reverse spell has stopped, due to her definite ending. The sisters' witches begin to speak at the same time, chanting these words.*

"You have killed our sister Yval, the High Witch, now we will take your essence for ourselves. We shall extract, extract, and become complete with both power and youth."

"Wow! Witches just do not give up; well, it is time to clean the fucking marsh!"

*Now the last three Witches of the Marsh are about to realize what real power and control can be. Chloe holds out her right hand and suddenly the 1634 Japanese katana blade given by Kensei Miyamoto appears in her hand. Chloe has just grasped how to control one of her dragon slayer blood superpowers. Chloe now realizes that if she focuses and thinks about a particular weapon of choice, it will appear in real form. It is now blade cutting time, and witches are not happy.*

*Chloe approaches them with caution, realizing they are witches and ruin, betrayal, and trickery can be extremely dangerous. Just as Chloe gets close enough to start cutting down this witchcraft. The fight turns from creepy to Dead Adrenaline creepy because the Dead Adrenaline infection has showed up in the Shrieking Marsh, and the eyes of the sister witches are blood red, they are now a host for this violent alien entity parasite.*

**DEAD ADRENALINE ZOMBIE WITCHES**

"Geez, really, you got be kidding, **Dead Adrenaline Zombie Witches!** Well one thing is certain, the DA entities have attached to their black hearts, so now it is time to search and destroy this evil, evil attached to evil; it does not get more death trap dangerous than this."

*With her Katana in hand, Chloe does not hesitate, knowing that the Dead Adrenaline infection has just taken over the sister witches and in seconds they will want to feed. As Chloe moves in for the kill shot cuts to their black hearts, the witches go berserk and start to howl like a savage banshee. The distorted screeching is a combination of witchery and alien invasion. This meant only one thing, death was on the menu, and humans are the main course.*

## DEAD ADRENALINE WITCHES ARE HUNGRY

*Unwittingly, these Dead Adrenaline Zombie Witches forgot the first rule in combat, never judge a book by its cover, if you do, you will miss the first block in your defense. Chloe is far more than just a human, she has dragon slayer blood power, and with this Chloe sparks the Katana sword she is holding off a large rock near the witches, The spark shoots towards Trahir and lands on this witch's hat. The moment the spark hits the*

*hat; a flame erupts on the top and Trahir's whole body goes up into a fireball from hell.*

*The flame ball is contagious, and Ryun also becomes affected by the fire. Soon the flame is covering both Trahir and Ryun's bodies, Artifice quickly backs away from her sister witches to avoid their melting bodies. As Trahir and Ryun are melting into skeletal remains, their black hearts fall from their chest cavity. Chloe blade cuts the black hearts, knowing the Dead Adrenaline entity is hiding inside, the black hearts beat for a moment and then become silent.*

*Both the witches and the Dead Adrenaline no longer exist; Chloe moves towards Artifice to finish her off and release her from her curse. As this is happening, Artifice does something very unexpected, this witch is known for her trickery by name and actions, but no human or supernatural being could have ever thought of this unusual step for survival by Artifice.*

*Artifice reaches deep into her chest, using her sharp, harden nails, cutting deep into her chest cavity. A slight, but loud screech comes from Artifice, and her chest opens with a puff of mud grey ash coming from inside. Artifice reaches into her chest and pulls out her black heart and throws it on the ground in front of Chloe. As the black heart hits the ground, her eyes turn back to the original gold, eye color. The black heart starts to beat as it lays on the mud marsh ground and for some unexplainable reason the heart starts to move on the marsh ground back towards Artifice. As this is occurring, Artifice starts to speak.*

"Go ahead Chloe, stab my black heart, kill this Dead Adrenaline entity inside, and break the curse, I will no longer exist as Artifice, which will be what I have wanted for centuries, ever since I was cursed to this marsh and witchery existence."

*Chloe takes a moment to hear what Artifice had just said, knowing that Artifice is known for her trickery. In those seconds of review, Chloe realizes what must happen and slices the black heart of Artifice in half. The heart stops beating and goes silent, the silence spreads throughout the marsh, even the marsh frogs are tranquil and quiet.*

*And like a medieval fairy tale, the Witch Artifice changes into young beautiful women with golden eyes and dark hair.*

**Golden eyed Beauty**

“You have broken the curse! Chloe, you are the one, thank you-thank you so very much. Imprisonment was the curse, punishment for centuries in the shrieking marsh, all because we wander into the marsh and met a dying old *Mud Grey Witch* who had hate towards humans, so she decided curse my sisters and me. The black heart with the Dead Adrenaline entity inside that you so skillfully destroyed was not mine, the Grey Witch's curse incarnated the black heart.”

“Now my real heart beats inside my body now with life and light and a new purpose, because of you. My Sisters, on the other side of the blade had no chance, because that was their black heart that changed, so they died with the curse.”

“Lady Chloe, you must understand my three other sisters were vicious people, evil, betrayal, and ruin did make up each one of them individually, it had been that way from birth, I was the youngest of the sisters and did what they told me, which lead me down a path of trickery. I knew it was wrong, but I did not want to displease them out of fear of losing my father or worst. We were from a very wealthy family in the land, but my father spoiled us and gave no guidance after the death of my mother. He was a broken man, my sisters hated me and treated me like a slave, because our mother had died giving birth to me. You see, I never met my mother in the land of the living, and they blamed me for her death. The witch we met in marsh knew this and cursed us to all eternity in the shrieking marsh.”

“You see , my Lady Chloe, the *Grey Witch* tried to take our youth for herself, but only had enough evil, ruin, betrayal, and trickery left in her wicked magic to change us into the Witches of the Marsh but was unable to take our youthful essence for herself and died before our eyes. Rotting, dissolving, becoming violent memory of the past.”

“The curse was of a hideous nature; our true personality traits exaggerated on a level of cruelty. Now even though I was a trickster by necessity, and not born with such deceit, the *Grey Witch* did not care and manifested this cruel curse on each of us. Bringing out the very worst in each one of us and making sure to trap us in the Shrieking Marsh forever.”

“The Witches of Marsh conjured by black violent magic from an old poisonous grey mud Witch that hated humans. After the Grey Witch cursed us, she began to cackle with a most violent laugh saying the curse is forever, and only she could undo the spell. Moments after saying this, the Grey Witch deteriorated from this earth and faded away like she never existed. Our bodies became the hideous Witches of the Marsh, and we soon discover that we had no control over our trickery, betrayal, ruin, and evil.”

“Over time the alpha witch order arrived and Yval appeared to have the most power and became the High Witch of the marsh and my other sisters and I knew this was the way of the curse, and the way of shrieking marsh.”

“I have to say, this is fantastic, anytime I can break a witch's curse and kill some DA(s), I am all in on helping.

Unfortunately, sacrificing your sisters was part of the process, not to sad about them, it sounded like they were not good people on any level. On a side note, what is your true name."

"Chloe my name is Guinevere; my father was King Leodegrance, and he was the King of Cameliard. You see Chloe, my sisters and I had this curse placed on us long ago, so our father is long gone from the land of the living."

"Wow! This is one interesting medieval shit sandwich, your name is Guinevere, now this rewrites the storybooks. Better be careful King Arthur, wait until he sees your beauty."

"King Arthur, I remember him cutting off one of the heads of the marsh creatures. You know, even as a witch in the marsh, I felt a compelling attraction to him."

"Oh yeah, I bet you did, well I am going to meet him, you are more than welcome to come with me."

"Yes, thank you Lady Chloe, it would be an honor to travel, with you, and I need a new kingdom to make my home, hopefully King Arthur of Camelot will welcome me."

"With a name like Guinevere, you will be simply fine, I have a way of knowing things like this."

"Chloe, follow with me, I know how to leave the marsh."

# MEETING ARTHUR

## 13TH CENTURY

"Here we are Chloe, the exit from the shrieking marsh, it is going to feel wonderful never to return to the marsh. I was a prisoner, the only time, my sisters, and I got to leave the marsh for short times throughout the ages was to spread our evil, ruin, betrayal, and trickery on the outskirts of the marsh. We trying to get fools and treasure hunters to enter the shrieking marsh. The spell was temporary, and we always had to return and live in the marsh forever.

"I understand Guinevere how good this must feel, knowing that the curse is over and you will never have to return to the shrieking marsh. Last time you were outside the confines of the marsh was to trick me to go with you. The witch Artifice is no more, now you can continue with your original life, but in a better way and better version of yourself Guinevere."

"Exactly Chloe!"

"Merlin, nice to greet us, the Witches of the Marsh are no more."

"I know Chloe, I had unshakable believe that you would destroy them, but you out did yourself and managed to save a young lady from her curse. Something of this importance does not happen in many lifetimes, but when destiny is in action nothing is impossible. Hello Guinevere, it is with magnificent pleasure to meet you, minus your witch's curse."

“You know my name, how could that be. Wait a medieval second, I remember you. You were a lot younger than, but you were my fathers first sorcerer.”

“Yes Guinevere, I knew your father King Leodegrance of the Kingdom Cameliard. I was his personal wizard back than, a young wizard learning my sorcery craft. Your father was a good man, a leader, but a father first. You see before you were born, he gave to the poor, always protected the less fortunate, both your father and your mother were giving and loving. They turned no person rich or poor away from their kingdom, but than a sad and diabolical thing happen to your father and mother. A witch arrived at their kingdom gate, asking that they show mercy on her and let her stay inside the walls of the castle over the harsh winter months. Your mother, Queen Vivian Leodegrance wanted to show kindness to the witch and let her stay inside the castle walls, but only for the winter. Your Father did not trust the witch and kept a close watch on her and went along with your mother’s wishes.

The witch used a small but comfortable room in the castle that King Leodegrance appointed for her accommodations. As the winter months, grabbed hold of the land of Cameliard, a sadness grew over the kingdom, and bad luck followed. Your older sisters were born and were remarkably close in age. The witch would return ever winter and stay at the castle. I tried to warn King Leodegrance that the witch was up to her wicked ways, but in a more silent way. King Leodegrance was too busy running a kingdom to listen, as the years went on your older sisters became absolutely corrupted by the witch within the castle walls. The final witches broom straw broke when the old witch decided to sweep all the kingdoms luck out of the castle. On that day, the evil witch began to sweep from the front entrances of the castle doors, completely to the back exit doors. King Leodegrance caught the witch in the process and managed to stop her before all the kingdom's luck got swept away by this witch. You see, one should never let a witch into their home willingly, because if a witch gets the chance with broom in hand, she will sweep all your luck away from your living life. King Leodegrance banished the witch from the castle and threw her back out into the frozen winter landscape, never to be seen again by King Leodegrance.

You may ask why I did not help get rid of this witch when all this witchery was happening. Little zap here, a little Merlin magic would have changed things, King Leodegrance asked me not to meddle with his affairs, which I honored, his love for Queen Vivian was great and when Vivian welcomed the witch, within the castle walls. King Leodegrance honored her decision because he loved her. You must understand, this witch was more than just a wicked old woman cursed by another's witchcraft. You see this witch, once was Queen Vivian's sister an encounter with an evil witch while traveling the countryside changed her sister forever. Much like you Guinevere when the witch cursed you and your sisters, this witch did a similar thing and placed a wicked spell on her that changed the Queens sister into a witch. Her cursed sister had no choice but to roam the countryside of this land, looking for a home but could never find one. Queen Vivian showed love, mercy and kindness and let her stay during the winter months, hopeful that some part of her sister would return, which never happened. In fact, the witchery grew stronger, and no human sign of her sister survived."

"Geez, that is an incredibly sad medieval story, well at least I was able to save Guinevere from her curse Merlin."

"You most absolutely did safe her, in the world of magic, spells and survival, destiny blade cuts everything. Now Guinevere let me clean you and Chloe up and make you two presentable to meet King Arthur Pendragon of Camelot. Time for slight improvement magic, you will not feel a thing, but your garments will shine."

*Merlin waves his hand slightly left and right, counts to five, and wizard magic happens, suddenly both Chloe and Guinevere are ready to meet King Arthur.*

**GUINEVERE**

**CHLOE**

"Wow Merlin! Now you are cooking with gas, Guinevere you look so beautiful, I love the gold dress it matches your eyes."

"Why thank you so much Chloe, I feel like a princess, and you are one astonishingly beautiful warrior."

"Well lady Guinevere and lady Chloe, I out did myself with my garment spell, now this spell is permeant, until you change your clothes. Ha!"

"Why Merlin, you clever Wizard, humor does the heart good."

"I believe, you are correct Chloe, now we will go meet King Arthur, so Guinevere you are a princess from the land of Cameliard, Chloe you are her traveling warrior protection. At least for now, because meeting Arthur is going to be a very delicate meeting, first impression means a lot to Arthur. I will let Arthur know that I met you in your travels, and that your Kingdom is no more, due to witchery and the passage of time. This is all so true, so Arthur will understand that you are looking for a new home. It would not be the first time a cruel curse has dismembered a kingdom, now we need some horses for the rest of the journey."

*Merlin waves his hand left than right and a mist, mixed with light suddenly materializes and fades away. Three horses with saddles and reigns appear, one Arabian gold, one Sky blue and one Emerald green.*

## Horses Of Camelot

"Holy medieval shit sandwich, now that is riding in colorful style Merlin!"

"No big castle idea, just a little Merlin magic, I painted each horse in our favorite color. Obviously, the Emerald green one is mine, the Arabian Gold one is Guinevere's, and the Sea blue one is yours Chloe."

"Prefect perfection Merlin, I guess you can read minds a little too."

“Most of the time, but sometimes it is a believe that becomes reality Chloe. Kinda like your destiny, but on an exceedingly smaller scale. Ok ladies, it is time to ride, Arthur’s castle is about two nights ride from here, and by my wizard’s knowledge these horses are extremely fast, so hang on. They know the way to Castle Camelot.”

*The horses of Camelot blazed a trail through the medieval landscape and made the ride in only one day. Merlin, Chloe, and Guinevere set up a camp to rest for one night, so they would be prepared for meeting Arthur.*

“Ok everyone, get some rest, we are about one mile from the Kingdom of Camelot as the Raven flies. Tomorrow will be an especially important meeting, either King Arthur excepts you into his kingdom or he tells you to leave or kills you if he feels you are threat to his kingdom.”

“I do not know for sure what will happen to me Merlin, but I have no doubt he will except Guinevere.”

“Oh yes, Guinevere is going to be fine Chloe, but you will have to proof yourself to King Arthur and the Knights of the RoundTable.”

“Merlin, did you say round table.”

“Yes, I absolutely did Guinevere.”

“My father King Leodegrance gave that round table to King Uther Pendragon, Arthur’s father. I remember it like yesterday’s breeze; it was a warm spring morning, and I went on a journey with my father and his warriors to meet King Uther. They were friends and had fought in the incredibly early crusades as young men. The *Round Table* was a gift to show appreciation to Uther for saving his life in battle. In return, King Uther told my father that no matter when, where or how life's journey takes over. King Leodegrance family will always be welcome in his kingdom and generations after. King Uther knew that my mother died giving birth to me and understood my father's suffering all to well, because he had also lost his Queen. I remember this conversation so vividly, and I remember a little boy who was a little older than me standing on the center of the round table with a look of amazement."

"Guinevere my sweet lady that was a noticeably young Arthur, who loved the round table, so his father, gave the round table to Arthur telling him to never forget the promise made to King Leodegrance and his family. Now this happened when Arthur was a young lad, but this Roundtable was the last gift King Uther gave to his son before he embarked on the fruitless quest to find and destroy the enemies that killed his Queen and people of his kingdom. Obviously, King Uther died in battle and lost his kingdom, and I brought Arthur to the far away family to protect him. As the story goes, Arthur reclaimed his Kingdom, which is now Camelot, and did find the *RoundTable* the last gift his father had given him before his death."

"Wow! You folks live in a small medieval world, but I must say, it would be easy to get lost in this world. The stories, the history, the fantasy, and action, no one can deny this to be true."

"Ok Chloe and Guinevere, I will see you in the morning, I have some Merlin mediation to take care of."

"Never question a wizard Guinevere, let's get some rest."

"I agree Chloe, morning comes fast in this land."

*As night falls upon the rolling hills of Camelot, silence becomes the music, suddenly aloud snarling sound echoes through the surrounding trees, which wakes up both Chloe and Guinevere, moments later a scream that sounded human pierces the air.*

"Did you hear that noise Chloe."

"I sure did Guinevere, and it came from that direction, just by those trees sitting at the bottom of the hillside."

"Should we find out who or what could of create such a loud horrific snarl and scream.

"Nope, my Dragon Slayer blood senses are telling me that it is an ambush. A sound that loud comes with two price tags, one is for **help**, and the other is for **harm**. I predict that **harm** is waiting at the bottom of the hillside by those trees, so let us make it walk up the hillside and spend a little bit of its violent energy."

"Chloe, but what if it is **help**, and someone needs rescued or saved."

"I will say this; we are no good to anyone if we became a victim, survey the scene before any action, my dad, the Man Called Clint always would say this. You see, my dad is a peacekeeper in my land, and would always say, look for the signs, no matter what the circumstances turn out too be."

"Your dad sounds like an incredibly wise man Chloe; I will follow your lead, Chloe."

*Chloe and Guinevere wait for the incoming danger; more snarls and humanlike screams begin to wail louder and louder, and than a bloody shadowy humanlike figure appears, the bright moonlight shines light partially onto this presence. The moonlight brightens and reveals who or what this could be.*

*A man, bleeding severely, with massive bite marks and flesh hanging from his body. The man's head is facing downward, in that moment, Guinevere starts to move towards the man, but Chloe stops her, because she knows what is coming. Guinevere looks at Chloe and asks her why they are not helping this man.*

"Guinevere that is no longer a man, dead adrenaline has arrived in Camelot, how do I know this you may ask, because these alien zombie beasts are hunting me and want to stop me on my quest to save the world. These savages are ruled by a leader called the Hive Queen, who happens to be from another world. She decided to invade earth and take control of humanity in the future year 2026. A lot to take in your mind right now Guinevere, but after what you have been through, I am sure you believe what I am saying."

“Oh yes Chloe, in a world of evil, anything is possible.”

“Guinevere wait for his head to rise, and you will see two blood red eyes, looking for a meal. A human meal is on the menu, and we are the prey, but have no doubt, Chloe the daughter of the Man Called Clint is nobody's prey.”

“By the blade of Camelot, this man’s eyes are blood red, and it looks like he has a couple of friends with him.”

“Yes, he does Guinevere, and by the looks of things, these Dead Adrenalines got into a vicious battle with the Wolves of Nightfall. Animals versus Dead Adrenaline-Alien Zombies, looks like the dead wolves lost the fight. Ok Guinevere, there are four in total of these Dead Adrenalines, stay back when they get close enough to blade cut. You see; to kill these Hive Queen minions of death, one must find the kill shot with their blade, which could be anywhere on the subject's body. On a side note, I bet these poor souls were local farmers in the area, when the Dead Adrenalines took their bodies and minds as a host.”

“I understand Chloe, but you need to manifest a sword for me with that Dragon Slayer blood superpower coursing through your veins. Kinda like when I was Artifice the witch in the marsh and you made a blade appear in your hand. I can weld a sword well, my father King Leodegrance, did have one enjoyment after the death of my mother. Teaching me the use of a sword for defense, he started instruction with me at an incredibly youthful age, so I became incredibly good at welding a sword. If possible, could you create me a Falchion sword, which I used when I trained with my father."

"Wow, like what I am hearing Guinevere, sword training, and European Falchion sword. Excellent choice, remarkably effective for slashing and chopping. Ok, here you go, take the sword, and remember, do not stop cutting until the Dead Adrenaline stops and drops."

"Thanks Chloe, and what a beautiful sword."

"You can keep the sword if you survive Guinevere! Now it is Time to Clean the Fucking Medieval land of Camelot!"

*Guinevere proofs her worth in battle and manages to kill one of the Dead Adrenaline's, after carving the hell out of the insane monster. Chloe makes short work of the other three DA(s) with only one blade cut a piece to each. Her superpower of finding the kill shot area on the Dead Adrenaline is unmatched. Long live the Dragon Slayer blood!*

"Believe it or not Guinevere, these Dead Adrenalines were in a weakened state, because they had just fought to the death with the Wolves of Nightfall. Normally they would be much more aggressive."

"I have to say Chloe, sword fighting for real is so much scarier than training, I got lucky today and survived."

"You did great, and you get to keep the sword, and you have a record of 1-0-0, win, lose draw."

"Ha! Medieval Battle humor, I guess, it keeps you going Chloe."

"Absolutely! Ok, I wonder where Merlin is, since morning has awakened."

*From the sky a falcon lands down beside Chloe and Guinevere, and a large misty cloud forms. Merlin appears from the mist bringing news and humor.*

"Good morning, ladies, I see you had a small battle for breakfast, I, myself enjoyed some nice, delicious chicken eggs from the local farm. Those farmers you both just ended will not be needing them anymore. Here are a couple of eggs for both of you, I cooked these eggs up with some Merlin magic to a nice, hard-boiled consistency."

"Thanks Merlin, Guinevere and I worked up a warrior's appetite this morning,"

"Oh, Guinevere my dear, I see your gold dress got some battle blood from that Dead Adrenaline you killed, here is a little morning magic to clean the dress up."

"Thank you, kind sir, I want to be my best this morning for the meeting with King Arthur."

"Well not even a drop of Dead Adrenaline blood touched your garments, Chloe."

"Yeah Merlin, a little luck, skill, and superpower took care of battlefield-business this time, but I am sure more bloodshed is on its way."

“Yes, Chloe your analysis is perfectly exact, more bloodshed is coming, in four days from now, violence, death, and mayhem will be on King Arthur’s Kingdom’s gates. Remember when I told you about the Saxon and Viking army teaming up and making a journey to the Land of Camelot with unknown evil traveling companion.”

“I do Merlin, did you have a vision that has given more information about this.”

“Not just a vision, a bird's eye view, last night, I decided to take a flight to their location, which is four days away. I used a little of my teleport magic, and shaped shifted into, the Falcon you happen to see this morning. They are most definitely on the move, and without a doubt the dead adrenaline infection is marching with them. Looks to be at least a mix of a 300 Saxons and Vikings all red eyed up and ready for carnage. King Arthur Knights & Knightesses max out around 150 of men and women. The 150 more warriors in the enemy's army does not worry me, because Arthur’s Knights are unmatched in battle, but the dead adrenaline aspect is a concerning matter.”

“Yes, the dead adrenaline infection is no joke, King Arthur needs to prepare and know exactly how to kill these dead adrenalines. It is nice to hear that King Arthur does not care if his Knights are all men, if they can fight, they a can become a Knight or a Knightess, so I guess the women can battle.”

“King Arthur is a great leader of his people, but he does have a certain way he decides if he is going to listen. Meaning, Arthur only will listen if he trusts you, which is ridiculously hard to earn from him, and I do not think four days will be enough time. Now about women becoming Knightesses, this happen 10 years ago when the Kingdom of Camelot was under attack, and more than half of his male Knights could not help in the battle, because a spell by a wandering Witch used by the enemy attackers, the spell paralyzed them. They were of no use, and the bloody battle was in full force. On that day he asked any woman that could hold a sword to help in the fight. Thirty women stepped forward and were prepared to die for the Kingdom. King Arthur knighted each one at that moment, and they held back the enemy attackers long enough, until I could break the spell and get the male Knights back in the fight. The Kingdom on that day survived and the women who fought, some of which did not survive, earned King Arthur's trust. I made out superbly that day and Arthur gave me my own chambers in the castle to study magic and sleep and relax. I use it from time to time."

"Sounds bad ass to me Merlin, ok, let us see if his trust and loyalty will be given."

*Merlin, Chloe, and Guinevere finally arrived at the castle gates of Castle Camelot, Chloe was amazed by the beauty and scale of the castle, King Arthur's Kingdom is spectacular.*

## CASTLE CAMELOT

"Something to see, what do you think Chloe."

"Merlin, it is everything the story books described wow! Amazement is not a strong enough word, is that silver armored plated stone walls."

"Yes Chloe, the stone outside walls have silver plated armor covering the Castle Camelot. This forms a solid shield for the castle, which makes Castle Camelot an unmatched fortress when war is at the gates. Also, the surrounding mountains and cliff sides protect castle from a rear attack. Now the silver that you see is like nothing ever discovered before, the silver can harden to steel if heated at the right temperature. In the time of Uther Pendragon, Arthur's father, he discovered the liquid silver just below the Cascade mountains in a creek bed. The Uther siphoned the silver liquid up and kept it in large barrels in a hidden location and never sold it or used it for any economical kingdom gain."

"Before he past on to the afterlife, Uther told Arthur about the liquid silver and where to find the barrels. King Uther also told Arthur about the Cascade mountains, and the legend of then Dragon realm, which is a real place where dragons live. Uther told his son to use the silver liquid for the benefit of the kingdom, but to never go to Cascade Mountain again in search of more silver. King Uther warned Arthur, and told him that the risk is too great, even though the silver was just outside the Dragon realms mountain, this was still too close and must never happen again."

"You see a human must never enter the dragon realm because it is certain doom. More about dragons later, anyways King Arthur decided to have his blacksmiths heat up the silver and coat the outside walls with the silver, which harden to a steel like consistency, which helps protect the Kingdom. There was enough liquid silver left over, so King Arthur had his blacksmiths use the castle's forge to heat up the remaining silver and coated his battle armor, along with twelve of his lead Knights and Knightesses armor. These Knights and Knightesses are his best fighters, eight men and four are women. The Roundtable is English aged oak and is a gathering place for King Arthur and his Roundtable Warriors to discus peace and prosperity, and war plans when the need arises. The Silver Castle and battle Armor was completed, shortly after King Arthur reclaimed his Kingdom and established the Knights and Knightesses of the RoundTable, and the Kingdom of Camelot as we know it to be today."

"Yea Chloe, the Castle appears even bigger and shiner then I remember as child, and usually that is the other way around. As an adult what you thought was amazing and bigger than life, becomes smaller later in life. Not this time."

"Yep Guinevere, not this time."

"Ok Chloe and Guinevere, we will be entering the gate, they will let me in because I am King Arthur's Wizard, plus, I could just zap myself inside if I need to, which they have found out on many occasions. Remember Guinevere, you are Princess Guinevere of the Cameliard Kingdom, which is no longer, and King Leodegrance was your father. All this is true, but we can leave out the details, like Guinevere becoming a witch and wanting to kill humans."

"Oh yes Merlin, I want that witch stuff to be forgotten for ever."

"It is my dear Guinevere, now Chloe, you are her warrior protection and were task with her safety, after the fall of the Cameliard Kingdom, due to a witch's curse. This is true, you have saved her from a witch's curse and are protecting her."

"No problem, Merlin man, I love your spin on the truth, it is true but depending on what part you read first. Sounds good to me, but I would say Guinevere can handle herself well with a sword, if necessary, so King Arthur better be nice."

"After being around so many centuries, Chloe, and Guinevere, it is fun to spin a little web to indirectly help the outcome. Ok, the Kingdom of Camelot will never be the same, but destiny is destiny."

*A Kingdom guard yells out to Merlin, Chloe, and Guinevere.*

"Cease your movement, or you will find an arrow in your direction, who is this wanting to enter King Arthur's Castle."

"Why it is Merlin Ambrosius, King Arthur's sorcerer, open the gate these women are riding with me. I bring news of an impending danger that will soon be approaching the castle walls."

"Merlin! I did not recognize you; it has been quite some time since you have visited the castle. Open the gate!"

*Merlin, Chloe and Guinevere ride into the castle grounds on the Emerald green, Sky blue, and Arabian gold horses, a crowd gathers around them, mixed with warriors, land farmers, bakers, blacksmiths, and teachers. Children are running around playing and seem to be the most amazed by the color of the horses. Suddenly, the crowd of people separates, and a large pathway opens. Merlin, Chloe, and Guinevere dismount their horses, and hand them off to the Stable Master, who takes them and ties them off. A man dressed in all black, approaches Merlin, Chloe, and Guinevere, he is the medieval guide of the King and knows Merlin well."*

“Hello, my friend, so nice to see you, it has been over a year.”

“Yes, it has Quintus, how are you this fine Camelot morning.”

“You know, shades of light and shades of dark, the kingdom is always evolving sometimes it is exceedingly difficult to keep the dark out. Merlin, I do love when you show up, because you always bring new Merlin magic into the castle, like solid painted horses that shine so bright. Looks like you brought some more light into today’s morning, who are these two beautiful women you have riding with you this morning.”

“They both have titles and extraordinary backgrounds that King Arthur’s ears must hear about before anyone inside the kingdom walls. Now the horses are old magic, I picked up during magic art class centuries ago.”

“Understood Merlin, no need to explain further, I will take you to him right now.”

*Quintus walks Merlin, Chloe, and Guinevere down a corridor and past four guards standing at the bottom of a set of stone steps. Quintus stops for a moment whisper something to the guards, and they step to both sides of the steps. Quintus motions for Merlin, Chloe, and Guinevere to follow him up the stone steps. Once at the top of the steps, it opens to a large area with what looks to be a a training room of sorts, with Knights and Knightesses practicing with some swords, upon closer look the sword blade usage appeared in action, real battle attack, and defense. Some of the Knights and Knightesses were bleeding, from non-life-threatening areas of their bodies. While some fighters were doing some full contact blade cuts, many others were standing guard in front and near a large wooden door found next to the training area. Quintus walks up to one of the Knight's and tells them Merlin is here with some visitors; the Knight looks past Quintus, sees Merlin, and quickly knocks on the wooden door, and opens the chamber door. The Knights step aside, and Merlin, Chloe, and Guinevere enter the chamber area. Upon entering this area, a Knight appears from behind a stone wall centered in the chamber area and begins to speak.*

"My name is Sir Bors, I 'am loyal to King Arthur and one of his lead Knight's of the Roundtable, what brings you to us on this fine day Merlin and by the way I gave my name and title for the benefit of these two ladies standing behind you."

"Good to see you Sir Bors, I bring news of an impending danger that is befalling this, Kingdom. I have with me two women, Princess Guinevere of the fallen Cameliard Kingdom, and Lady Chloe, who is her traveling protection. You see a Witch had cursed the Cameliard Kingdom and King Leodegrance is no longer, but Guinevere his daughter managed to survive, and Chloe became her protector. Chloe has taken and vow to never leave her side, until Guinevere was safe from outside forces of this cruel land."

"Mmm, interesting story to say the least, but give me a minute and I will pass this information onto King Arthur, who sits just beyond this stone wall."

“Ok, Sir Bors may take a few minutes to enlighten Arthur, Bors is very faithful and loyal to the cause and King Arthur, and his swordsmanship is better than most, but not the best. Bors would take a blade for Arthur because a Knight of the Roundtable serves the Kingdom of Camelot without hesitation.”

*As Merlin, Chloe and Guinevere are waiting for Sir Bors to return, a loud voice echos from behind the stone wall. It is a voice of a King, and Merlin hears the voice and knows it is King Arthur calling out to him.”*

“Merlin! Merlin! My friend, I hear you have brought visitors to my kingdom and treacherous news that is on the march to this land. Please come fourth and we will discuss your discovery of enemies preparing to cause bloodshed in the land of Camelot. And yes, most definitely bring the ladies with you, I want to meet them.”

*Merlin, Chloe, and Guinevere move forward and walk around the stone wall. On the other side is a sight of pure medieval perfection, the man himself King Arthur, and his Knights and Knightesses standing comfortably behind a fantastic Oak wood Roundtable. A sight plucked from the pages of the storybooks and legend that would leave any warrior or non-warrior amazed in positive fashion.”*

**King Arthur & the Knights & Knightesses of the Roundtable.**

"Merlin, you crazy wizard, where have you been, you have been away for a year, and who are these beautiful women with you on this brilliant morning."

*"Guinevere smiles at King Arthur and wonders how a man in charge of such a powerful kingdom, can be so positive and uplifting, knowing death is marching towards his kingdom.*

*Guinevere turns to Chloe for a moment with a look of uncertainty. Chloe looks at Guinevere and says something that catches King Arthur's ear.*

"Guinevere a man like King Arthur and his Knights and Knightesses want peace primarily, but the warrior spirit does invite another test of true battle. So, news of an army of pain, suffering, and death eclipsing on their land is a challenge to test their *skills."*

"You are precisely correct, lady with the blue eyes and blond hair. What a warrior mindset of wisdom you have just spoken about. What is your name and who is the enchanting beauty you were talking to.

*Chloe looks at Merlin, smiles and starts to talk to Arthur without hesitation or fear.*

"My name is Lady Chloe of Beaver County, Pennsylvania, which is a far-off land, not on any of your land charts or maps for this region. King Leodegrance called upon me and our kingdoms warriors to help his kingdom, which was under attack by violent raiders that a witch was helping to overthrow. I am the only remaining warrior left, and entrusted to protect Princess Guinevere, until she could find safety and a new home. If Camelot is everything, we believe it to be than Guinevere has found her new home and place of safety."

"Well said Lady Chloe, Merlin, you sly wizard, this one has a fighting spirit. Chloe you and I will need to talk further, but for now have a seat around this glorious Roundtable, and we will discuss together the violence coming our way, and how to best defend the kingdom and my people. Princess Guinevere come sit by me, I want to hear your story, and about your father King Leodegrance, my father King Uther was fantastic friends with your father, and they would meet at warriors' gatherings to discuss the state of the lands. I was just boy during those times, but I remember it vividly. In fact, this amazing Roundtable was a gift from your father to mine. Obviously, my father had passed on to a higher plain, and I did not know about the attack on your kingdom, or I would have sent help."

"Yes King Arthur, the witches magic was powerful, and no word of the attack got out. A memory spell caused any messenger to forget the message of help when they made it to your kingdom. And during the days of warriors gathering, I was just a little girl too, but I do remember the meetings and seeing you as a boy. I was there the day my father gifted your father the Roundtable.

"Makes total sense Princess Guinevere, we have history from an incredibly early age. Now let us all sit and enjoy some morning breakfast, as we discuss the current events on the castle walls. Make room for our guest, Knights and Knightesses grab three chairs for them to sit. Merlin, describe to me the threat coming our way, and Lady Chloe, and Princess Guinevere fill any blanks in the story, because at my table everyone's opinion matters."

*And on this Medieval morning the meeting of a King and his Knights and Knightesses of the Roundtable, a woman named Lady Chloe from a far-off land called Beaver County, Pennsylvania, and a Princess from the Kingdom of* Cameliard, *along with the Wizard Merlin discuss the evilness coming to the kingdom. Merlin explains how he visually did see this army of death with red eyes and the taste for human flesh on the march. He explained simply that this demon death had taken over the bodies and minds of the enemy, so they are even more powerful.* Merlin goes on to explain the army is a mix of a 300 Saxons and Vikings all red eyed up, ready for carnage, and about four days away from the kingdom.

*Chloe decides to give details of where this possession, manifest from, stands up from the Roundtable and begins to speak, and the fire and brimstone in her voice made everyone silent as she revealed the source of the Dead Adrenaline invasion.*

"This force is not of this world; it comes from a far-off universe beyond our believe system. It is not human, it is not animal, but it is alien to our world! The evil entities inside these enemy forces want nothing more than to destroy humanity. You see, I come from the year 2086 in the future and have been sent back in time, to gather knowledge of fighting, wisdom to think through this conflict, and travel back to the year 2026 to help my father, *The Man Called Clint* end these alien creatures once and for all in a final battle. This is the only way; we can stop this madness from continuing. One last thing, there is a certain way to kill these Alien-Zombie humans, a blade cut to their weak spot where the alien entity has attached."

*Silence comes over everyone sitting at the Roundtable, when suddenly, King Arthur erupts in laughter, along with his Knights and Knightess's. Arthur looks over at Merlin and tells him that this Chloe is one great storyteller, but laughter is a much-needed friend when death is knocking on the castle gate. King Arthur's smile leaves him, and he starts to give orders to his lead Knights and Knightesses of the Roundtable.*

"Spread the word of the traveling raiders advancing towards the castle, explain to the other Knights and Knightesses that these are both human and evil. Fortify the castle line of protection, send scouts out to see where these enemies are and how close they are to our land. Once we know this, we will take the battle to them, this fight must end on the medieval battlefield and not within our castle walls. The castle walls will be our last resort, but failure is not on this Roundtable. Put these orders into place, and let me know the outcome, then we will go to battle."

*Each Knight and Knightess understood completely and left the chamber to fulfill their medieval orders. King Arthur stood in the chamber with Merlin, Chloe, and Guinevere, at that moment Arthur walks up to Chloe and places his hand on her shoulder and makes a statement that proves he is the King of Camelot.*

"Lady Chloe, I do not fully understand what you have just said to us, but I believe you. Truth comes in many forms but believe is believe, and I know death is coming to Camelot, and we must be prepared. You will train my Knights and Knightesses on how to kill these demon dogs, or like you said, Dead Adrenalines."

"Thank you, King Arthur, trust me when I say this, knowing how to kill these savages will give your kingdom a fighting chance, because this battle will be like nothing you have ever encountered or will again."

"Time for me to tend to a few castle things, make yourself at home, Quintus will show you to your chambers Chloe, along with Guinevere. Merlin you already know where your place in the castle is my wizard friend. One last thing, I need to say, Guinevere your beauty is overwhelming in an incredibly positive light, it is so wonderful I got to see you standing with us in Castle Camelot. Ok, I will meet you in our fight yard in a couple of hours, Lady Chloe bring that fighting knowledge with you, because you are going to need it. My twelve lead Knights and Knightesses will get the training, and they will pass it down the castle line."

*With those words, King Arthur quickly walks out of the Roundtable chamber.*

"Well, Ladies the message we brought did not fall on closed ears. Arthur has heard and believes in the cause; now we have a fighting chance."

“Sure do, Merlin, Guinevere looks like you caught King Arthur with a positive light of beauty. Also, nice story telling Guinevere, memory spell, brilliant thing to say. Ha!”

“Yeah, guess, I still have little trickery left in me, but only for good of humanity. I am not going pretend; Arthur is one handsome King, and from where I was sitting, he was great listener too.”

“Ok, ladies, Quintus will take you to your quarters, we will meet in the fight yard in a couple of hours. Now I have some Camelot Castle business to take care of, a Wizard’s work is never done.

“Yep, sounds like a solid plan of action Merlin, see you than.

*Chloe and Guinevere settle in for a couple of hours in visiting chambers; Guinevere decides to take a nap to catch on her beauty rest. Chloe focuses on her blade cuts, preparing to train the Knights and Knightesses of the Roundtable in a couple of hours.*

# PREPARING FOR VIOLENCE

## 13TH CENTURY

*King Arthur stands at the top castle tower, overlooking the land of Camelot, knowing that death is on the march and his kingdom is directly in its path. As Arthur stands there focusing on his battle strategy, a white mist suddenly appears, Merlin materializes before his eyes, and Merlin looks at Arthur and begins to speak.*

"Arthur my friend, you are troubled, as you should be. Death on the highest evil level is coming to Camelot. I can only tell you that Lady Chloe of Beaver County, Pennsylvania is our salvation, she speaks honestly and is a great warrior in her time and other times on earth. Chloe's ability to kill these Dead Adrenaline is unmatched, she is of a supernatural realm, like me, but on a far deeper level that travels beyond our realm. Her destiny lies in the Dragon Realm, so this battle against these savages must happen, and death is the only outcome for them. Chloe needs to fulfill the prophecy she was born to do. Arthur, do you grasp what I am saying."

"Merlin, a wise man once told me to believe, know, understand, prepare, and let your blade speak for you when the time is right. You see that man is me, no one else, it is time to let my blade speak! Lady Chloe will train my Knights and Knightesses on how to kill these Dead Adrenaline warriors, and our Kingdom will not fall, and Chloe will fulfill her destiny for the good of all humanity! For on this day, the Kingdom of Camelot's sword blade will speak!

"Well, Arthur, it sounds like you found your voice again, and I did not even have to cast a happiness spell."

"You crazy wizard, you always know how to make me laugh!

*Laughter echoes through the valley of Camelot, a King, and a Wizard, finding humor even as death is creeping closer.*

"OK Guinevere, Sir Quintus has just brought us to the so-called fight yard. I do not see any Knights or Knightesses yet, but I do hear laughter in the air echoing. It is Merlin and King Arthur I believe, having a good healthy laugh, nice to hear, humor keeps a person going as my dad the Man Called Clint has said."

"Wow, even King Arthur's laugh sounds kind and wonderful."

"Geez Guinevere, you got it bad, Arthur better be ready."

*In orderly fashion, the Knights and Knightesses of the Roundtable slowly trickle in like a consistent flow of water in stream. Three female Knightesses and nine male Knights, each with a look of disagreement on their faces. Finally, King Arthur arrives with Merlin, Arthur walks up to a female Knightess and asked her if the kingdom defenses are in place. She nods her head signaling everything is in place, Arthur turns to Chloe, and draws his blade, tells Chloe with a slight smile, let us begin, death is marching, and time is always leaving, no matter how much we try to stay in the moment. Chloe draws her sword, which is her katana blade, but decides to transform the blade into a more efficient medieval Falchion sword for the blade fight ahead. Chloe looks at the warriors and tells them it is time to prepare for violence. They look on in astonishment of this magic, Arthur laughs and says, she is the prophecy!*

*King Arthur and each of his Knights and Knightesses realize that Chloe is not your average swordswoman, she brings smoothness and power behind every movement. Each individual fighter starts to pick up the movements and technique, realizing that quick speed and power combined will help the process of finding a week spot on the Dead Adrenaline. The learning process went fantastic because Chloe is a great teacher, but each Knight and Knightess, including King Arthur posses a quality that makes the perfect student. No ego or jealousy.*

*The days training was complete, the Knights, Knightess's, and King Arthur learned how to find the blade cut kill shot, and how to remove the armor of their opponent quickly with each cut, so no armor protection would be in place. Even Guinevere got training, which impressed and delighted King Arthur. Chloe had completed her task of training King Arthur and the Knights and Knightesses of the Roundtable. King Arthur was pleased and had his Chevaliers and Dames spread this training throughout the Kingdom, because he knew not only his lead warriors should have this knowledge, but the whole entire Kingdom family. The King thought, anyone able to hold a sword would learn these techniques, some will be less effective, but better to have a defense and attack than to have no knowledge to survive. Chloe agreed and now understood why he is the King of Camelot, and his kingdom is strong.*

*Two days passed, and King Arthur lead warriors were able to train the rest of lower-level Knights and Knightess's. The kingdom is 150 strong with men and women ready to face the march of Dead Adrenaline enemy warriors heading towards the kingdom. Also, the commoners inside the castle walls and surrounding the kingdom were taught how to kill a DA. King Arthur has a conversation with Sir Gawain, who is a trusted and relied on Knight in the kingdom."*

"King Arthur, the Knights and Knightesses are ready for battle, 50 will stay back with Castle Camelot to protect it, along with our community of people, which include men, women, and children. This leaves us with 100 strong for the field of battle."

"Yes, Sir Gawain, this is a solid battle strategy, we will leave the castle with 100 of my finest warriors, which includes you and nine of my lead Knights. Sir Bors and Dame Fay that are lead Knight and Knightess will keep order in the kingdom, while we are gone to end this attack. While I got your attention, where is my thirteenth Knight, has he returned from the woods, which he so enjoys. He always tells me it keeps his skills sharp to be with nature."

"Actually, your thirteenth Knight has returned and is waiting to get some Dead Adrenaline training in the fight yard."

“Well, he should pick the sword wielding moves up quick, because he is one of our best swordsmen’s in Camelot, aside from me.”

“Very true my King.”

“Ok, I will have Lady Chloe train him, and this should be something to see. Have Quintus, get Lady Chloe and we will meet at the fight yard.”

“Already taken care of King Arthur, she is being escorted to the fight yard as we speak.”

“Excellent, let us head down and get a front row seat, inform the other Knights and Knightesses about this training / match of sorts. I do enjoy good blade cutting fun, and my thirteenth Knight does not like to lose in training or anything.

“Thanks, Quintus, for bringing me to the fight yard, King Arthur must want me too personally train this last Knight on how to kill a Dead Adrenaline. Interesting, Quintus, what is this Knight’s name.”

“Hello, Lady Chloe, here comes King Arthur and his twelve lead Knights and Knightess’s, also, it looks like our friend Merlin just misted into the fight yard with Guinevere. Now about this thirteenth Knight’s name, King Arthur can tell you this Knight’s name. Looks like you got a captive audience Lady Chloe, a large crowd is gathering.

“Hello Chloe, one last Knight to train up, he is my thirteenth Knight and is my best sword fighter in Camelot, here he comes now, you can not miss him, he is the one dressed in gold armor. Be careful this Knight has never lost in battle, in truth, not even a cut from blade."

"Wait a medieval minute, he is the thirteenth Knight, Holy Grail shit sandwich, why it is Sir Lancelot."

"Yes Lady Chloe, it is Sir Lancelot, my best Knight in the kingdom, I will not ask how you know his name, but I must warn you, Lancelot is a different breed of Knight, he fights with his King and Kingdom but has a stand-alone attitude. Meaning, he will kill you if he gets the chance, so you better be prepared when the training begins."

*Chloe looks at King Arthur, and nods her head with approval, then she glances over to Guinevere and does see a slight glimpse of excitement in her eyes as she is looking at Lancelot. Chloe thinks to herself, this could be bad if the Arthurian legend is true. Guinevere marries King Arthur, and Lancelot seduces Guinevere and betrays Arthur. Although the Dead Adrenaline soldiers on the march could change the outcome of coming events, so Chloe gathers her thoughts and focuses on Lancelot who is walking up to her.*

"Well, it is nice to meet the lady who has trained my brother and sister Knights and Knightesses of the Roundtable. I heard you speak my name, so no need to waste time on introductions, but know this, I will not lose today, you will either yield to my blade or die here and now in front of the gathering audience."

*Chloe laughs and than says something the medieval world has not heard in this speaking fashion.*

"Let us do this Lancelot, and "Don't Be a Dill Weed!"

*Merlin smiles and tells King Arthur, a Dill Weed is an herb, but in Chloe's land dill weed means begin. Arthur begins to laugh and tells Merlin, I know it is an herb, but Chloe just insulted Lancelot. Good for her, sometimes the first blade cut is words, and with this exchange, Merlin and Arthur sit back to watch the match unfold.*

**Sir Lancelot**

*Chloe squares off on Sir Lancelot, already knowing this man did not come here for practice, but for real-medieval battle. Guinevere looks at King Arthur and asked him a concerning question.*

"I thought this was just practice and training, both Chloe and Sir Lancelot looked prepared for war."

*Arthur looks back with a gentle smile and tells her something remarkably true.*

"Not on this day, you see Lancelot is a warrior that will not bend with the wind, he as never lost and if someone is going to train him. This person must proof worthy to be his teacher, unfortunately for Lancelot, Lady Chloe of Beaver County, Pennsylvania is not from this land, and she is bringing a windstorm, so he better start bending."

Sir *Lancelot moves in quickly and closes the distance on Chloe with a lateral line of attack, his sword techniques are impeccable, Chloe's left rib area feels a slight sting of the blade. Lancelot was going for deadly blade cut and wanted to slice through the ribs to a vital organ, now there is no doubt he is trying to kill Chloe. During this deadly sword attack, Chloe manages to deflect the sword blade of Lancelot, so she could avoid death, after this deflection, she, quickly sliced a-crossed Lancelot right sword hand, causing a massive blade cut opening, which begins to spray blood from a damaged artery. Lancelot sword falls from his grip onto the blood-stained medieval dirt. Chloe side steps and resets with her sword, normally she would continue the attack, but today is for training purposes, even-though Lancelot is fighting for a kill. Lancelot quickly wraps his right hand with a torn piece of his inner garment. Chloe looks at Lancelot and gives him a chance to stop his violent behavior, so she can teach him how to fight Dead Adrenalines and kill them.*

"Sir Lancelot, I am no ordinary women! I have Dragon Slayer Blood coursing through my veins, so know this, you are fighting with a warrior that not only has fighting skills but also has supernatural abilities. My Falchion sword cut through your gold-plated armor, now your sword hand is useless. I have powers that are hard to explain but explanations do not change what just happen. Yield to my warning because I will not give another."

*King Arthur watched in amazement, as did his Knights, Knightess's, and people gathering in the fight yard arena. At that moment, Arthur realized what Merlin has been saying was true, Lady Chloe of Beaver County, Pennsylvania is the prophecy.*

*Sir Lancelot, looked over to King Arthur and than back at Chloe, he smiled and laughed with confidence. Reach down and pick up his sword with his left hand and started to speak.*

"I will say this, Lady Chloe, you are fast and exact with the sword, but I did cut your rib area, and I do see some blood coming from your side. You should be the one thinking about stepping aside and backing down from this frenzy fight. I out match you; I am going to let you in on a little secret, my best sword arm is my left, but I can wield a sword blade with either.

Now think about this Lady Chloe, if I cut you with my weak sword hand, what could I do if I used my more powerful, fast, and exact left hand. You believe you have bested me, but the match is not over, until only one stands."

"Oh boy, really Lancelot, you want to continue this sword fight to the death, even though you are going to bleed out if you do not get that hand injury cauterized. My injury is minor, but yours is a lot deadlier, your choice, so make it."

*Sir Lancelot starts to stumble slightly from loss of blood, but is still ready to advance towards Chloe, because he will not yield, even though the odds are against him. One, then two steps towards Chloe, when suddenly he looks past Chloe for a second and sees a vision of the most beautiful lady he has ever had the honor to lay eyes on. Under his breath you could quietly here him say, so you are Guinevere, and as the words gently rolled out of his mouth. Sir Lancelot collapsed and passed out from his injury onto the medieval ground. At that moment, King Arthur, ordered two of his Knights to lift Lancelot up off the ground and get him to the barber-surgeons for now, and find the Master Surgeon for the castle. But, as the Knights were removing Lancelot, something horrific happened.*

*Sir Lancelot, no! Stop! What are you doing, the crowd of common folk gathering begin to scream at what they were seeing. Lancelot had just bit both Knights on the throat and tore out their windpipes, blood splashes out of there necks like a waterfall of red medieval wine. As the Knights collapse to the ground, Sir Lancelot stays standing, his eyes are blood red, and his hunger is on full display.*

**Sir Lancelot has Become a Dead Adrenaline**

*King Arthur draws his sword and moves towards Lancelot.*

"Wait Arthur!"

"No Merlin, Sir Lancelot has become one those Dead Adrenaline beings, which is now inside Camelot's Castle walls. This should not be, I will be the one who kills my thirteenth Knight. No one else, not even you Lady Chloe."

"King Arthur, I understand, but you must realize that these alien Dead Adrenaline entities are cunning beast that always, I mean always have a reason for everything they execute. Lancelot is now a Dead Adrenaline host, but his body is dying, due to the wound he suffered, too much blood loss, so this DA entity will want to leave his body and find a stronger more suitable host."

*Suddenly a distorted hideous voice begins to echo through fight yard arena. It is Lancelot, or what used to be him, now the Dead Adrenaline speaks for him.*

"Chloe is right, my King, Hahaha! You humans will parish and our species will remain; nothing will stop us. Come to me King Arthur, we were brothers in the crusades and have fought side by side over lands and beyond. I have saved your life, and you have saved mine. You know this to be true, where is your loyalty to me, has it faded away like the passages of time."

"Loyalty is a word only used by Knights, and you are no Knight, Lancelot once was my thirteenth Knight, but now that is no longer, on this day."

*With those words said by King Arthur, he steps back, hands Chloe his sword, and nods for Chloe to finish the training session. The Knights code requires the sword of a King to end the life of a Knight that is no longer with them, due to unforeseen consequences.*

"I will make it quick, out of respect for your Knight, King Arthur, especially this one."

*Chloe looks directly at Sir Lancelot and does not say a word. Her actions decide his fate, and like an unexpected sting from a wasp, her sword blade with one movement, cuts both hands off, and than pierces underneath Lancelot's chin and up through his skull. Chloe retracts the sword; Lancelot begins fall to ground and is no more. No signs of life, the Dead Adrenaline is dead, along with Sir Lancelot, the thirteenth Knight of the Roundtable.*

**THE ENDING OF DA LANCELOT**

"Ok my people of Camelot, nothing more to see here, the match is over."

*King Arthur's Knights and Knightesses all start to yell out.*

"King Arthur has spoken! Everyone, leave the fight yard now!"

*As the common folks start to disperse and leave the fight yard, Chloe starts to yell for them to stop, she has something to say and wants everyone to hear her words.*

"Now you all know what we are dealing with! Be ready because this evil will not stop, until each and everyone of your human bodies become food or an alien entity host! This force of Dead Adrenalines hunger for the taste of human flesh, and need bloodshed, and suffering to survive. As you have just seen, a Dead Adrenaline entity will take over your mind and body if your will to survive weakens. You will become a shit sandwich of evil and death, Sir Lancelot has proven this, in his wounded and weaken state the Dead Adrenaline captured him and took control of him. Remember this day, this fight, this savagery, because what you have just been a part of is nothing more than a minor blade cut compared to what is coming."

*And, with those strong words from Chloe, the crowd of people slowly started to chant, "We will fight for our people, for our King, and for Camelot! Camelot forever!!!!*

*At that moment, King Arthur walked up to Lady Chloe with a profoundly serious expression on his face and held out his sword and pointed it towards her.*

*Chloe looked over at Merlin, and realized what she needed to do, looked back at King Arthur, and than kneels at his feet.*

*At that moment, King Arthur tells Lady Chloe to stand, and unlike past dubbing ceremonies of a Knight or a Knightess's, King Arthur is now standing eye to eye with her and then begins to speak.*

"Lady Chloe, you are beyond anything or anyone I have ever seen in my kingdom. Your ability to fight, blended with supernatural powers, means only one thing. The prophecy has arrived, and it is you, Merlin told me one day a women would arrive in the Kingdom of Camelot for righteous reasons and survival in her eyes. You are that woman, and now has you stand before me, with the power of my Kingship, I dub you to be my thirteenth Knightess of the Roundtable."

*With those words, King Arthur places his sword on Chloe's upper right shoulder and neck, and speaks these words, **"Be Thou a Knightess."***

**CHLOE IS KNIGHTED BY KING ARTHUR**

*The people of Camelot erupted with cheering and excitement in the fight yard arena, now Chloe, will be the Thirteenth Knightess and is forever part of Camelot! And with those words the people of Camelot slowly start to disperse and prepare for the battle that is coming. King Arthur tells his Knights and Knightesses to assemble at the Roundtable for one last conversation, before they embark on the journey to meet the Dead Adrenaline Saxon-Vikings and take the battle to them.*

"Chloe! Chloe! Wow, and I did not see this coming.

"Guinevere, I do not know why I am going to say this, but sorry about Sir Lancelot, I saw how you were looking at him."

"Oh, you mean 'Sir Lance-a-not!' Trust me that would have been a big medieval mistake, I think he might have been into his gold armor more than anything else. Although, he did protect the kingdom, until his ego took over and clouded his judgement."

"Guinevere, glad to hear you say this, because had Lancelot survived, this kingdom would have changed in a betrayed way forever."

"Knightess Chloe, come with me for moment, I would like to speak with you before you meet at the Roundtable with our King.

"Absolutely Merlin."

"Guinevere, I will talk with you later."

"Ok Chloe."

"What is on your wizardry mind Merlin?"

"Oh, you know the normal, kingdoms, witches, medieval battles, dragons, and prophecies, with occasional time travel twist. You see Knightess Chloe; I can indirectly help along future events in this time, but you Knightess Chloe can directly alter or change future outcomes. This is a powerful elixir that one must never drink all the time, or it will consume your existence. Do you understand what I am saying?"

"Yes, I do, and you are so correct, a King and a Kingdom would have shattered, if Sir Lancelot had not fallen in the fight yard. I am not going to lie about this, Lancelot was not a good person, and his ego consumed him, in fact I believe after I injured him in the match, and this dead adrenaline arrived, he gave his mind and body to the evil entity, because he could not live with losing to me.  At that moment, I did not care to save such a selfish traitor to Camelot, not to mention the affair that would have happened in the future with Guinevere."

"Chloe, you have seen the future too, Arthur and Guinevere get married, and Lancelot betrays his king and steals Guinevere's heart."

"Yes and no, these future events are promises that could happen but sometimes promises can break. Meaning if Arthur marries Guinevere and makes her his Queen, no Lancelot is around to fuck it up, which is a wonderful thing. However, like I have said, promises of future events my never happen if we fall on the medieval battle ground against the Saxon-Viking Dead Adrenaline forces, then another future awaits. Anyways, this medieval love triangle is intriguing but is a tiny blade cut compared to the bloodshed of humankind. I need to stop the Dead Adrenalines, in this time and mine."

"I agree with your foreshadowing Chloe; the future holds the outcome of the Dead Adrenalines, and you are moving forward through the future to directly affect the outcome. Now this battle talk we speak of, keep your mind focused on the violence in the pathway ahead, which is something a true wizard always does, thinks, talks, and acts."

"You see Chloe, you have been giving many titles in this land of Camelot, in such a brief period. Let us list the titles, Chloe the daughter of the Man called Clint, Lady Chloe of Beaver County, Pennsylvania, and the Thirteenth Knightess of the Roundtable. As I speak to you Knightess Chloe, I will say you have powers far beyond this realm, sorcery will come easy to you through out the ages, and to infinity. Even with all the titles given, based on birth, location, proven battle record, and honor. There is still one more title you will obtain, and it will shape you for all time. This is your destiny and not even you will know the future outcome of this, because it will happen in the Dragon Realm. You will survive or you will parish that is the way of the dragon doctrine."

"Wow! Merlin, you just got medieval on me with destiny and dragon realm, sounds scary but intriguing at the same time. Once we kill off the Dead Adrenaline Saxon-Vikings on the march, and when the time is right, you can show me the hidden dragon realm location, and I will be ready to fulfill the prophecy."

"Absolutely Knightess Chloe when the time is right you will fulfill your destiny. Anyways, I do sometimes get into the prophecy stuff a little too much, but on a lighter conversation note, I never liked Lancelot, what a medieval donkey's ass, he never followed the Knights code of ethics and always was self absorbed. Arthur knew this, but felt obligated to Lancelot, because during the crusades, they fought side by side and saved each other's life on many occasions. Arthur knew Lancelot had many faults, but also knew that when war was happening, Lancelot would fight for the Kingdom of Camelot."

"Yep, Lancelot was shit sandwich, enough said bout this, ok good talk Merlin, catch you on the medieval battlefield if you are coming with us. I must go to a stupid meeting at the Roundtable, too many meetings about the same thing. Somethings never change, whether it is the 13$^{th}$ century or the year 2086, people are always having these fucking meeting. Funny, oh well."

"Ok Chloe, hope you have fun at the fucking meeting, I will see you in the future, and remember, a good sorcerer, thinks, talks about it, and acts."

"Your right Merlin, that makes perfect wizard sense, bye."

# MEETING AT THE ROUNDTABLE

# CLASH AGAINST THE DARKNESS

## 13TH CENTURY

*The Knights and Knightesses all gather at the Round Table and King Arthur starts to discuss the battle plan against the impending evil coming to their land. King Arthur explains in detail how the fight strategy should unfold but also discusses 2nd and 3RD medieval warfare if needed. Every warrior, including Chloe, who is now a Knightess, all have their voices heard and a complete plan of attack and defense is now sharper than a medieval blade. Chloe is extremely impressed with the outcome and believes now there is a chance to defeat the Dead Adrenaline Saxon-Vikings marching towards the kingdom. King Arthur says one more thing before they all step away from the Roundtable.*

"Defenders of Camelot, before we leave on our journey, we will bury our dead Knights, each of these Knights lost their lives by the hands of a dead adrenaline, including Sir Lancelot, this evil caused his actions and death. I will not make a speech, to engulf your spirit to go to battle, their dead bodies are that speech and a reminder we are battling an alien species!"

*With those words the Knights and Knightesses began to chant long live our King, long live Camelot!*

*A brief but meaningful ceremony for the slain Knights takes place and the fallen Knights are brought outside the castle walls to sacred blessed soil. A Knights and Knightesses cemetery nestled behind the castle with the backdrop of cliffs and mountains. Blessed soil from the waters of the Lake of Avalon, during the crusades King Arthur brought this water back from the mystical lake, legend speaks that the Lady of the Lake gave Arthur water from Avalon and a few of her tear drops from her eyes. Arthur brought the water mixed with the tears back and had Merlin and his religious priest named Saint Derfel Gadarn complete a blessing with the water and tear drops, which combined religious faith and mystical magic, "so it shall be, from life to death, to eternity, a Knights and Knightesses honor will never die."*

*With completion of the burials, King Arthur, and his men and women go to the armory to gather their weapons and protective gear. A former Knight, Sir Perceval one of King Arthur's oldest Knights, who is semi retired from being a Knight on the medieval battlefield and is now in charge of the armory and keeps track of all weapons taken and returned. One must, make no mistake, once a Knight always a Knight, a Knight never loses his edge, especially one of King Arthur's Knights. Sir Perceval starts to hand out armor, swords, and shields, along with other weapons such as the longbow and crossbow. Chloe discovers another reason the Knights and Knightesses of Camelot have an edge in battle, because one would believe that their swords blades are unmatched, this is true, but their armor is something made from Arthurian legend. A bright silver shine of light comes from the armor, which can blind an enemy in battle. Silver taken from the silver waters of the Cascade falls and forged into silver-plated armor that will only effect and attacking enemy. The Knight and Knightess of Camelot will not be hurt by the bright glare from the blinding light, and only an attacking enemy will feel and see the power of this light. Chloe remembers the story from Merlin and how King Uther, Arthur's father brought the silver laced water back from an area just outside of the Dragon Realm and how Arthur coated the castle with the silver and had his blacksmiths forge silver plated armor.*

*"Knightess* Chloe, here is your battle armor, it is protective but light weight, which helps each of us Knights and Knightesses in battle. Plus, the bright reflective light the silver armor gives off is an advantage in battle. There is magic in this silver, because only a true enemy of Camelot is in danger of temporarily blindness by the bright shine it gives off. Remember this, the illuminating light of the silver armor is mystical and manifest when it chooses too, as if the silver armor is alive."

"Absolutely astonishing to say the least, Sir Perceval."

"Yes, Knightess Chloe, we are a blade cut above any of our enemies, and they will soon find out that Camelot's Knights and Knightesses are battle tested."

*One hundred of King Arthur's best fighters ride out on horse-back to meet the Dead Adrenaline Saxon-Vikings and end these savage aliens from a far away universe.*

*Knightess Chloe rides next to King Arthur towards the Dead Adrenaline threat, and he tells Chloe the Kingdom is protected by a mixture of fifty Knights and Knightesses, and his people will fight til the end if necessary. Also, Arthur tells her a secret about the silver coated Camelot Castle.*

"Chloe we are a proud people, and have battle scars running through our veins, this makes all the people of Camelot love and appreciate what we have and and we will never give up what belongs to us. Also, if for some reason, these Dead Adrenaline Saxon-Vikings slip past our battle line, the Camelot castle will defend until the end, meaning the castle's silver coated stone will light up like a Medieval Christmas tree and blind the invaders, which gives my people an advantage."

"So, what you are saying Arthur, the Kingdom of Camelot does celebrate a Medieval Christmas!"

*King Arthur erupts into a loud proud laughter, which becomes contagious and the Knights and Knightesses of one hundred strong begin to laugh down the line. It was something to hear and see and Chloe starts to join in on the laughter.*

"Chloe! you are so very humorous, and most definitely, my people celebrate Christmas. I love your humor and your way of easing tensions before battle. Really good stuff!"

"Why thank you King Arthur."

*And as quickly as the laughter begin it abruptly stops, and Chloe sees a transformation of warriors, the one hundred strong have a look of serious confidence on their faces, as if the battle as already started in their minds. King Arthur is silent as if he as already made his first blade cut in battle. At that moment in this medieval time, Chloe realizes these Arthurian Warriors are true fighters that have Burendo(blended) their mind and body together for the battle ahead, just like a Burendo Shotokan Warrior would do in battle. The battle line has been set, now the cannibalistic Dead Adrenalines will realize for every action is a consequence. Let the battle for Camelot begin!*

*The one hundred strong of Camelot fighters have the Dead Adrenaline Saxon-Vikings in their blade edge sights and the DA Saxon-Vikings do not hide. For they have no fear and believe in their black hearts they will win the day, the one hundred strong Knights and Knightesses know this, and are ready to cut out their black hearts. King Arthur directs his lead Knights and Knightesses to spread out and assemble the battle plan.*

"My lead Knights and Knightesses you know the plan, take the long bows to the high ground on the cliff edges, and have the crossbows up front, when ready let the arrows fly, then have the crossbow line fall to the sides, and we will appear. Like death itself, we will cut down these enemy invaders like the sunrises with its bright glow of righteousness. Some Knights and Knightess follow behind on foot, place the animals in a safe location in the back. Make it happen and may your sword blade find its enemy on this day of victory!!!"

*Chloe follows King Arthur's lead, and knows he is the king, because he does not just tell his men and women to go into battle, he rides in first on his horse and starts the blade cutting festival! A true leader of his people, no fear of death, just embracing victory!*

*Body parts are falling from both sides of the battling medieval field, blood is spilling out like a water fall of death, such carnage and violence, no shield can protect the eyes and mind from such a brutal massacre in this thirteen century. Not a fairy tale story, just guts, blood, body parts and unimaginably pain and suffering.*

**Medieval Battlefield Runs Red**

*The Dead Adrenaline Saxon-Vikings are winning the battle of carnage, the Knights and Knightess are either dying on the mediaeval stage or changing into a dead adrenaline, which is adding to the enemy army of DA(S).*

**CLASH OF GOOD AND EVIL**

*Then it happens, like a burst of energy light, the silver armor worn by the Knights and Knightesses of Camelot begins to shine and the onslaught of Dean Adrenaline Saxon-Vikings become stunned and pushed back by the light of righteousness. In those brief seconds, the Knights and Knightesses react and start to take apart the Dead Adrenalines one cut at a time, looking for the killing blade cut. As this is unleashing, Chloe finally sees the Alpha leader of the Dead Adrenaline Saxon-Vikings and knows destroying the DA leader will confuse and weaken the enemy. It was unknown if this leader was a Saxon or Viking before the Dead Adrenaline took hold of him.*

## DEAD ADRENALINE SAXON-VIKING LEADER

"Arthur you must kill the leader of this evil Dead Adrenaline force, if the leader falls, this will weaken the enemy, and we will win the day! You are the King of Camelot, and it must be your blade cut that ends this."

"So true Chloe, and I would not have it any other way, this evil leader is mine, and I will cut him down, for I am the King of my people, and we will win on this day!"

*As King Arthur is making his way to face the evil leader, Merlin suddenly appears and throws out a spell making an opening through the wall of Dead Adrenalines standing in the way of King Arthur. Now a clear path is open for King Arthur and the Evil Leader, who has just now removed its war helmet to face off without interference. As Merlin's magic is indirectly helping, both the Saxon-Viking Dead Adrenalines and the Knights and Knightesses to stop battling each other to watch their leaders fight. It is a normal custom for battling forces to stop fighting if the leaders of both medieval tribes are facing off, so it was understandable that Arthur's men and women would stop, but the infected Saxon-Vikings must have reached down into their human memories and honored this custom. Strange, but it is happening, and King Arthur is about to clash with darkness.*

**KING ARTHUR VS DA VIKING-SAXON LEADER.**

*As everyone on both the good and evil side watch the clash of light against the darkness unfold, Merlin has positions himself at the top of a cliff edge, directly below him is the last remaining, 200 of mixed Dead Adrenalines, some Saxon and some Vikings standing there, looking at King Arthur and their evil leader in a bizarre blood thirsty way, as if they are ready to erupt like volcanic lava and scorch the earth. The Knights and Knightesses of Camelot managed to kill 100 of these dead adrenalines, but at tremendous cost. Merlin knows that if King Arthur falls in battle the blood frenzy feast will begin again, and if Arthur does kill the evil leader, these left-over Dead Adrenalines will be confused, but still very hungry for human flesh. As Merlin looks over the medieval battlefield, he realizes only a mix of fifty of the King's Knights and Knightesses remain, the rest have died or changed into dead adrenaline soldiers for the other side. The one hundred strong is now only half, which means an overwhelming outnumbering of evil is about to unleash.*

*Merlin starts to think, talk and act, just because that is what wizards do. At that moment, he decides to test out a crumble spell, which uses the ability to harness the wind and let it lose in a gusting fashion towards any object he chooses. On this day, on this battlefield, Merlin sends this bad ass wind power directly at the cliffs edge. Slamming down and chipping away enormous sized rocks and dirt and sending it downward onto the Dead Adrenaline enemies. Covering each of their bodies, fast and deadly, no signs of life remain. Eighty or so Dead*

*Adrenalines avoid the rockslide and start moving towards the King's men and women.*

*As this Merlin Magic is going down in Medieval town, King Arthur is still blade cutting away, and the Dead Adrenaline Evil leader still has not fallen on the battlefield. Both Arthur and the Evil leader have taken some cuts from each of their blades, but no fatal sword cut has landed. Arthur knows he must find the weak spot on this Dead Adrenaline and shut him down forever. As the sword cutting continues, Arthur's Knights and Knightesses care for their wounded, and his lead Knights and Knightesses assembled to cut down the Dead Adrenaline Saxon-Vikings coming there way, now the odds are better, thanks to Merlin, 80 Dead Adrenalines against a mix of 50* Knights and Knightesses, *which includes one badass fighter Chloe the Thirteen Knightess.*

*At that moment, Chloe looks at the fifty remaining Knights and Knightesses and tells them her superpower senses have just notice something that is a fantastic advantage in a way. She quickly tells them that the weak kill spot on the remaining 80 Dead Adrenaline Saxon-Vikings is all the same, and Chloe yells out. "Cut each Dead Adrenaline behind the left ear!" And with this, like a well-oiled Medieval war machine, the Knights and Knightesses of Camelot begin to systematically end the dead adrenalines, knocking their war helmets off and slicing behind the left ear. One by one the Dead Adrenaline Saxon-Vikings fall, until only one is standing, a vicious hideous looking female solider, this one is different, it waited and did not run into battle with other dead adrenalines. Chloe senses something unusual about this one, something toxic and intelligent, Chloe approaches with caution, and is ready to cut this dead adrenaline down, and than it begins to speak.*

"Chloe! Chloe! You are the daughter of the Man Called Clint, and you will pay the fatal price for the sins of your father. You will die on this medieval battlefield and will never travel to the year 2026 to help your father. If I were you, I would lay down your blade and just give in to this future fact. If you do this, I will show mercy when killing you and end your life quick, from one warrior to another."

**THE DEAD ADRENALINE VIKING WOMEN**

"Geez, every time I am just trying to save the world a dill weed shows ups, rambling on about how I will not survive, what a bunch of shit sandwich talk. No I'am good, evil bitch, my sword will stay with me, and you will find out why I'am the Man called Clint's daughter! Fellow Knights and Knightess, stay back! This one is mine to end, she just made it personal, bringing my dad into the conversation."

*With that Chloe, approaches the Evil, preparing to cut the dead adrenaline down. When suddenly, something sad an unexpected happens, the evil dead adrenaline lays her sword down and kneels and extends her neck out, as if to say please end my suffering. Emotions are present and tears are running down this Dead Adrenaline's face. Chloe is wondering two things, is this an alien entity trap, or somewhere in the recesses of this dead adrenaline soldier is her human side asking for me to end her pain and suffering. At that exact second of thought, Chloe places her left forearm directly in front of the dead adrenaline soldier's mouth, and without hesitation the dead adrenaline bites down on Chloe's forearm, a small but definite bite has happened.*

*Chloe steps back from the Dead Adrenaline Viking women, and she yells for the other Knights and Knightesses to stand back and watch. This reminds Chloe of an Incredible Hulk transformation, from Hulk, back to David Banner from the TV series, or Bruce Banner if your more of comic book person. Now this Dead Adrenaline soldier is shapeshifting from a hideous cannibalistic savage infected by and alien entity, back to her original mind and body state of living.*

*A beautiful Viking female woman stands before Chloe, and she is confused where she is and what has just happened.*

**VIKING WOMEN**

*As the Viking women is released from her alien host prison, a small lighted orb leaves her body, and is heading straight towards Chloe, Chloe holds out her right empty hand and suddenly a Katana blade materializes in her hand and once the light orb is close enough, Chloe blade cuts it in half, and the light goes out. Chloe turns and looks at her fellow Knights and Knightesses, smiles and says the Sword Saint Miyamoto showed me that blade cut.*

*Chloe has one of King Arthur's Knights speak with this Viking Women, who just so happens to speak the Viking language. He gives an explanation and communicates to this poor soul about what just happened to her. As Chloe hears them speak to each other, her mind as already grasp the Viking language and understands what the Viking women is saying. Just another Dragon Slayer blood superpower that Chloe gets to use, the power to understand any language only after a few moments of someone or something speaking.*

"Ok, everyone, no worries, see my forearm has healed up already, just another one of my superpowers as some of you know. This Viking women, now has dragon slayer blood coursing through her veins, which cured and healed her from the alien entity infection. This sometimes works and sometimes it does not, but this woman genuinely wanted to return and some how managed to control the alien entity taking her has a hostage host, and here we have it. She will need some time to accumulate back to being human again, but she is Viking and enemy of Camelot, so be careful.

*Chloe looks at the saved Viking women and asked her, what name does she go by and the Viking women response.*

"My name is Ingrid; my father is King Ragnar Lothbrok!"

"Like I said everyone, be careful, she is a Viking and now we know she is a daughter of a Viking King, none of us would have guessed that one.Ok, it looks like our King is still battling that damn Dead Adrenaline Viking-Saxon leader, what a fight, neither will yield."

*Just as those words are spoke by Chloe, King Arthur finally ends this Dead Adrenaline Saxon-Viking leader with a slicing cut a-crossed the eyes of this evil leader, cutting the pupils of both eyes. The evil leader collapses grasping his eyes, blood is spurting out from his eyes onto his hands of this abomination. Slowly the life leaves the body of this leader, and the dead adrenaline dies with the body and mind of its host.*

## THE DEAD ADRENALINE SAXON-VIKING LEADER IS DEAD

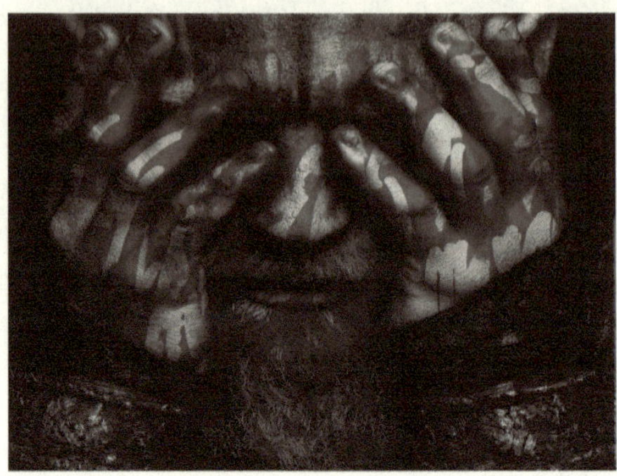

"It is over now! Death to our enemy, Camelot is safe for now, my men and women we are victorious, let us go home. We will bring our dead with us and salvage everyone from the battlefield and rock covered landscape. Chloe my thirteenth Knightess, your knowledge and fighting skills, saved us from destruction, I thank you.

Merlin, nice indirect help, you are one clever wizard.

Lastly Knights, and Knightess you are why Camelot will always exist. Long live the land of Camelot and our kingdom!"

*With those words, they all head back to Castle Camelot, and some medical treatment occurs with the wounded Knights and Knightess to keep them alive. When they arrive at the castle, Chloe shows the Medicus physician, Barber - Surgeon, and the castle Apothecaries how to heal the wounded and use her Dragon Slayer Blood to battle the Dead Adrenaline bites. Chloe explains that a dead adrenaline bite will cause a blood infection, and they will not survive, so her Dragon Slayer Blood needs administered. Just a drop of Dragon Slayer blood, under their tongue and it will absorb into their system. Chloe informs them a violent reaction of body movements will take place during the healing process, but they will survive. As the process is occurring, Chloe realizes that her dragon slayer blood is immensely powerful and might be more important than Austin* Maximillian, *Gordon Scott, and Sullivan believe it to be. Time will tell the tale as the present leaves second by second, minute by minute, and hour by hour.*

"Quintus, let my Knights and Knightesses know we can clean up and rest, but only after we bury our dead in the sacred soil."

"Absolutely, my King I will gather the men and women."

*"They bury the dead Knights and Knightesses, and King Arthur begins to speak in their honor.*

"This Kingdom we call Camelot has survived because of men and women like the ones who died, every time our blades cut, and our bodies hurt, we will remember these warriors who have gone before us, for they will live on in our memories, until we meet them again in the afterlife. Now rest my people, for a celebration of the living and the dead will be here in the coming days."

## *CELEBRATION AND DESTINY*

### 13TH CENTURY

*A couple of days of healing and rest has past, and tonight a celebration of life and death, and destiny will be echoing through the Camelot Castle walls. The people of Camelot are a proud, generous tribe that will fight and love on elevated level. For as much as the Knights and Knightesses love to battle, they love to enjoy the fruits of their labor. King Arthur knows enjoying some Ale, delicious food, music, friends, love, and stories is just what the Medieval Witch Doctor order to take the edge away from past, present, and future battles.*

"We assemble here in our Kingdom to honor the Warriors that have left the land of living, but tonight our destiny is different, the outcome of our world's life is on Knightess Chloe, my thirteenth warrior, may her sword and shield protect us all. She has chosen the path to be human-kinds salvation from an enemy far greater than the evil Dead Adrenaline Saxon-Vikings that battle us just but a few days ago. Everyone within the sound of my voice! Knightess Chloe's destiny has been prophesies; time will reveal her destiny. But tonight, we celebrate and honor us and our fellow men and women that have passed on to a higher place of existence.

*And with those words, the festivities began, and the family of Camelot celebrated late into the medieval hours of the morning. Chloe was now part of the Camelot family and knew this time would pass in the 13th century, but for now she was in full medieval glory, and took none of this journey for granted.*

*The years pass, King Arthur takes Ingrid Lothbork hand in marriage, and she was now Queen, which made the kingdom even stronger, and became a bridge of peace between the Vikings and Camelot. The years continued, because time never yields, more battles, more fighting knowledge, and more sword cuts through the years. Some of those battles involved Dead Adrenalines and some were just humans against humans. King Arthur never wavered, nor did his Knights and Knightesses, Chloe discovered varies medieval sword wielding techniques and strategies that were savage in nature, but battle worthy against dead adrenaline and others. A mind set that if a warrior died on the battlefield today, tomorrow or in the future Camelot was worth it, the world was worth it, the human-race of good people was worth it!*

*Thirty years had passed, and with the passage of time, things change, time does not care, and will never stay in the moment, for time is a living thing that surrounds us. Time is a god given right, but everyone's time is not the same on earth.*

"Good morning, Merlin, I have not seen you around much in the last month or so."

"I know Chloe, but as you know thirty years has past, and the kingdom is aging, along with its people. You have been patient and devoted to your training, hell fire, you are the best fighter in the kingdom, because no one can blend magic and brutal warfare together like you. You are both sorceress, and Knightess, which will be of skillful use in the coming days. The time has come, the dragon realm is waiting for you, and destiny or death awaits. I have been what you would say in your time, in talks with the Dragon King for the past thirty years, trying to convince this medieval power that you are here in Camelot waiting, and wanting to speak with him. Dragons are very doubting creatures when it comes to humans, but for some reason after thirty years the Dragon King decides he will see you, but make no mistake, dragons have an evil side, and are clever crafty beast that hate humans, and believe that they are the superior species. Fair warning, you will be entering their world, their realm, and they have the high ground."

"Wow! Merlin this Dragon King really does not give a shit, oh well, it is time for him to listen, and for me to fulfill the prophecy. It is sad to leave Camelot on a level, I would have never imagined, but if I do not act now, the Dead Adrenalines will win the day. I must tell you for the past thirty years, I have loved this medieval world, it has been fantastic. This will be sad to leave because this Kingdom has been my second family."

"Yes Chloe, it will be hard for you to leave, but time has not aged you, and you are now stronger than ever, this is your time to claim Excalibur from the Dragon Realm, this will be the final test in this realm. If successful, you can travel to the future year of 2026 and help your father cut down the Evil empire of

Dead Adrenaline forever and save everyone, no matter what century we exist in."

"I know Merlin, what I must do, just getting a little nostalgic about my past experiences here. I will say, I do miss my dad, my mom and brother Luke tremendously, but I stayed focused these thirty years for them and humanity.On another note, just a little magic knowledge from one wizard to another, you see everyone here realized after ten years or so, I was not aging, which is true. How that works is, I will age the time I live in, but if I take quick time travel trip, just passing through the year 2086, which is my true year I should be living in, my body and mind reboots to age 23 again. Through the past thirty years, I would seek out of this Medieval century and pay a quick visit to the year 2086, just pass through, and reset my age back to the age of 23. I wanted to keep my youthful edge, while I continued my medieval training.

"That is simply amazing to hear this, even for a Wizard with my abilities. When it comes to aging, my body and mind, age at extremely slow rate, a little Merlin magic if I say so myself, but I have not perfected the age thing yet like you though."

"Maybe Merlin, you need a little dragon slayer blood coursing through your veins."

"Oh Chloe, as you know, I have vial of your blood, as you would say, if things turn into a shit sandwich, I might just take some and see if my magic mixes with your magic."

“I love it Merlin, keeping things real and true, while I guess, I better say my goodbyes to the King and Queen, and everyone.”

“Yes, most definitely, I must say Chloe, as you have proven, changing the future by alternating the past, and present which quickly becomes the past, does work. Think about it, thirty years ago you cut down Lancelot, who would have had an affair with Guinevere, who would have been married to Arthur at the time. This would have shattered the Kingdom, on an internal level of betrayal. Obviously, no affair occurred, because Lancelot did not live, but Guinevere never married Arthur.

Arthur married Ingrid the daughter of King Ragnor Lothbrok, the King of Denmark. You saved Ingrid by letting her bite you and have a chance to come back to the land of the living. By doing this, now King Arthur and King Lothbrok are allies. Vikings and Arthurian's working together based on a marriage, you see one thing is true about Viking women, they only marry for love, and not political power and status. A Viking women could never be ordered to marry someone they do not love. Crazy how things work out, now Guinevere did find love with one of King Arthur's Knights, and it worked out for the best. Just out of an old Wizard's curiosity, why did you never find love Chloe.”

“Oh well, I had my relationships and built great friendships along the way, but I always figured, I have time, I am only 23 years old.”

“Well said Chloe, no wizard could argue with that. Before you leave and if you survive the dragon realm, Excalibur is pure silver, harden steel, and has magical powers infused into the heart of this sword. Being the wizard that I am, I discovered something in the future that came form the past, something that will be a battle changer. I will tell you a little secret that when the time is right, this secret will be unbelievably amazing to know.”

*Merlin leans into Chloe and whispers the secret to her and tells her to only reveal the secret when the time is right.*

“Yep Merlin, I will keep that secret safe until needed, now it is time to focus on saving the world, bye Merlin, thank you for everything. I am going to get ready for my journey to the Dragon Realm and say my goodbyes.”

*Chloe is prepared for her journey and meets King Arthur and Queen Ingrid to say goodbye.*

**King Arthur and Queen Ingrid**

"Hello, Knightess Chloe, by the looks of your dress attire and weapons, you must be going on a journey. You see Kings know these things, if you need any help, it would be my honor to aid you."

"I know King Arthur, you would do anything for me, and I know I can say this in front of Queen Ingrid, for her love is true for you, as you already know. Anyways, the time as come, I must go to the Dragon Realm and fulfill my destiny, if I survive this, then I have a chance to save the world and our species. I will leave quietly, just tell everyone, I went on a quest by your order, no one will question this."

"My face is older, and my hair is grey, so I am grateful that you have been with us for thirty years, time goes fast, memories of this time will never leave. Go fulfill the prophecy and know the people of Camelot love you and will never forget your time with us."

*And with those words from King Arthur, Chloe leaves the Castle quietly, so no one is aware she is leaving for all time. As she is exiting the rear gate, Guinevere walks up to her and gives her a hug, and tells Chloe thank you for everything. Chloe smiles, and thanks Guinevere for being such a great friend, and walks quietly from the Castle Camelot to begin the journey to the Dragon Realm.*

**Chloe and Guinevere Say Goodbye**

# UNTOUCHED BY HUMAN BREATH

## 13TH CENTURY

*It has been ten sunsets and eleven sunrises, and on the eleven sunrises, Chloe reaches the base of the Cascade Mountains. A generous size creek is flowing around this mountain, and according to Merlin near the top at the cliffs edge is the entrance to the Dragon Realm. A tremendous climb, but Chloe is up for the challenge and is ready to get this bullshit over with. Within an hour, Chloe scales the mountain side and makes it to the cliffs edge where the entrance to the Dragon Realm exists. She takes a moment to catch her breath, think things out, and starts to make her way into the entrance.*

*Chloe is halfway through the entrance, when she does see the partial Skeletons of a dragon and a human laying beside each other. Now she sees the truth Merlin had told her, King Caliburnus and Dragon Invictus died together halfway in between the human realm and dragon realm. The cave entrance helps preserve the bones, but time always wins. Seeing is believing, and there can be no doubt that Excalibur is waiting for her to claim within the Dragon Realm.*

*Finally, Chloe sees the end of the tunnel to the Dragon Realm. She takes a deep breath and steps out into the daylight. What Chloe sees is amazing and powerful, stone-rocks intertwined through a maze of trails and cliffs. The sound of waterfalls splashing in the distance, and the water running down the cliffs is clear, and has a visible silver shine to it.*

*Chloe realizes she is looking at the pure silver water of the Dragon Realm, which is untouched by human hands. The silver water leads to a center where a rough roundish shaped rock-stone is found, and the silver water and rock-stone surround this roundish object.*

*In the Center of this rock-stone is a sword, not average by sight, but neither spectacular, just a medieval sword forged into the oval shaped rock-stone. Chloe senses a power coming from the sword and knows never to judge a book by its cover, or you will miss the first block, as Master G would say. What looks to be frozen silver water holds the sword in place. At that moment, Chloe knows with all her believe that she is looking at Excalibur, the mythical, legendary sword of Camelot. The sword is no longer just existing in her imagination, and she must claim the sword.*

## EXCALIBUR

*Suddenly her amazement is shattered, by the sound of deep roars and screeching sounds, similar to a bat with a Lion as its back up. The screeching roar stops, and Chloe begins to feel the wind pick up and she hears a loud flapping sound, and Chloe knows the Dragons have arrived and the winged beast are surrounding Chloe.*

*Chloe knows she is outnumbered, but with unflinching focus holds her hands out and a medieval cross bow appears, which is a viable choice against dragons. Chloe is ready to go to battle, because with her powers, she can keep the arrows materializing and loading. Unlimited arrows ammunition is a powerful thing when dragons are breathing down on your destiny.*

*Chloe starts to yell out and is speaking dragon-tongue, suddenly the surrounding dragons' throats start glowing a red amber, and flames of death are ready to be release. As this is manifesting, Chloe says something that stops the actions of the dragons surrounding her. The dragons start to listen to Chloe's words and understand that this woman is more than just a weak human wondering into their realm.*

**THE DRAGONS ARE LISTENING**

"I come for Excalibur, let the judgement test begin!"

*With those words, the dragons slowly circle, but do not attack, in the distance a hissing sound is heard, and the sky of dragons open, and a blood red dragon appears, and lands on the cliffs edge. It is the Dragon King, Chloe's judgement test truly will begin now, the Dragon King begins to speak with a voice of delight and dreadfulness.*

"So, you are the so-called prophecy that Merlin Ambrosia has been talking about for many centuries. You come to claim Excalibur and fulfill your destiny. Really do you think that you can win this day and survive the judgment of the Dragon Realm."

"Well for starters, I have Dragon-Lord magic, which gives me an ability to communicate with dragons and in some case command them."

"Oh yes, you are a laughable at best, communicating with our species you have proven, but you will never command a dragon. We are the most powerful, proud, intelligent species in this world, and if you think for one moment that a human can control our species, you are pathetically mistaken. I must say, Merlin really talked you up, but this dragon is not impressed, and so you know, us Dragons can also use materialized magic to create any working weapon or object that exist in our time. See now, I changed your crossbow into a longbow, and I gave you a red cloak. Us Dragons really have no use for this kind of magic, but it is amusing to our species."

*Chloe looks in her hand, and a longbow is there now, also, Chloe realizes a red cloak is now attached to back. The Dragon starts to laugh in hideous fashion and tells Chloe that blood red is the favorite color of the Dragon King. Chloe and the Dragon King begin to just stare at each other as if they were sizing up each other's next medieval move. Silence and the background sound of waterfalls is the only thing heard. In that moment, Chloe decides to say what she thinks aloud.*

**The Dragon King Sizes Up Chloe**

"Ok Dragon King, let me say it my way, my name is Knightess Chloe, I am the daughter of the Man called Clint, I have trained with my father, Master G, Kensei Miyamoto Musashi, King Arthur and the Knights and Knightess of Camelot, along with Sorcerer Merlin, my training is not restricted by time or space. So, make no mistake, it is **Time to Clean the Fucking Dragon Realm!"**

*With those unexpected words said by Chloe, the Dragon King continues being silent, recoils back and reveals a very sinister smile, then speaks.* ***Let the Judgement test begin!!!!"***

*From the left of the Dragon King, a scrawny looking dragon flies up and lands near Chloe. This dragon is like a King's Jester, giving off vibes of amusement. Chloe quickly realizes this boney thin looking dragon is serious.*

**THE DRAGON KING'S JESTER**

"The test will begin with this pathetic human battling one of our elder dragons, the hate towards humans has festered for centuries, so this human called Knightess Chloe will soon see the fury of a dragons hate. Knightess Chloe, climb down to the stone ground just below, but be prepared because this elder dragon will not give you any advantage."

*Chloe makes her way to the stone floor below and realizes a mountain wall surrounds the back of her, human barbecue is on the menu and Chloe understands what is about to happen. A piercing sound is echoing off the stones in the Dragon Realm, the elder dragon slumbers over towards Chloe, scraping its talons across the stone floor. The hate in this dragon's eyes is for real, as this is occurring the mountain wall begins to rumble, a large crack forms down the Center of rock-stone wall that sits behind Chloe. Both halves begin to open inward like giant doors, and stone steps are on the other side that go upward to the top of the mountain.*

*Chloe quickly enters the doorway and goes up the stone steps, upon reaching the top something beyond believe is waiting, a large stoned floored octagon, carved out on the mountain top. Open sky is above, and jagged rock edges surround the outer rim of the octagon. The ultimate fight yard at the top of the Cascade Mountains, where feuds and battle tests are decided. Dried up sections of blood are scattered on the rocks and stone Octagon floor, which tells Chloe, past judgements have taken place. Chloe begins to talk to herself out-loud and is thinking about her dad.*

"Well Dad, I made it to the last lap of my training and testing with the Dragons, now I need claim Excalibur and get back to you in the year 2026, so we can destroy the Dead Adrenalines. You would love this fighting arena in all its glory, but I am not going to lie, this is a scary shit sandwich. No time to doubt, it is time to put my fight face on.

## DRAGON OCTAGON OF JUDGEMENT

*Chloe steps out onto the Stone Octagon and prepares to face this old elder Dragon. As she waits, she can here the spark of talons striking the outer rocks of the Octagon platform, like a steel match getting lit. Out of the misty sky a green reptilian like object is seen coming closer, than this beast of the sky lands. It is the Elder Dragon, with a calling card of talons striking the stone and rock, which might be a just nervous habit or just a way to let its prey know death is coming.*

## ELDER DRAGON

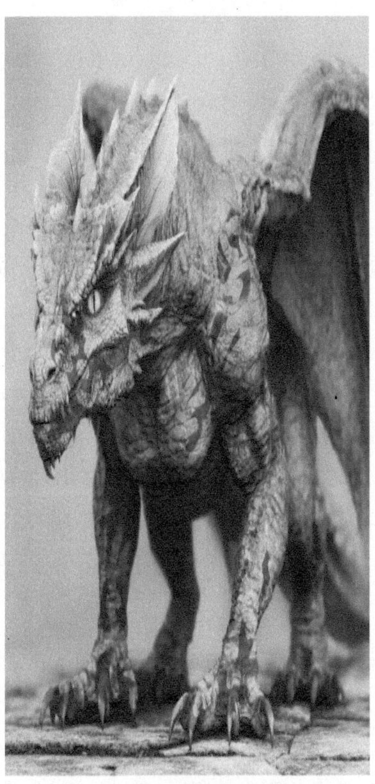

"So, you are the prophecy, Merlin has been talking about, I hope you do not waste my time, because you interrupted my meal. I was feeding on a giant mountain salamander, they taste surprisingly good, but nothing compares to the taste of human flesh, and here you are, Chloe is it, what a small little name you have, you must know pain is coming. I will end this meeting quick, but painfully, and so you know if I were the Dragon King, humans would have been exterminated from their realm long ago."

*Chloe decides not to return any conversation with the Elder Dragon, for the beast has a mind set that is caged with hate. Like Great, Great Grandpa at the family picnic, listen to him but stay away from the stupid talk. As Chloe sizes up the situation, she notices that most of this dragon's weight is on the front legs, and truly little on the hind legs. Meaning I bet this old dragon has back, leg, hip, and knee problems. The front legs look more built up from carrying most of the dragon's weight when moving. This leg positioning is not a 60 /40 Burendo Shotokan fighting stance, which means sweeping the front legs is a choice. As Chloe is deciding quickly on a good weapon to materialize to fuck up the front legs of this dragon, the Elder Dragon continues to talk.*

"Chloe, if I want to, I could merely flap my wings and peel the skin and flesh from your bones, and leave you to cook in the dragon sun, then I would come back later and consume you. Lucky for you, I am not patient enough to wait for my meal, so I guess I will just eat you raw, which still taste delicious! Although a little flame will crisp you up, and I will eat you whole."

*The throat of this old dragon begins to glow red, which means it is about to let loose dragon hellfire! Chloe materializes a stainless-steel Kite Shield, which offers good body and leg coverage, which she places on her left hand/arm.*

*In her right hand a doubled headed Meteor Hammer, which is a long chain with two spherical shape weights on the ends, this weapon is Chinese in origin that dates to the Ming Dynasty, and it is perfect for what Chloe is about to try. The Elder Dragon lets loose a full gust of flame, which blast towards Chloe. Chloe holds the Kite Shield in place and curls up into a ball and waits for the fire storm to stop. As the last flame is spit by the Elder Dragon, Chloe returns to her feet and starts running full speed towards the dragon with the Kite shield in her left hand and the Double headed Meteor Hammer in her right. Rotation of the Meteor Hammer has begun, and Chloe is waiting for the hellfire to release a second time by this dragon. Chloe is about ten feet away, when the flame burst happens again, but this time, Chloe is ready and catches the bottom edge of the flame and moves behind and under it. The force from the dragon's flame thrower propels Chloe towards the dragon at a powerful speed, Chloe releases the Meteor Hammer, aiming for the right front leg and left rear leg of the Elder Dragon. Target placement occurs and the one weak rear leg and one strong front leg get entangled. Chloe manages to Judo roll off to the side of Elder Dragon and returns to her feet, and still has the Kite Shield, and materializes a cool ass Medieval Long Sword, and with sword and shield in hand she waits.*

"Mmmm! What is this, you have done, A pathetic chain with two weighted ends wrapped around my front leg, and back leg. This really does reinforce my thought that humans are so very unintelligent, I will snap this chain like a blade of grass."

"No, you old dragon, the way I see it you have three choices now that you could try. The first would be to snap the chain with your legs, but you have a problem, one strong front leg and one weak back leg connected to the chain. If you place any kind of pressure on the chain, whether you pull or push sideways or up and down. You will fall to the stone floor, and I will close the distance and gut you open like a Medieval Christmas Turkey. If you move your mouth towards the chain, and try to bite through the chain, your neck will be a perfect target for my blade to cut your dragon head off. Now you do have a third choice, fly up and away, which would mean you gave up and I win the first round of judgement of the dragons, so what is it going to be old Dragon."

*The Elder Dragon pauses for a moment than begins to grin and starts to speak.*

"Oh, you foolish human, your sword blade can not cut through my armored scales or even my underbelly. A dragon's body is like one big shield, I will wait for you to move in, and you will feel the wrath of my dragon power and unrelenting fortitude. The chain will break one way or another, then I will crush your bones inside your body, and you will die a painful death."

"Ok than, let us do this old dragon, but just one more thing, I did not mention, I know where your weak soft spot is under your scale. It is just behind your dragon knee on your left rear leg, so get ready because I am coming for it."

*The Dragons grin changes to slight panic, and in a crazy frenzy the Elder Dragon frantically tries to break the Meteor Hammer chain, first by forcefully moving its legs , but collapses to the stone floor, at that point, the old dragon attempts to bite at the chain, but the chain is out of reach. The dragon looks back for Chloe and realizes she is standing next to its left rear leg, with the sword blade seconds from cutting the soft spot behind the knee. In those brief seconds, the Elder Dragon, takes flight, and knows the test is over. As the Dragon, flies away, it realizes, Chloe could have blade cut sooner but did not. The extra seconds she gave, let him fly away, and on this day, a human showed mercy. The completion of the first judgement test is over, and mercy was shown by a human to a dragon.*

*"Geez, what a dragon shit sandwich that was turning out to be, so glad that old dragon decided to fly away, or I would have cut this bitter old dragon down. Yes! That is right dragons, I am talking aloud, I am ready for my next test!"*

*Suddenly, the Dragon King's Jester Dragon appears perched on top of the rock edge of the Octagon and begins to speak.*

"Well done, Chloe, you showed mercy, which has never been seen by a dragon when a human is involved. Now, now, do not get overconfident, because you have seen nothing of what the dragon realm can offer when it comes to death. Be ready and be prepared because it is time for you to battle a young stronger dragon."

*With those words the Jester Dragon flies off.*

"Ok, it is time to break out my Kanta sword, and I think I will keep this Kite Shield up and ready, because those darn dragons love to flame throw."

*In the distance sky above, Chloe can hear something yelling her name, Chloe! Chloe! And like a sledgehammer hitting steel, a bright orange colored dragon with hate in its eye's lands on the stone floor of the octagon. This dragon does not stay stationary and keeps moving right and left, like a snake getting ready to strike.*

**THE ORANGE DRAGON**

*Quietly the Orange Dragon, begins to speak, and tells Chloe, that no flame will come from his breath, the test of Mercy involving fire has happened with the Elder Dragon, but unlike the failure of the old dragon. A human will die today in the dragon realm, and fulfilling the prophecy will not happen.*

"Chloe, I am too powerful and fast, your skills will never match my ability, I fight for the dragon world, and no human will stop this."

"Ok, let us do this, Orange Peel, yep, that is right, I just gave you a nickname, so let us see what you got."

*The Orange Dragon did not like the nickname given by Chloe and became very enraged that a human would even dare to say such a thing. With that angrily thought the Orange Dragon starts to circle Chloe, waiting for an opportunity to strike.*

"Ok, time to materialize a polearm weapon, how about a nice Halberd, which has a great spear point, ax head, and hook to do the most cutting and puncturing damage. Yep, that is right I am saying it aloud Orange Peel, so you know exactly what weapon a human used to kill you!"

*With Halberd weapon in hand, the battle begins, a human, against a dragon, it does not get anymore medieval than this. A quick flick of the dragon's tail cuts Chloes left front leg, blood begins to gush out of it, luckily it is not an artery, but a vein has been cut. A second flick of the dragon tails occurs, and this time Chloe's ax cuts the tip of the dragon's tail completely off, which causes the Orange Dragon to recoil the tail in pain. Orange blood is dripping from the tail because all dragons blood is the same color has their scale skin. Chloe sees the blood and is amazed because no one every knew this, until now. Without hesitation the Orange Dragon charges forward than moves to the left quickly and whips its body towards Chloe with both front talons out, Chloe manages to send the spear head of the Halberd through the right talon forepaw of the Orange Dragon. She continues thrusting forward with the weapon and breaks through the talon forepaw further, sending the entire spear, ax head, and hook under the right shoulder, slipping under the scales into the soft spot of the Orange Dragon. As the kill spot lands the Orange Dragon, manages to open its jaw and bite down on Chloe's upper torso, clamping down trying to bite Chloe in half, Chloe's spine and back are damaged and she passes out, but is still breathing.*

*Blood starts to release from Chloe's injuries, orange and red blood cover the stone floor of the octagon. The Orange Dragon falls to the stone floor and dies, unable to bite Chloe in half. Slowly the Orange Dragon's bite releases, and flops forward onto its stomach with its head stretch out and passes away. Chloe falls to the stone floor near the dragon and is still breathing but the wounds are severe, she has a broken back, and a severed spine.*

**The Orange Dragon Vs Chloe**

*The King's Jester Dragon flies down from above and lands next to the Orange Dragon and Chloe. As he watches the red and orange blood mix on the stone floor, The Dragon Jester waits for Chloes last breath. Suddenly, something amazing happens, Chloe's breathing becomes stronger, and she starts to awake, miraculously her body his healed, no more severed spine or broken back, her blood regenerates back into her body and Chloe stands up and speaks to the Jester Dragon.*

"Well, that was extremely painful, and never want to go through that again, but I live, and the Orange Peel does not."

"Yes, indeed you do, and the young dragon does not, you have completed the test of no mercy given. Now the 3rd test will begin if you win this test, then you will speak with the

Dragon King, he has a question to ask you. Let the final judgement test begin."

*With those abrupt words, the Jester Dragon flies off, and as Chloe's waits, she can hear a sound of heavy footsteps coming up the stone steps to the stone Octagon. Then it appears as it comes walking into the Octagon to do battle. Chloe has never seen such sight and knows now the Dragon King is using some dragon magic to even up the odds against her. Standing before Chloe is a warrior, mostly dragon, but standing up right with a body shape of a human, a weapon of death manifested from the Dragon Realm.*

*Chloe prepares for this death match and knows this judgement test is no joke, and the dragon realm is playing for keeps.Chloe does a quick scan of this beast, to tries to find the soft spot, but no kill spot exists, which means their may be no way to kill this creature from the dragon realm. A slight concern travels into Chloe's mind, but she quickly discards any doubt that she will lose and prepares to battle this weapon of death. A Buckler shield made of steel materializes, along with an Arming sword, Chloe knows this will be close combat, so she chooses weapons that can match her opponent.*

**A WEAPON OF DEATH**

*The Weapon of Death does not speak and goes to work viciously with sword attacks against Chloe, steel is sparking, and it echoes through the Dragon Realm, the clash is unrelenting between both warriors. One from the human realm and one from the dragon realm, both battling for their realm. A battle that will end with only one victor, or could that outcome change, could something unexpected happen. Then after hours of fighting and blade cuts being handed out, a blade cut slices Chloe from her shoulder to wrist, causing her two drop her sword, as the sword is falling, Chloe quickly completes a Mae Geri Kekomi (Front Thrust Kick) catching the back handle*

*of the sword, causing it to flip in mid-air and projectile upward, straight towards the Weapon of Death. The tip of the blade punctures through the black armor and directly in and up, through the solar plexus of this creature. Only one inch of the sword blade has cut into the area, damaging a network of nerves and disrupting the nerves. The Weapon of Death drops two its reptilian knees and loses grip of its sword and shield.*

*At that moment Chloe looks at this dragon-warrior that the Dragon King created and tries to show mercy, by telling this Weapon of Death to surrender. Suddenly, the throat of the Weapon of Death starts to turn bright red and is heating up. The Weapon of Death stands up, this could mean only one thing, a hellfire is about to show up. Like a person turning a light switch off, Chloe completes a Kaiten Ushiro Geri (Spinning Back Kick), driving the sword straight through the body of the Weapon of Death and out the other side. As this is occurring, Chloe, materializes a broad ax in both hands' steps into an X-stance and spins out landing the broad ax right a crossed the neck of the Weapon of Death, cutting the head clean off. Chloe yells the words " No Mercy!" Chloe is victorious, and the King's Jester shows up.*

"I must say, the outcome of this battle is not what I thought would happen. You have achieved victory three times, mercy, no mercy, and both mercy and no mercy displayed in this third test. Now you will meet the Dragon King again, he has a question for you, so it is time for you to return to the center of the dragon realm, where Excalibur awaits you, along with the Dragon King."

*Chloe leaves the octagon and walks back down the stone steps, back into the center of the dragon realm. The heart of this realm where the final judgements will happen. Chloe realizes whatever question the Dragon King will be asking will be the final shield against completing her destiny. As Chloe enters the heart of the dragon realm, she sees the Red Dragon King, standing behind Excalibur, with its wings spread open. A sinister smile painted a-crossed its dragon face as if this beast of the dragon realm knows something. At this point, all the other dragons arrive on the outer rim of the dragon realm center, as if they know something unimaginable is going to happen.*

**THE DRAGON KING HAS A QUESTION.**

# THE QUESTION

## 13TH CENTURY

"I am the Dragon King, all knowing, all powerful, and I have no weakness, I see you have the power to find the weak spot on my species, but unlike other dragons when I became the Dragon King, the soft spot under my scale became strong and no longer a weak point. This is the magic of the dragon realm, and that is why I can never die. You come here from a far-off land, battle my dragons in the octagon, and become victorious, which has brought you to this point Chloe. You have showed mercy, showed no mercy, and both mercy and no mercy at the same time."

"This is a very unusual quality for a human, I only seen this one other time when King Fortis Caliburnus, showed mercy and Dragon Invictus became allies in their concluding moments alive, which formed a bond between a dragon and human, which created Excalibur. Great Dragon Power and Divine Kingship blended to make power and righteous in one, which is Excalibur. Only a species with those true qualities can remove Excalibur from the forged silver water and rock-stone. We will find out if you are the prophecy and this is your destiny, but first before you even try to remove Excalibur from its resting place, you must answer one question."

"Ok, what would that question be Dragon King"

“Chloe you will never know the answer, and why would you, you are a human first, and your power and magic come second, but a dragon’s power and magic are born first. Chloe from a far-off land beyond, “what is my true name! “

*And with that question the dragon recoils back, ready to strike Chloe down if she answers the question wrong. Chloe knows she must answer only once, and the name must be correct, or the wrath of the Dragon King will happen. Speaking the name in dragon will be easy for she speaks dragon-tongue, but saying the correct name is an undertaking that may not happen but must. Then Chloe begins to focus on the Dragon King, who is waiting for an answer, she begins to stare at the eyes of this dragon. Looking past the Dragon King’s outward features, but deep into the dragon's mind, at that moment she realizes that her superpowers let her look at many types of species, and reach deep into their thoughts, which could be past present or future. Chloe is unable to reveal the name from the Dragon King’s present or future thoughts, as if the dragon as blocked out any memory of its true name. Silently, but quickly Chloe travels backwards into memories the dragon has lived, clear back to the birth of this Dragon King.*

*There it manifested, a dragon egg lying just beneath the surface of a silver laced spring, below the Cascade mountains, this egg had washed down from the mountain from its dragon nest and was now outside the dragon realm, and in the human realm. The dragon egg begins to hatch, and a bright blood red dragon appears from the shell and is underwater. The dragon’s starts to breath and inhales the silver laced water, begins to glow a bright silver, and than returns to the blood red color. In that moment, the dragon begins to fly from the silver water and back up to the dragon realm. The Dragon King was born that day in time and did fulfill its destiny to become the King of the Dragons in the future. This image became clear to Chloe, and she knew the true name of the Dragon King, and like a blink of a dragon eye, she was back in the present time staring at the Dragon King again.*

"So, Chloe do you have an answer to my question!"

"Yes Dragon King, your true name is **ARGENTUM!** You were born in the silver waters, but outside the dragon realm on that day, your egg hatched in the human realm, and you became the Silver Dragon, your outer scales are red, but just like your true name you are truly a silver color, which indicates your bond with the silver waters of the Cascade mountains where this Dragon Realm exists."

*The Dragon King recoils back even further and its red color scales, suddenly change to a bright shinning silver. The Dragon King is ARGENTUM, the silver dragon once again.*

## ARGENTUM THE DRAGON KING

"Chloe, you have spoke my true name, since my birth, I was waiting for my true name to return and the power of the silver waters that not only course through my veins but coat my outer scales. You see, on that day I flew back to the dragon realm as newborn dragon, my parents found me and told no other dragon what had happened in the human realm. My parents told me that my scales would remain blood red and would only return to silver if a human would say my true name, ARGENTUM! My body never had a weak spot under any scale area, but my punishment would be to remain blood red in color, as a sign of hatred towards all humans, and even if I did not want too, my desire to hate all humans would be uncontrollable. I forged this hate in the dragon realm, even if I did not want too, you have released me from this punishment, and now I can create a different mind set in my dragons. Even if humans hate us or live in fear, us dragons will show mercy when we can and no mercy when we can not.

All my dragons will obey this law from this day forward, now Chloe claim Excalibur if the sword excepts you and not the other way around."

*With those final words from Dragon King Argentum, Chloe walks over to EXCALIBUR and can sense the Dragon Power and Divine Kingship surrounding its resting place, born of both human and dragon blood, and only a righteous powerful species can claim. With this thought, Chloe reaches down and grabs the sword handle with both hands and gets ready to find out if the prophecy is correct. Chloe pulls Excalibur from the rock-stone and a bright light with silver glow begins to cover her body, her armor becomes a living thing with powers to adapt and protect her, she feels this power within her mind and body. Slowly the silver glow starts to fade, and Chloe is standing there with Excalibur in hand, and the Dragon King Argentum looks at Chloë and begins to speak.*

"From this day forward, you will be known as **The Samurai-Knightess** in all realms of this world and others. Your armor will be just like my silver scales in nature; it will adapt and change depending on your need in battle. Your power to materialize weapons of choice is unmatched, but now you can summon Excalibur the most powerful and divine sword to ever exist. It will rest in the dragon realm, but when every you are of need of it, the sword is yours to use. No one ever really owns this sword, but you have the righteousness to wield it against evil. Before you leave Samurai-Knightess, I have a gift for you, a gift of a dragon. This dragon will help you, in your quest to save humankind and all species for that matter. I hear the Dead

Adrenalines are fucking up the world, so it's time that you return to the year 2026 and help your father the Man Called Clint end this treachery, and in case you are wondering how I know all of this, Merlin has kept me pretty informed. Merlin also said your dad will call you the Silver-Samurai and think that he created a name for you. When get a chance, you will have to let him know the name was wrong and you are 'The Samurai-Knightess!"

"Got to love Mr. Merlin, and yes, my dad would think he created a cool warrior name, and I have to say, I never thought I would hear a dragon say the word fuck. Nice to hear, you are keeping it real, so where is that dragon you speak of."

"As you have seen, us dragons do have emotions, happiness, sadness, and angry, so we know when something is fucked up. We will say goodbye than Samurai-Knightess, the dragon that is a gift from the dragon realm is waiting at the top of Cascade Mountain, this dragon shows mercy and no mercy when needed. It is a gift from us, but it will be up to this dragon to decide if it will accept you as its leader. This dragon has no name it will be up to you to name it, now go, and remember you are wielding great power Samurai-Knightess, which carries mercy and no mercy."

*Chloe the Samurai-Knightess makes her way to the top of the Cascade Mountain and meets this dragon with no name. They look at each other, an unspoken conversation takes place, similar to the unspoken conversation that Dragon Invictus and King Caliburnus had when they met each other centuries ago. The Samurai-Knightess and this dragon would not lead each other but would be allies in the fight against evil.*

*Chloe names the dragon YOSAI, which means FORTRESS in Japanese, and on this day a friendship is forged on top the Cascade Mountain top. The Samurai-Knightess and Yosai the Dragon are the team the world needs.*

**THE SAMURAI-KNIGHTESS AND YOSAI BECOME FRIENDS**

*The Samurai-Knightess materializes a saddle that just so happens to fit a dragon, she looks at Yosai and tells the Dragon that they are about to time travel back the year 2026, and help her father, the Man Called Clint with destroying the Dead Adrenalines that have invaded mother earth. Yosai understands the dragon-tongue Chloe is speaking, looks at Chloe and is ready for the adventure. Yosai flies off with the Samurai-Knightess riding, and they both disappear in the sky together.*

“Ok Yosai, my outer silver armor will change and adapt involuntarily to protect me has needed, as will your armor like dragon scales. I will materialize weapons of choice as needed and will break Excalibur out when the time is right and needed. Get ready because we are about to enter the year 2026, in the land of Beaver County, Pennsylvania. A full-on war is going down in Dead Adrenaline town, so be ready, we will accumulate slowly in this year of 2026, which will help our bodies with time traveling, even though I do not believe I need to accumulate anymore when I time travel.”

“Yosai, when we hit the mark, and I find my dad, The Man Called Clint, you will fly down there and drop me off, and than fly back up into sky and wait for me. Once I have help destroy these DA savages and know my dad is safe, come back and pick me up. We will leave this time and get you accumulated and return, find my dad again, and we will join this battle permanently, and be there for the decisive battle.”

**THE SAMURAI-KNIGHTESS & YOSAI TIME TRAVEL.**

# IT'S GOT FANGS, THE FINAL BATTLE

## YEAR 2026

*The Samurai-Knightess (Chloe) and Yosai (Dragon) have arrived in the year 2026, and they understand that time is a very uncontrollable thing, different timelines can happen, just by the smallest change in the past, present, or in some cases the future, which can alter what reality will be. Meaning they both must be very methodical and nonsystematic to confuse the Dead Adrenalines, the entire killing of these alien invaders must take place, so no remnant is left that they ever existed.*

*Chloe, AKA the Samurai-Knightess has found her dad, who just so happens to be getting attacked by 100 or so red eyed Dead Adrenalines in the exceptionally large gravel parking lot of the Daughtery Township Fire Hall in Beaver County, Pennsylvania. Yosai drops Chloe off, she materializes the Haja-no-Ontachi (Great-Evil-Crushing Blade), which is the longest sword in the world.* Blood, blade, and silver are all that the Dead Adrenalines see. The Samurai-Knightess *manages to help save her dad from the onslaught, but does not stay or speak with him, because she needs to leave this year of 2026, which will help Yosai accumulate to the year 2026. Before the Samurai-Knightess leaves, she bows her head and says a merciful prayer for all the human blood spilled on this day, knowing that now they are free from the bondage of the dead adrenaline infection.*

## THE SAMURAI-KNIGHTESS PRAYS FOR THE DEAD

*At an abbreviated time later, both Yosai and Chloe return, and fly down from the sky, the Samurai-Knightess and Yosai make a grand entrance and land in the parking lot of the Beaver County Radio station back in the year 2026. Chloe,* ***The Samurai-Knightess*** *and her dad,* ***The Man Called Clint*** *reunite and talk about Kim and Luke, and how the family is surviving. Irish Warrior and the last remaining Burendo Warriors are present and ready for battle. Chloe also explains briefly about why she could not stay with her dad, after she helped save him from the Dead Adrenaline attack in the Daughtery Fire Hall lot. Unfortunately, the battle to save the world is happening, so there was no time to get into detail about how she became the Samurai-Knightess and how she got a dragon.*

*Also, Chloe does not tell her dad, her name is not the Silver Samurai just yet and decides to let him run with that name for now. The Man Called Clint realizes that Chloe, his daughter, might be the game ender against these Dead Adrenaline savages. Especially against this Dead Adrenaline-Alien Emperor, Vlad the Impaler that has showed up in Beaver County, Pennsylvania and is the ruler of all the Dead Adrenalines.*

*The last stand has arrived good vs evil, time will reveal the victor, but blood will be spilled, because the battle for humankind is bitting down with full force. The battle unfolds, and The Man Called Clint is confronting the Vlad the Emperor of the Dead Adrenalines, Clint is standing outside the radio station face to face with this evil presence. The Samurai-*

*Knightess posts herself on the roof top of the radio station and is sitting on Yosai, ready to advance and attack. Vlad the Impaler, this evil twisted Dead Adrenaline Emperor begins to speak and is getting ready to show its true self, and* ***ITS GOT FANGS!!!***

**VLAD THE EMPEROR OF THE DEAD ADRENALINES**

**THE FINAL HUNT HAS COMMENCED**

"Let's start with my name, I am known as Emperor Vlad, which is true, but I go by many names, which usually change based on the host body I invade. I have what you humans call a spaceship, spacecraft, or UFO, and yes, I do prefer to travel by ship, instead of what you like to call a light sphere, which is actually what we look like without a human, animal, or creature shell host. I have the ability to time travel, which has taken me all over the universe.

I have been to the past, present and future, so my knowledge gathering has been exceptional. But, on this day, I will obtain a most extraordinary gathering of knowledge, along with the blood and flesh of you and your followers, including, your daughter Chloe and her Dragon. After this deed is done, I will continue my wrath, and leave Beaver County, PA, only to continue my hunt. You see, I will kill every living species on this planet and leave extinction behind. Now that you and your followers know what is about to befall, I have one more gift of knowledge to offer you, before I commence with the hunt.

My name is Vlad, and I am the Emperor of my species, but I go by another. A name you will know Clint, a name that will make you understand what is about to happen. My name is Vlad the Impaler, born in Sighisoara, Transylvania, and ruled in 15th century Europe, my methods of destroying my enemy are vast. You see Clint, I traveled to the 15th Century Europe in the year 1476 and located Vlad.

He was evil, powerful, unrelentingly, and craved death and violence on a gigantic level. I respected this and knew at that very moment; I would take his mind and body as a permanent host. One would think, his will to survive would not make him an easy takeover, but it was the opposite. Vlad The Impaler embraced the opportunity to become greater and eviler, so he willfully except my alien entity into his soul.

In the year 1476 Vlad the Impaler was documented in historical records that he had died, but don't you see evil never really dies, Vlad the Impaler, became Emperor Vlad on that day, and evolution took over. I control, him, but he is part of my genetic makeup, and now his evil is my evil, and my evil is his evil.

I do have one more thing that must be mentioned and shown before the hunt begins. Vlad goes by one other name, and this name will make you understand what is coming. **Dracula**! And just so you are not wondering, yes, he is now an Alien-Vampire! Prepare for the wrath of evil, the time of humans is over, I will give you a few minutes to realize I am death, and life cannot exist in the realm of death, and then the hunt will commence."

Ok, Burendo Shotokan Warriors come outside, and take your position. Spread out and keep alert, this is it.

Irish where is Chloe.

“Oh, she has already exited the building and is sitting on Yosai, on top of the roof. Clint, this is some really scary fucked up shit. Vlad The Impaler, who is Dracula, and Alien Emperor blended (Burendo) together into one complete package of Medieval-Nosferatu-Extraterrestrial origin, which is really messed up shit. I guess Vlad the Impaler, really did drink blood.”

You are so right Irish Warrior, so when we survive this, I will not mind watching the 1922 silent German film, Nosferatu: Symphony of Horror, or at least watch the iconic scene where Count Orlok ascends a staircase in a shadowy form. Anyways, Irish that was highly creative Nosferatu usage in describing Count Vlad Dill-Weed.

“Clint if this is the end, remember you have always been a top shelf friend, but you have issues.”

Right back at you Irish.

Burendo Shotokan Warriors, it is **Time to Clean Fucking Dojo**, one last time! Count Vlad Dill-Weed has just returned, and that is one ugly ass Alien-Vampire. What a hideous sight to behold!

Chloe! Or should I say, The Silver Samurai, are you ready to launch.

“Yeah, Dad! The Samurai-Knightess and her trusty Dragon Yosai are ready and prepared to face death.”

Wow! That is a cool ass warrior name, far better than the Silver Samurai name, I assigned you Chloe. Ok than, the Samurai-Knightess it will be.

I hope the Samurai-Knightess and her trusty Dragon Yosai are prepared for everyone's sake because death just arrived, and **it has fangs!!**

**DEATH HAS ARRIVED, AND ITS GOT FANGS!**

*The fist and fangs begin to fly, along with a dragon named Yosai, The Man Called Clint somehow manages to avoid the fangs and claws, biting and swiping at his throat and face. Emperor Vlad is trying to tear Clint's face apart but is unable to land even a tiny cut. Clint gains a little distance, which puts him in a perfect kicking range, at which time he unleashes a perfect textbook Yoko Mawashi Geri (spinning side kick), crashing into Vlad's pelvis area. The kick was extremely powerful, knocking Vlad back several feet, and onto the concrete parking lot of the Radio Station. As Clint is spinning out from the kick, he dawns his katana blade and is ready for some more.*

*The Army of Dead Adrenalines who are waiting in the distance, let out a painful scream, and begin to run towards the radio station building They are coming in full force for Clint, and his Burendo Warriors. As this is happening, the Hive Queen separates from the hoard of Dead Adrenalines and manages to scale the back side of the Beaver County Radio station. The Hive Queen is coming for the Samurai-Knightess at an extremely fast-paced run on the roof of the radio building, but just as she is ready to pounce on top of the Samurai-Knightess. The Samurai-Knightess and Yosai launch and are flying towards the hoard, as this is happening, Yosai turns its dragon head back towards the Hive Queen and lets out a controlled flame burst. Engulfing the entire body of the Hive Queen causing this alien evil to fall from the roof top and hit the ground like a pile of rotting ash. The Hive Queen is no more, and the Samurai-Knightess yells out,* ***that's my dragon!***

*As the mayhem is violently erupting, Sandra, Olivia, and Irish Warrior are outside the radio station and are standing next to the Man Called Clint waiting to fight to the death along side him. Irish Warrior tells Cool Blue 2026 to start running towards the Dead Adrenalines, find their kill spot, and start blade cutting with a sword like blade that is retractable and detachable. Irish Warrior installed this blade on Blue 2026 right android hand, just moments before this alien invasion took a major fucked up turn. Irish Warrior also did a quick modification to Cool Blue 2086, now both hands have sharp dagger like spikes on them that are like spiked brass knuckles. Cool Blue 2086 knows what to do and flies towards the Dead Adrenalines, and while hovering above, Blue 2086 starts to dart down like a bird of prey, looking for the kill shot. As this bloody mix of science fiction, horror, action-adventure, and fantasy mayhem is unfolding, Clint tells Irish Warrior that Vlad is a very clever evil leader because of what just happened.*

*Yep,* Irish, things are about go down in Dead Adrenaline town, Vlad the leader is just playing with us like weak humans. I do not believe my *Yoko Mawashi Geri (*Spinning Side Kick) would have just knocked Vlad back so easily. This Alien-Vampire-Dead Adrenaline is pretending to be injured, so the Dead Adrenaline minions become enraged about this, and come for us. Look Irish, just as I suspected, Vlad is standing up and looks like a proud parent watching his children doing well in life. In this instance, it is not doing well in life, but in death.

"This is true Clint, but I am done fucking around, it is time to break out some Irish Warrior ass kicking, because I am sick of these Dead Adrenaline games these evil alien creatures are playing. Looks like, Blue 2026 and 2086 are taking out many of these DA(s), which helps in the fight."

That's, the spirit Irish Warrior!

Sandra, get ready to kick some alien ass, use all your fighting skills, and any weapon of choice you chose. Remember, look for the kill shot, and make it happen quick because they outnumber us.

Irish Warrior, please go with Sandra, kill as many dead adrenalines as you can. Also, nice modifications on the Cool Blue brothers."

"What can I say, it is what I do! Anyways Clint, time to end these savages finally, and looks like Sandra got her Han'i Ha weapon of choice ready to takeout some zombies, nice to see the future guys used my design. I am going to use a collapsible double spiked bow staff; I brought with me, the spikes break off, and new ones will appear, like magic, ha! I feel weaponized since the dragon slayer blood became part of my DNA, plus, my bow staff skills you showed me Clint in the past feel ready to go."

I Like what I am hearing Irish, you technologically genius creating a battle-ready collapsible bow staff with spiked ends, you always surprise me Irish Warrior. Now go kill some Dead Adrenaline Zombies, I will take care of this fucked up, dill weed Vlad guy!

Olivia, go back in the radio station and wake that survivor up that managed to make it back to the land of the living, after changing back from a dead adrenaline. The Dragon Slayer blood really worked well on him, and he had been a dead adrenaline for a while. Usually if a human stays taken by the alien host too long, they will not survive, even if they get dragon slayer blood.

"Sensei Clint are you thinking what I am thinking."

Yes, Olivia, this survivor's blood might be even more powerful cure. The fact that he returned to human form, and for some reason the Dead Adrenaline Zombies did not attack, this tells me they did not want to bite him even though he was human again. It might have looked like he survived by luck, but I believe the Dead Adrenalines, let him go because of fear.

Ok, let us move quick, because the DA(s) are closing in, but lucky for us the Samurai-Knightess just dropped into the center of the hoard and doing some killing, also, it looks like her dragon YOSAI is making barbecue of some of these dead adrenalines. Dragon's breath of fire is a bad way to go.

*The Samurai-Knightess tells her dragon Yosai to fly around the outer circle of Dead Adrenalines and flame torch the shit sandwich out of them. When this is happening, she drops into the center of the hoard and goes to work slicing and dicing. The Samurai-Knightess knows she must move quick, because a dragon can only breath fire for an abbreviated period, then it needs to recharge its dragon flame. Double sword blades are out, and the Samurai-Knightess is going to war.*

## THE SAMURAI-KNIGHTESS GOES TO WAR

*Irish Warrior and Sandra, join in the fight and are battling the Dead Adrenalines, minor bites do happen, none are fatal so far from the Dead Adrenaline. This causes these Dead Adrenaline host to slowly change back into human form, unfortunately these humans get chomped on by the raging Dead Adrenalines around them. Feeding time is back in the game of life and death. Irish Warrior and Sandra seize the opportunity to find the kill shots on the feeding Dead Adrenalines to end their suffering, along with the humans on the menu. Blood is everywhere, death is part of war and on this day, only one species can be the victor.*

*The Samurai-Knightess is making quick work of the Dead Adrenalines she encounters, knowing where to find the kill shot is speeding the process up. Yosai flies down and begins to claw with its talons and swipes with its long tail, cutting down many Dead Adrenalines. Once Yosai's dragon flame is reset, an above attack of firestorm will continue. The Samurai-Knightess starts to make her way back to her dad to help fight Emperor Vlad. The Man Called Clint is moving towards Vlad but must fight some Dead Adrenalines that broke from the hoard, because the Dead Adrenalines are very protective of their leader, even though Vlad needs no protection. A painting of blood and flesh is covering the concrete parking lot; nothing is stopping Clint from getting to Vlad.*

*Finally, the last protective Dead Adrenaline falls, and Clint decapitates this one, and kicks the head right towards Vlad's chest. Vlad reaches out and catches the Dead Adrenaline head and crushes the skull like grape full of blood and brains.*

*Vlad gives Clint an extreme look of hate and begins to speak. As Vlad starts to speak The Samurai-Knightess arrives to their location and stands beside her dad, The Man Called Clint.*

"I see your daughter has your back, how heart warming it must make you feel Clint. Family does matter in times of pain, suffering, happiness, and joy. I to understand this and respect this. So, it shall end for the last time with you and your daughter, The Samurai-Knightess and The Man Called Clint battling my immediate family member and I."

What the Fuck are you talking about Dill Weed!

"Clint, easy now, I will call off my Army of Dead Adrenalines and than you tell your people to stand down. We will battle here and now, and the winner will be the supreme species, and the loser will parish as with any war of pure violence. No middle ground, no compromise, just death."

*And with this, Vlad gives a signal to cease, and the remaining Dead Adrenalines stop attacking and form up behind Emperor Vlad, a short distance away. Clint communicates with Irish and Sandra to stand down and get back over to him, along with Cool Blue 2026 and 2086. The Samurai-Knightess lets Yosai know to hold off on the flame broiled barbecuing for now. Yosai flies over and lands on top of the radio station. As this is going down in Dead Adrenaline town, something horrible, and unimaginable happens, the glass doors to the radio station shatters outward and out walks a the most hideous looking zombie dressed in gold armor. This Zombie is holding Olivia violently in its grasps, twisting her body, almost in-half. Olivia is conscious and utters the words,* ***The survivor is a*** **Shapeshifter***; we were all fooled. As Olivia barley finishes speaking, and Emperor Vlad starts to yell out!*

"I would like everyone to meet my son! The prince of my kingdom and will be the ruler of planet earth when I leave to continue my conquests, Olivia is correct, a Shapeshifter he is, and they do exist, and are very evil. My son made a fantastic choice to take over this shapeshifters body, during our travels throughout this universe. What a perfect weapon to blend into the crowds when, as you say Clint the shit sandwiches start to fly! And yes, it is a Zombie, since you humans affectionally are calling us some sort of Zombie, my son decided to shape-shift into one, just for the fun of it."

Tell your dill weed son to let Olivia go, if it is a fight to the death, you want Vlad, then let us finish this because I'am more than ready to cut that vampire smile off your face.

"Now we are getting somewhere, a challenge, from a man who actually cares about saving humanity. I see you hold a special place in your human heart for this pathetic woman you call Olivia. Now we will fight to the death, but your daughter, the Samurai-Knightess will also fight my son, and he is very hungry. As far as Olivia living, that will not happen, you see my son always finishes a kill, plus, the Samurai-Knightesses' dragon vaporized my Queen, or should, I say Hive Queen. One species life for another seems like a fair solution."

*And with those words from Vlad, the Shapeshifting son of Emperor Vlad begins to change again, but this time into something unspeakable, something only believed to exist only in mythology. As the transformation begins and ends, Olivia's body becomes a scrape of meat, no time to react and safe her.*

*The Man Called Clint, and the Samurai-Knightess know this to be true, sadness and than angry comes over them. Now standing before them is a bloodthirsty Werewolf, tearing Olivia almost in-half, blood, internal organs spill out, and Olivia falls to the ground. The Alien-Werewolf bends down and looks over Olivia and is satisfied with the kill.*

**Alien-Werewolf-Dead Adrenaline is Satisfied with Its Kill.**

# PAIN, SUFFERING AND SACRIFICE

## YEAR 2026

*Clint yells out to Vlad;* ***It's Time to Clean the Fucking DOJO!*** *With those words, his team of a Burendo Warriors knew what needed to happen. No compromise, and no one would be standing by while the leaders of each species battled to death. Everyone would be involved in the killing, even Yosai the dragon was on board, and let out a flame throw of hellfire, destroying many Dead Adrenalines standing by waiting for a command from Emperor Vlad to start killing again. As the flames from Yosai hit its intended target, Irish Warrior and Sandra start to take out dead adrenalines again, knowing this would be the last battle with the dead adrenalines, so they both gave everything they could offer. The Cool Blue brother androids continued with their onslaught of death, trying to thin the hoard.*

*This took Emperor Vlad, off guard, he did not expect this reaction and thought that The Man Called Clint, and the Samurai-Knightess would be the only ones fighting, while the Dead Adrenalines and Clint's team watched for an outcome. Vlad did not like this at all, he wanted it to be a spectacle of power over one species and wanted an audience. A moment of confusion set in, and Emperor Vlad just could not wrap its alien mind around this. As this moment of confusion was occurring with Vlad, the Man Called Clint, closed the distance, and cut Vlad's right arm completely off.*

*Vlad swiftly reacts, and swipes at Clint with the remaining arm, cutting Clint a-crossed his chest area, Clint steps back and drops with a Ura Mawashi Gedan Ashi Barai (Spinning Low Leg Sweep), knocking Vlad onto its back. Without hesitation, Vlad bounces back onto its Alien-Vampire-Dead Adrenaline feet and moves in for the kill. Clint Judo rolls out of the direct line of attack, regains his footing, blood is seeping out of Clint's chest, the wound was deep, and might be fatal, Vlad and Clint continue to fight, and Clint is managing to avoid anymore major injuries, but the blood loss is starting to affect him. As this is going down in Dead Adrenaline town, the Samurai-Knightess is trying to get close enough to this Alien-Werewolf-Dead Adrenaline, but for some reason this beast is avoiding her and not fighting back. Then the Samurai-Knightess hears the voice of Vlad, yelling out!*

"Destroy her, I command you! Also, my children your Emperor commands you to fight the human enemy!

*With the sudden attack and confusion, Vlad forgot to command his son, and dead Adrenaline minions to resume fighting. This was a good thing, because Irish Warrior, Sandra, and Cool Blue 2026 and 2086, along with Yosai were able to kill a ton of Dead Adrenalines that were not fighting back. This really thinned the hoard, which only left about 30 or so Dead Adrenalines, but now they were fighting back, and the team needed to be precise with every kill.*

"*Ok*, you fur bag shit sandwich, now we are going to battle to the death, and you will feel the power of the Samurai-Knightess!"

The *Samurai-Knightess is ready to kill the wolf, and with light speed, materializes a silver bow staff, which is light weight, but should do the trick to kill a wolf creature. She searches quickly, but cannot find the kill shot spot, meaning that this Alien-Werewolf-Dead Adrenaline is somehow masking the location or does not have a kill spot. This must also mean that Vlad is immortal and has no kill shot either, like father, like son.*

"Dad! Vlad has no kill shot spot, you need to just slice and dice, kick, and strike, until this alien bitch weakens!!!" I am going to annihilate this wolf-dog son."

"I hear you, Chlo! And my will to survive that has kept me alive from day one of this Dead Adrenaline-Zombie apocalypse will win the day, because I will not be eating this shit sandwich!

*Vlad begins to cackle a loud shrieking sound and tells Clint that he understands the love of family and finds it quite sweet that he calls her Chlo, then with vicious intentions, he reaches out and grabs, Clint's throat, snapping Clint's neck. Upon releasing Clint's throat, Clint crumbles to the ground, and drops his katana sword, blood pulsing from his neck area. The concrete becomes painted with the blood of Clint's body; he has bled out.*

"You pathetic weak humans, do not still understand, I am the superior species!"

*As Vlad starts to speak his bullshit soap box speech, the Samurai-Knightess is trying to hold back her emotions, knowing the Man Called Clint, her dad is dead, she is still battling the son of Vlad. Hitting and spiking this beast with all, of her strength, mixing in materialized silver throwing stars and knives, but nothing is putting down this Alien-Werewolf, The Wolf, does land several painful, and bloody claw strikes at the Samurai-Knightess, penetrating the armor into the flesh.*

*The Silver armor adapts and changes, even adding head and face protection when needed. During the claw and mouth bites given by the Alien-Werewolf Dead Adrenaline savage, the Samurai-Knightess realizes that the wolf is shrieking out in pain with every attack, and it is not from her attacks, but when this animal claws or, bites the armor. This could mean only one thing; the silver laced armor of the dragon realm is deadly to this Werewolf.*

*Vlad is still standing there talking a lot of bullshit alien craziness, when Yosai fly's past and lets out a huge gust of dragon fire hitting Vlad directly, apparently, Yosai got sick of the bullshit coming from Vlad's mouth and let him have it. As the flame and fire fades away, and smoke clears, Vlad is just standing there, like nothing even happened, and begins to speak again.*

*"Dragon flame can not destroy me; in fact, I happen to love fire and brimstone. You must know by now, I can not die, yes,*

*this Man called Clint did cut my right arm off, but it will grow back in time. I am all powerful and the time of humans existing is over, it is the time of my species. Now I will end the rest of you with my alien powers, because I am growing tired of this planet, but some of my remaining Dead Adrenalines will spread this infection in Beaver County, Pennsylvania, and our species will own and inhabit this world, in this present time and future!*

*Irish Warrior and Sandra realize Clint looks to be dead but keep fighting the remaining Dead Adrenalines. Sandra knows that Clint has escaped death before and holds out hope it happens again. Irish Warrior knows Clint, always finds away back to the fight, but sends both Cool Blue 2026 and 2086 over to check for signs of life. Both scan Clint, but no signs of life are present. Vlad looks at the androids and starts to laugh and starts to speak again.*

"He is dead, your hero, The Man Called Clint is dead! I know this to be for certain because I am a God! Soon the Samurai-Knightess will be dead, my son is ready to end her life. Do it son, kill the Samurai-Knightess, do it now!"

*The Samurai-Knightess is in pure fighting mode, as the claw swipe, almost takes her head off. The battle rages on, the Samurai-Knightess remembers something Merlin told her, a secret that will be revealed, when the time is right. And with that thought, the Samurai-Knightess summons Excalibur the sword of Dragon power and Divine Kingship.*

"The time has arrived, Silver can kill, but only silver from the Cascade Mountains where the Drăgon Realm exist. Pure untouched silver laced waters forged into the Sword Excalibur!"

*With those words, the Samurai-Knightess blade cuts the Alien-Werewolf-Dead Adrenaline from one to seven has the clock turns, cutting the wolf in-half from its right shoulder to its hip bone. The body of this Alien creature separates, and each half fall apart. As Shapeshifter's body dies, a dead adrenaline light sphere appears from one half of the body, the Samurai-Knightess blade cuts this light sphere with amazing speed and destroys it. The Samurai-Knightess, turns and looks at Vlad, and says these words.*

"Your son is dead, deal with dillweed, now it is your turn to die."

"This can not be, no silver of the human world can kill a werewolf, shapeshifter or even alien entity that does not have a weak spot."

"Your right dip shit, no silver from the human realm, but from the dragon realm, now that is a whole different fairy fucking tale!"

"Now! You humans will know the full wrath of my hate for weaker forms of life, especially humans!"

*Emperor Vlad lunges towards the Samurai-Knightess and starts to reach out to grab hold of her, as this movement is happening, it suddenly stops. A solid Mawashi Geri*

*(Roundhouse Kick) lands squarely on Vlad's deformed chin, knocking the fucking fangs right out of this evil abomination's mouth. The power of the kick was incredible, knocking Vlad's head backwards, and sending this leader of the Dead Adrenalines stumbling uncontrollably. Finally, Emperor Vlad regains its footing and looks in vicious anger to see who had kicked him. Standing there is the Man Called Clint, alive and well!*

"What is wrong Vlad, did you just find out you are a pathetic weak alien species. Yes, that is right, I live, survive and I am still kicking alien ass. A no-fang Vampire is not a good look for you."

"Dad, your alive, thank the heavens above, I thought I lost you."

Dragon Slayer blood honey, which gives me a superpower to survive, just like you, although this time took a bit longer to recover. Broken neck, severed spine, and I lost all my blood. Really painful and dreadful way to go, now let us end this Fangless evil, here and now Chlo.

*At that moment, Vlad starts to send a surge of deadly energy light towards Clint, at which time, Chloe steps forward and lands another round kick to Vlad's face, which throws off the landing of the evil light surge. Clint moves at an angle and avoids the deadly power surge. Then it happens, the Samurai-Knightess and the Man Called Clint start unleashing and complete arsenal of hand strikes and kicks. Sometimes at the same time, and sometimes opposite of each other. Vlad tries to stop the onslaught but just can not seem to get focused and drops to its knees. Vlad the Impalers body is breaking down from the punishment, the Man Called Clint steps back and the Samurai-Knightess takes over with the sword Excalibur and begins to speak.*

"You waited too long to use your alien power on us humans, your arrogance, and believe that we were the weaker species was your downfall. Thinking you could just destroy us with the power of Dracula, under your control, and human host with cannibalistic Dead Adrenalines inside them. Now it will soon be over, and may you go back to the pit of hell your species climbed out of. The sword Excalibur, I hold is a Holy sword, which shows mercy or no mercy, on this day no mercy is on the menu. Oh, one more thing, Excalibur is pure silver from the Dragon Realm, and it kills Vampires, Werewolves, Shapeshifters, and Dead Adrenalines to, you evil dill weed. Remember this, good always wins because evil believes it can never lose!!!"

*With those final words, the dethroned Vlad is a destroyed mess of disbelief, knowing that his species are losing the invasion. A powerful silence surrounds everyone, and then the Samurai-Knightess uses Excalibur and cuts the head of Vlad the Impaler clean off, Emperor Vlad is no more. The body of Vlad turns to bloody ash and falls to the ground. Within the ash a purplish, reddish, and bluish light sphere floats up above the bloody ash. It is the King of the Dead Adrenalines, and like a shooting star it flies upward at a fast speed.*

*The Samurai-Knightess reacts, calls for Yosai, catches a ride and with Excalibur in hand, is in hot pursuit after this evil. The Man Called Clint yells out to his daughter, and tells her, she is the salvation of humanity, and to kill that alien dillweed!*

"I got this dad, ok Yosai keep that evil sphere in your sight, we need to stop it before it leaves earth, we got one chance, if it gets out of earths atmosphere, we will lose it. Prepare your battle scale's, make sure it is the toughest you can transform to. Once we get close enough, take a swipe at the Evil light sphere, I want to knock it off its escape course, and than I will cut this Sphere down with Excalibur, I will also change the shape of Excalibur when needed to give us the best blade cut possible.

**YOSAI AND SAMURAI-KNIGHTESS PREPARE TO END THIS.**

*As they get closer to the Evil Sphere, Yosai takes a swipe with its dragon tail, suddenly and unexpectedly Yosai and the Samurai-Knightess realize this was a major mistake. The Evil light sphere is now trying to suck them into it, like an anaconda devouring its prey.*

**The Evil Sphere vs Samurai-Knightess & Yosai**

"Shit Yosai, the Evil Sphere is absorbing us, it is starting with your tail. We need to break free and fly above it, and than I will jump from you with Excalibur in hand, if I time it correctly, I can blade cut this evil sphere, which is growing larger, by the second. One cut from Excalibur will end it, but first I will try to move to the back of your body Yosai and try take a cut with Excalibur!"

*As the Samurai-Knightess starts to move to the back of Yosai, the Evil Sphere lets go of Yosai's tail and continues to fly upward.*

"Get your compass back Yosai, plan B, let us fly above the sphere and I will jump from you, and if I time it correctly, Excalibur will do the rest. Either the Evil Sphere let go of your tail because it realizes there is silver coursing through your dragon veins, or it knows Excalibur will end it. Either way we still need to stop it before it gets to space, so let us fly past the Evil light Sphere and above it, fly Yosai, fly Yosai!!!"

*The Samurai-Knightess flies around the Evil Sphere, and gets above while riding Yosai, and tells Yosai to fly down and catch her when it is over, and leaps from her dragon. She begins her descent towards the Evil light Sphere with Excalibur in hand, timing is everything, because there only will be time for one blade cut. The Samurai-Knightess position herself as she is falling and transforms Excalibur to a sleek style sword that still has the pure silver of the dragon realm and carries Dragon Power and Divine Kingship. The time has come and the salvation of the humanity rest solely on* **The Samurai-Knightesses** *ability both mentally and physically, one blade cut, one chance, one destiny. No one person could have trained for this moment in time, but Chloe has, and she is the Samurai-Knightess for all time!*

## The Samurai-Knightess Last Chance

“Ok Chloe, slow your thoughts down because we are about to hit our mark, Crazy, I am falling to my death and I’am talking to myself, or at least in my mind. **God**, I know you are here with me, I place my fate in your hands, and my skill set in mine. The time for Dragon Power, and Divine Kingship is upon us.”

*The Samurai-Knightess prepares for the end, grasp Excalibur with both hands, speaks to **God,** and is ready to cut down this Dead Adrenaline Evil entity that has been destroying Beaver County, Pennsylvania, and the world in the past, present, and future.*

**The Samurai-Knightess says a prayer & prepares to end Evil**

“Oh shit, here we go, Excalibur do your magic!!!!”

*The Evil Sphere is just seconds from the Samurai-Knightess blade cutting it, as Excalibur blade cut begins to happen, the Dead Adrenaline Evil Sphere attempts to spin in a counterclockwise direction, hoping to avoid the blade cut, and maneuver away from the Excalibur blade partially, but the tip of the blade slices into the sphere. The impact of the Excalibur blade cutting into the Evil Sphere was powerful and earth shattering. At that moment, Excalibur cut the sphere, the Samurai-Knightess and the sword become one weapon of Dragon Power and Divine Kingship, and the pure silver of the Cascade Mountains and the Dragon Realm bleed into the Evil Sphere.*

*Time stops for an abbreviated moment as the Samurai-Knightess removes the blade from the Evil Sphere. As the Samurai-Knightess continues to fall, she sees the Sphere turn solid silver on the outside and the inside. It has turned to rock-stone-silver, just like the dragon realm's landscape, suddenly the dying Evil Sphere stops it movement, and freezes for a second, but than starts to fall at an extreme high rate of speed towards the Samurai-Knightess, who is still falling below the Evil Sphere. This could be by accident or by design, a final effort by evil to destroy good, either way, the Sphere is falling and on a direct collision course for the Samurai-Knightess.*

"Now this is a shit sandwich because what I see is the Evil Sphere that should be dead or dying heading right towards my body. Come on Yosai, where are you, time is running out!"

*The Samurai-Knightess gets ready with Excalibur and is going to take another blade cut at this Evil Sphere boulder falling towards her, but there is no way to avoid the round evil paperweight from striking her. The Samurai-Knightess can regenerate back to live, but a fall from this distance and impact from this Dead Adrenaline object might be too much to survive. Plus, at this speed and impact, the Samurai-Knightess will be nothing but bones, blood, and body parts.*

*Five seconds, four seconds, three seconds, two seconds, and finally one second. The completion of the blade cut happens, just has Yosai flies' underneath of the Samurai-Knightess and places his back under her feet, which gives a solid base for the sword cut. Yosai, grips the Samurai-Knightesses feet in with a transformation of its scale armor, which will be enough to hold. The cut is powerful, and Yosai flies from underneath the Evil Sphere, cracks the sphere with his tail, and flies away with the Samurai-Knightess.*

*Yosai swiftly maneuvers back around, and The Samurai-Knightess takes a seat to look at the dying evil sphere, and than it happens, the sphere explodes into dust particles of death.*

**The Evil Dead Adrenaline Sphere Leader Is Dying**

**The Evil Dead Adrenaline Leader Explodes and Dies**

*The Evil Entity leader of Dead Adrenalines is no more, and because the leader has died, hopefully the dead adrenalines soldiers will fade away and not survive. The Samurai-Knightess and her trusty Dragon Yosai have killed the Alpha Alien, and humans rule the earth again.*

# ONE WILL REMAIN

## YEAR 2026

"**That's my dragon!** Thank you Yosai, your help is like no other, you are the best, we make a wonderful world saving team. Yep, Yosai I'am glad I did not get to test out if I could survive such a violent fall, now let us fly down to my dad and tell them the good news, and see if this made a complete difference to end this alien-dead adrenaline invasion."

*The Samurai-Knightess and Yosai fly back down to see what the outcome will be, as they land back in the Beaver County Radio station parking lot, they see something very unusual and stunning. The remaining dead adrenaline entities have left their host body and released their minds. The Dead Adrenaline spheres are floating about 6 feet in the air spinning in small circles in a confused manner, unfortunately the human host were too far-gone when the Alien Entity-Dead Adrenalines left their bodies and minds. They looked to be just a lifeless bag of skin and bones, blood, and flesh, even at the very end, these Dead Adrenalines manage to kill humans.*

*The Samurai-Knightess lands with Yosai and walks up to her dad, Irish Warrior, and Sandra, who are ready to end the last of the dead adrenalines. Also, Cool Blue 26 and 86 are in the area waiting for the next move.*

“Chloe (Samurai-Knightess) these are the last of the evading cannibalistic aliens, so there is a part of me that wants to be the one that cuts them down. I was the first human to kill a dead adrenaline, so maybe, I should be the person that kills the last dead adrenalines on earth.”

“Or dad, we could just let Yosai ham barbecue them with some dragon fire.”

You know what Chlo, turn your dragon loose, what do you think Irish Warrior.

“Yep, time for the last ones to find out what rights they do not have, torch those alien asshole!

“I agree so very much, Sensei, time to end this.”

Yep Sandra.

“Ok, Chlo, do your magic!”

*And with those words from the Man Called Clint, The Samurai-Knightess looks at Yosai, smiles, and Yosai launches into the air, and flies above the dead adrenaline spheres. Yosai circles the Dead Adrenaline spheres, which are about 15 of them, and lets out a large flame breath, which evaporates them into ash. The Dead Adrenalines have lost, and the human species are the victor.*

*Or so they believed in those moments of triumph, until something alien evil and bizarre happens, the ash cloud starts to turn blood red, and the ash pieces become alive. A swarm of ashes that look like bats in the red sky, this can mean only one thing, Emperor Alien Leader is still alive, and somehow it kept Vlad the Impalers vampire powers, along with his own alien bullshit.* **Dracula** *and* ***Dead Adrenaline*** *have merged permanently. The Samurai-Knightess and the Man Called Clint, along with Irish Warrior and Sandra, do not like the looks of this shit sandwich.*

"Well, this battle is not over yet Clint!"

Yep Irish, this dead adrenaline leader is a clever, sinister one, just does not die easily. I bet it switch places with those 15 dead adrenaline entities, as it was flying to the sky, pretending to escape, except it was all 15 dead adrenalines in that big ass evil sphere. Old Vlad took over each human host individually, and killed each human, then exited their bodies, and each one of the 15-light spheres were one evil entity leader trying to survive. Not sure how this happens, but the proof is flying in front of us.

**The Alien-Vampire-Dead Adrenaline Leader Has Survived**

Chlo, what do think about these dead adrenaline events.

"Dad, I do believe it is Emperor Vlad, but in this form my sense for danger coming from this alien leader in this state is harmless. However, we can not kill it while it stays these flying blood ash bats, but it can not do anything to us, except leave. Both Yosai and I know this to be true, plus, my silver armor, and Yosai's scales have not changed into battle ready form. Although, it will eventually change into something dangerous, and humans will be back on the menu, but it wants to flee and go hibernate for another 60 years. Meaning in the year 2086, the dead adrenaline infection will resurface and complete the invasion. If this happens, we did not save our civilization."

Sounds bleak and unacceptable, so what you are saying Chloe, it is time to call the leader out for one last fight to the death, which is getting so old.

"Exactly dad!"

*The Man Called Clint steps closer to the blood ash bats and yells out. It is time for one last kumite (fight), so figure out what form you want to take, and let us do this dill weed!*

*The arrogance, hate, and over confidence of the Dead Adrenaline alien species is uncontrollable. Evil will never yield, especially to the human species, but it knows it should leave and hibernate for another 60 years, which would only be 60 minutes for their species. The year 2086 would be the year in time to continue the invasion of planet earth, and nothing done today by the Man Called Clint and his band of warriors would change that outcome. The intelligent move in this war would be to leave and return with the Dead Adrenaline infection in the year 2086, but the internal drive of this alien entity wants something different. It believes that its species can never lose, and must kill Clint, the Samurai-Knightess, Irish Warrior, and the Burendo Warriors, to satisfy its existence.*

"Dad, if this Alien leader exits the area, it will be near-impossible to track it down, especially if hibernates in the earth. If that happens the dead adrenaline infection will show up in the future year 2086, meaning we have changed nothing."

Ok than, it is time for me to really confuse this alien shithead Chloe!

*The Man Called Clint, knows just what to say to this Alien Leader, and begins to speak, but what Clint starts to say shocks everyone except the Samurai-Knightess.*

We were wrong, we were so wrong, your species are the superior organisms in this world and others. Please let my species understand your ways, our intelligence is minimal compared to yours. You are a mighty force of nature, beyond humans' ability to comprehend, show mercy towards our species, or at the very least, mercy to the last surviving warriors. You are a King, and we will be your followers.

*The Samurai-Knightess knows what her dad is doing, the bait has been set, and the ego of this alien entity is unmatched in this world and others. Also, Irish Warrior and Sandra start to understand what is about to happen, now it is up to this dipshit*

*Dead Adrenaline to decide its fate. Minutes pass, and finally it happens, the alien leader makes its choice and speaks. A Voice from above in the swarm of alien vampire ash bats addresses Clint.*

"So, you finally understand something clearly, the light of evil burns bright and is everlasting. Clint, I will show mercy on you and your followers, prepare yourselves, because I am about to show you what our species truly look like. Yes, we can take many varied species bodies and minds as host, and my kind can enter their bodies in a light shaped sphere, which I use for a purpose and for time traveling a cross the universe and hibernating in the earths crust. All of this serves us and is our way, but I do have a true form of existence, which is my true self. If you want to truly except our existence and your fate, then I will reveal my true self to you and your following warriors Clint."

*The Man Called Clint, does not speak and waits, along with the others, then it happens, a transformation of the Alien leader, which leaves everyone grasping for a logical thought, because what is standing before them is both shocking, unimaginable, and mind blowing beyond words. The true self of this Alien Entity can not be unseen or put back in its evil bottle, a complete image of Evil stands before them, and nothing can every change this optic. A being that is both psychotic and extraterrestrial in nature, pure evil that has infested earth on level never seen before. An invasion that has left death, destruction, pain, and suffering without remorse or conscience.*

*Now this humanoid alien is standing before the defenders of the earth, ready to except their defeat, or so it believes.*

**The True Self of the Alien-Dead Adrenaline Leader**

"I know earthlings, I am a fascinating sight to visualize, but understand, our kind are the first organisms to ever exist, and we are the dominant species in the universe. Yes, we have destroyed worlds and other species for the grand concept we believe in, which is to make all life bow to us. My ability to survive will never be in jeopardy, as you see by my image here today. I am both unique and a glorious King of the universe, so why would I let other species survive. Oh, by now Clint, you are wondering what is going to happen next or hoping for my mercy. The mercy you and your followers will receive on this day, will be a slow death. You see, by dying slowly, you will realize that your death was for the good of our species, and our survival!

Now this is a gift I am giving all of you from my species to yours, pain and suffering is that gift that will release you from your pathetic, weak, unfortunate existence. Now I know, you are not giving in to me, and you will never join our cause for totalitarianism, but this is so much fun to have an opponent that just does not want to yield to my power and control. In my existence, it does not get any better than this, and with every breath of my beautiful lungs, I know I am the most powerful species in the entire universe."

"Dad, can we put this evil Einstein back in its A-Hole spaceship, and blast it off to a universe far, far away."

Now that is funny Chlo, humor keeps us going, nice blend of Einstein with a touch Star Wars. This Alien dillweed is no genius, but does come from a universe far, far, away. Ok, now it is time to end this, and I know what I must do.

Hey, I'am ready to except defeat, your greatness is overpowering, what was I thinking King of the Universe!

"Clint! I just knew you would understand that this battle you have been waging is all for not. It is quite refreshing to meet a specimen like you that truly realizes what I'am trying to carry out. When I finish with all of you, my spaceship awaits and I need to launch more of my alien species into the world and crush this place called earth, some now, and some in 60 years. This is so extremely exciting and gratifying, knowing that nothing can stop me."

*(The Samurai-Knightess whispers to her dad) "Wow, this evil asshole ego is off the charts with delusion, enough so, that this dill weed revealed that inside the spacecraft, there are more dead adrenalines that will release into our world again.*

Delusion is exactly what I am counting on Chloe, now use your magic, then send it my way and I will give this delusional dill weed the gift that just keeps on giving.

"Oh yes, now you are speaking my language, and I will have Yosai take care of the dipshit DA(s) aboard the spacecraft.

*The Samurai-Knightess sends a signal to Yosai, who silently launches into the sky, waiting for things to unfold. Yosai, will be unleashing full dragon freeze breath at the spacecraft to exterminate the last of the dead adrenaline entities. Now Yosai waits and holds back on releasing this ice ammunition, knowing this ice-storm will be a deep freeze of death. After all this dragon species can release flame or ice, which is inherently natural for dragons from the dragon realm. In battle mode a dragon will not wait to release its flame or ice, but in stealth mode a dragon will wait, until the time is right. The dragon will fly silently above, watching, waiting, and than acting on its enemy. While Yosai waits, Sandra and Irish are trying to figure out what is about to go down in Dead Adrenaline town, and Sandra is not happy with Sensei Clint.*

"What, the hell are they talking about, it looks like Sensei Clint, wants to just walk up to this alien leader with out a hand weapon. The only thing that will kill this thing, is a particular silver."

"No worries, Sandra, I have known my friend Clint for along time, heck, he even gave me the nick name Irish Warrior. As you have seen, every move he makes is for a solid reason."

"Your right Irish Warrior, I am just worried about the outcome, and Sensei Clint.

"Sandra, Clint's next move will be unpredictable and only one will remain and I believe with total confidence it will be Clint. Cool Blue 2026 and 2086, video this from all angles, because the world is going to want to see this ending."

***The Man Called Clint** approaches the Evil leader of the Dead Adrenalines, who has now transformed into ceremonial attire.*

**Evil Leader is Ready to Be Victorious**

*The Alien Leader is blinded by its delusions of control over the human spirit, thinking in its twisted mind that the human's fortitude to survive has collapsed. Especially, because this human leader,* ***The Man Called Clint*** *has given in. With that ominous thought, the Alien Leader reaches it creature like hands out and places them on Clint's shoulders and begins to speak.*

"I will take you as my human host, a complete human with a powerful mind and body, which is suitable for a King to use. You must give in and know this is for the higher species existence and the lower species extinction."

*As this is going down in Dead Adrenaline town, the Man Called Clint places his hands behind his back, making the Alien Leader assume that Clint realizes the battle is not winnable, and surrendering is the only thing left to do.*

*The process begins, and Clint's body starts to shake slightly, and starts to metamorphosis into something human and alien in nature. As Clint begins to change, he suddenly pulls away from the Alien Leader, who now only has half of its alien entity life source in its alien body. Meaning, it is so much weaker now, but Clint is stronger, but can he harness the evil energy for a good purpose and blend his strength with this foreign organism. The Dragon Slayer blood and some of the past superpowers he acquired, during the fight with the Hive Queen, along with his skill set and total will to survive the entity infection are helping. Clint is finding his way and controlling his own body and mind but does fill the evil force breathing down his neck.*

*Clint's nerves are on fire, and the evil entity is trying to smother him, and take over his mind and body. The struggle is real, and full contact Kumite(fight) is going on within Clint's mind and body. This evil infection is trying to force Clint back over too the Alien Leader to complete the evil entity transfer. Fortunately, Clint is no average human host, and his mind and body chooses to stop and fight this darkness infecting his life force. The Dead Adrenaline infection is now part of him, and Clint must use this evil power for good and knows what he must do.*

**The Man Called Clint is now Part Dead Adrenaline-Alien**

*Now Clint is ready, and the game board has been set, and circles the Alien Leader, who is now confused and trying to grab back hold of Clint. At that moment Clint, understands completely what this Alien Leader needs to do, take him as a permanent host body, because the true self body of the alien leader must be dying, because of the break in the evil transfer. A weak pathetic Alien body stands with deadness in its eyes, and is wilting away, like an evil creepy purple flower.*

**Evil Alien Leader is Dying**

*With that thought, Clint unleashes a crowd pleasing, crushing three combinations of kicks, consisting of a left Soto-Uchi Jodan Geri( Inside-Outside High Kick) to the head, following up with a right Mai-Keage-Geri (Front SnapKick)to the solar plexus and ending with a left turning Mawashi-Geri (Roundhouse) to the back of the alien's head. The rapid kicks knock the Alien Leader to the ground, but this time the alien was hurting, and not playing alien possum. Clint knows that in this state the Alien Leader is vulnerable, so Clint makes his last two final moves, knowing it had to happen now. Clint grabs hold of the Alien Dead Adrenaline leader, holding it up by its alien shoulders.*

*While holding up this alien garbage, Clint starts to transfer part of evil dead adrenaline entity that he had received back into alien body. Once Clint completes this, he implements a solid Koshi-Guruma throw (Hip-Wheel throw), sending the alien dill weed crashing to the concrete lot, using a grasping headlock, combined with the hip wheel throw. After throwing the Evil DA, Clint takes a couple steps back, looks at the alien dipshit and tells him he sent some dragon slayer blood back too, knowing that this dragon slayer blood is like holy water to this evil abomination. The Alien Leader starts to shriek out in pain because its blood is boiling internally, Clint who has totally returned to his human form, looks over to his daughter Chloe and yell's out to her.*

*Chloe, do what you do!*

*"You got it dad!"*

*And with the speed of a cheetah and power of an uncaged bear, the Samurai-Knightess materializes Excalibur again, and blade cuts from the right side of the alien's waist, completely through and out the left side of the waistline. Cutting the Alien dill weed leader totally in half. The Alien Leader tries to morph its body into a more protective skin and head covering, but it is to late.*

**The Samurai-Knightess Blade cuts down Evil.**

*As the Alien's body slides apart, a silver-colored liquid mixed with gold pours out, and like disintegrating magic, the silver liquid evaporates the body of this Alien evil, like acid burning through metal. The Alien's body is turning silver and slowly melting away, and the pain and suffering from this invasion are now no longer part of this world. Only death to this evil alien infection, and humanity has conquered the enemy from outer space.*

**The Evil Alien Leader is Melting Away.**

# IS THE WORLD SAFE

## YEAR: 2026, 2086, 1634, AND THE 13TH CENTURY

"Well dad, the world is safe for now, in the past, present, and future, and only one remains, the human species."

Yes, we did Chloe, it was at a cost, but I want to thank you my daughter, the Samurai-Knightess, because your set of skills are far beyond anything in this world and beyond. You were the master key to unlock victory, and your dragon Yosai is one bad ass warrior too. Kinda reminds me of Dragon Heart with Dennis Quad as the hero, and Sean Connery, as the voice of the dragon, so does your dragon speak. Chloe.

"Oh yes, but only I can understand him, because I speak dragon, and Yosai kinda sounds like Sean Connery, which makes for a cool listening experience."

Nice, I got to learn the dragon language someday because that is incredible, ok, Chloe, I going to say my goodbyes to Sandra, because she will be going back to the year 2086, which should be dead adrenaline alien free, based on the ass kicking that took place in this year of 2026.

"Yep dad, the timeline we are in will be Dead Adrenaline free, along with other timelines, if you understand what I am saying. The alien invasion might have creeped into different timelines, but because I killed the alpha alien, no Dead

Adrenaline will survive long, in such a confused state. The warriors or hopefully heroes in those timelines will take care of the leftovers if that makes sense. And truthfully, the Dead Adrenalines will just die on their own, because they have no guidance without a leader, which makes them really a weak species if you think about it. Unlike our species, which will fight until the end, and find away."

"Yeah, that sounds timeline correct Clint and Chloe, so based on the Alien infection originating by borrowing underneath the earth's soil in the year 1969 and hatching loose in the year 2026. The Killing of the Alpha A-hole leader in this year of 2026 does mess up everything for the aliens."

Exactly, Irish Warrior.

Chlo, Irish Warrior has spoken the truth, and it appears, we have conquered and fixed the trauma inflicted on earth and humanity. Just like in every war, people die, which is always unavoidable, but we minimized casualties, even though death took a lot of human life still, along with other creatures.

"Yep dad, Irish Warrior is correct."

Ok, I am going to send Sandra and Cool Blue 2086, back to the year 2086, If you want to say goodbye to Blue 2086 Irish, now is the time.

*Irish Warrior walks up to Cool Blue 2086, along with Cool Blue 2026. The Cool Blue Androids, reach their hands out towards each other, and Irish watches them shake hands, almost in human like fashion. The android's nod their heads at each other as sign of approval. Irish Warrior tells Cool Blue 2086, to keep the future safe and they will work on keeping the present save. Irish tells Sandra to have a save trip forward to the year 2086, and to keep Cool Blue 2086 out of trouble, Sandra smiles at Irish Warrior and tells him she will take care of it.*

"Ok Clint, Cool Blue 2026 and I will make it back to my house, and I will send out an audio and video message that the Dead Adrenaline infection is over. Once's they see this, they will send in the United States Controlled Military, Scientists, and Doctors, which will confirm the truth. Also, when you show up outside the terminal realm Clint, they might find out the full story of details from you. I will wait here for now, until things calm down.

Yep Irish, you are spot on with your thought process, sounds like a plan. I will be seeing you soon my friend, along with your cool ass robot. Also, I bet you need to rest, this has been a pretty big outing for you Irish.

"You mean Android, and with friends like you Clint, ha ha, who needs future ones. And yes, you are correct, I do need some rest and relaxation, because being your friend and helping save the world can wear a person out."

Good one Irish, nice to see things are getting back to normal, and we still can be friend's, ha, ha! I will be seeing you later.

"Bye Chloe from the future."

"Bye Irish Warrior, tell Kitty, I said hello.

"I will Chloe, and when I see my wife, I will tell her the Samurai-Knightess says hello."

Ok Chloe, give me a minute to say goodbye to Sandra and Cool Blue 2086.

"Ok Dad."

"Well, I guess, this is goodbye Sensei Clint,"

Sandra, you, and Sullivan are the last of the Burendo Warriors, so when you return to the year 2086, and you meet up with Sullivan. Tell him, I said thank you for finding my daughter, Chloe, and sending her in the right direction to fulfill her destiny. Also, thank you Sandra for never giving up and fighting ever treacherous step we had to take on this mission. It will be up to you and Sullivan to train future Burendo Shotokan Warriors, so America and the world can be a safer place. I wish Olivia had survived but bring her body back to her family. As you know war is hell, but you did survive and are the future."

"I will Sensei Clint, and I will never forget your teachings and thank you for everything, and on another positive note Sensei. Cool Blue 86 did a more detail life scan of Olivia body. Olivia has a very faint heartbeat and brain function, so we will bring Olivia back to 2086, and see if future medicine can do its magic. Right now, I placed her body in a portable life support system that Olivia had brought on this mission. The fact that Olivia is still alive, might have something to do with the dragon slayer blood, Irish Warrior, and you gave us, to help with the reverse age issue."

*Clint looks at Sandra and tells her absolutely, and with those final words, Sandra walks up to Sensei Clint, gives him a hug, moves back a couple steps, and Cool Blue, Sandra, and Olivia time travel pod away to the year 2086.*

Time to get the hell out of the ex-terminal realm /Dead Adrenaline free zone of Beaver County, Pennsylvania and go see our family, Chlo.

"Yosai and I are ready to go dad."

*The Dead Adrenalines were exterminated, and the world did reset, The Samurai-Knightess did get the Man Called Clint back to the family, it was fantastic reunion. The Samurai-Knightess did not go with her dad, knowing that her younger self was waiting with her mom and Luke, it would have been kinda cool to meet herself in the year 2026 age 16, but time traveling is a delicate thing and must be respected. The timeline will be different for young Chloe, but the the Samurai-Knightess will have a different timeline when she returns to the year 2086. The Man Called Clint, understood this, said his goodbyes, knowing that Chloe, the Samurai-Knightess has further quest to fulfill and will be the worlds protection from this day forward. Now Clint, did not know how long he could live because of his superpowers and dragon slayer blood, which is another tale for another time, but for now he was going to enjoy the time with his family, and see where life takes him.*

*The Samurai-Knightess decided to take just a quick time traveling dragon flight to the future, about one month out into the future, to see if the government did the right thing.*

*The Leader of America and the United States Controlled Military, along with other officials, finally admitted that Alien invasion was the cause of the Dead Adrenaline infection. Pressure from within the United States and other countries forced this admission to happen. Also, the release of video footage from Irish Warrior, courtesy of the Cool Blue 2026, help force the hand of our government. Shortly, after this release the government removed Beaver County, Pennsylvania from the terminal realm list. A recon mission occurred, which proofed suitable safe conditions in Beaver County, Pennsylvania, so eventually the residence returned to their homes. And, life resumed, but it was a new normal after this horrific event that originated in Beaver County, Pennsylvania, but the human species have a* ***God*** *given ability to survive and stay the course. This is why they are the greatest species that* ***God*** *ever created.*

"Well, Yosai the world is safe from the evil dead adrenaline invasion, and hopefully no more of those dill weeds are out in the far away universe plotting something. My believe is that we took out an alien race that found out they were not the higher species. Plus, it is never a solid thought process to take on Americans, especially ones with a set of fighting skills, weapons of choice, political view, humor, nostalgia, and love for family, friends, and **God.**

*And with those words of truth, the Samurai-Knightess and Yosai, time travel back to 2086, just to make sure everything was Dead Adrenaline free. Austin Maximillian and Gordon Scott were her first stop, and they both told her that whatever happen in the year 2026, totally ended the events in 2086 involving the Dead Adrenalines. They went onto say that by killing the Dead Adrenalines off in the year 2026, a positive result in the year 2086 happened, which just caused the DA(s) to fade away and vanish as if they never existed. Some of the human's taken over by them survived, but most died due to long term Dead Adrenaline infection. Both Austin and Gordon were extremely grateful and thanked the Samurai-Knightess for killing off this alien invasion. The Samurai-Knightess went onto tell them that her dad, the Man Called Clint and his team were also the reason it was successful. Austin was glad that Clint was still kicking and survived.*

*The Samurai-Knightess thanked Gordon for his masterful genius that made time travel possible and gave her the 23-year-old healthy body to complete this mission to save the world. Also, she told Austin that his guidance and friendship with her dad, The Man Called Clint and kindness towards her helped both through the time traveling process.*

*The Samurai-Knightess introduced them to Yosai and told them she would be in touch from time to time but would not be staying, because the world needs help. Both Austin and Gordon understood, knowing that Chloe, who is now the Samurai-Knightess would be the protector of the world. Before the Samurai-Knightess left, Gordon Scott told her that the transmitter that he had placed behind her left ear at the beginning stages of her quest, can send an alert signal. No matter what year she is time traveling in, including different timelines for that matter. Gordon told the Samurai-Knightess that the fact she has superpowers, it only makes sense to be the universes protector. The Samurai-Knightess smiled at Gordon, and laughed, and told him that Yosai and her will be in touch.*

"Ok, Yosai, time to visit Mom and Luke before we leave, I know mom is wondering if dad, the Man Called Clint survived, and I now realize altered timelines can happen, so by changing or ending the alien invasion in the year 2026. A branching timeline has happened, meaning time will move forward at its normal pace, and the future will be different from that time on. The wonderful thing about this is, Dad, Mom, Luke, and my younger self will be together into the future in a new alternative timeline if **God's** will allow's this to happen. The sad thing is that my mom and Luke, in this timeline, will not see him again if that makes sense Yosai. It is for the simple reason that the Man Called Clint, my dad only existed in this timeline once, back when he was found by Austin's recon team, and then sent back to his existing year to start saving the world. Timelines can be a blessing or curse, but at least the world is safe, no matter what paradox in time a person is living in, or at least for now."

*Yosai looks at the Samurai-Knightess and tells her that what she just said was a deep time-travel shit sandwich of thought.*

"Sorry Yosai, ha, ha! I went down the time travel rabbit-hole, which can turn into a black-hole if you let it, which I will not. Time is time, past is past, present is present, and future is future."

*The Samurai-Knightess meets with her mom and Luke, not as the Samurai-Knightess, but as the 23-year-old Chloe, who is a daughter and a sister. Surprisingly enough, her mom understands with complete confidence and is glad the world is safe, her husband is alive. Chloe's mom's eyes shine with the brilliance of that love and she is glad that her and Luke's past self are with him.*

*Also, Luke is right there on the same reverse age time travel page, I guess with age comes wisdom and calmness. Luke really gets a Burendo Shotokan karate kick out of seeing Yosai, the Dragon. Chloe tells her mom and Luke that she will visit from time to time to see them, and make sure, they are safe and taken care of as they age through life. Mom is now 114 years old, and Luke is 75 years, life in the future prolongs ages, but the longer a person lives, more memories are created, some good, and some forgetful. Chloe believes that* ***God*** *will bring forth goodness for both her mom and Luke and says goodbye for now, and leaves with Yosai, as the Samurai Knightess!*

*Before, the Samurai-Knightess and Yosai leave this timeline in the year 2086, they stop and meet Sullivan. The Samurai-Knightess, thanks him for everything, and tells him that Sensei Clint thanks him for being a solid Burendo Warrior and finding his daughter (Chloe)to help start the throwing star in motion to save the world from the dead adrenaline invasion. Sullivan is appreciative of this and tells the Samurai-Knightess that the Burendo Shotokan training will not be forgotten, and the training of new students will continue to make the world a saver, and better environment for future generations. Sullivan also, tells the Samurai-Knightess, that he is not alone in this mission, because Sandra, and even Oliver that Sensei Clint sent back from the year 2026 to 2086, by way of a throat punch-choke and a time pod vessel are here.*

*With an incredibly happy smile on his face, Sullivan tells the Samurai-Knightess that Olivia is alive and well, thanks to the dragon slayer blood in her system, along with a few cyborg modifications that helped her make a full recovery.*

*Lastly, Sullivan looked at the Samurai-Knightess and the dragon Yosai, and tells them, they are here if she and her dragon ever need help in any form of battle in this world, and any timeline they are needed. Sullivan starts to smile again and tells them after all, some of us do have Dragon Slayer blood.*

*The Samurai-Knightess gives a nod of approval, smiles, and tells Sullivan with great confidence, to be ready.*

"You never know what the world will need, I will tell my dad, Sensei Clint, or as the world nows him "**The Man Called Clint,"** that Olivia survived and is well, and you and the Burendo Shotokan Warriors are ready when needed. Also, I have no doubt my dad will be continuing the training of old Burendo Shotokan Warriors and new ones in the year 2026 as time moves forward. Goodbye Sullivan, and stay well my friend, I am sure we will meet again, time will tell that tale."

*And with those words of truth, the Samurai-Knightess and Yosai vanish into the time traveling air.*

*The Samurai-Knightess decides she needs to make sure that her past instructors were okay, so she passes through the year 2026 in Charleston, South Carolina about one day after she had left Master G, to continue her quest. Hoping Master G, had survived and not encounter any major problems with the Dead Adrenaline infection, after she had left. A quick glance in that time revealed the reason Master G is unstoppable, a battle had played out between Master G, and the Hive Queen, which had happened before the dead adrenaline infection had officially ended in the year 2026. Master G had ended Hive Queen -2086, and the Samurai-Knightess believed the proof was absolute. Master G was holding the skull of the Hive Queen in his hand, which means he snuffed out the dead adrenaline evil light, but also means that Liz Granite was also dead. Sacrifices happen in war for the good of the many, and Liz was one of those sacrifices. Liz's dramatic storytelling was the catalyst that brought The Man Called Clint's Journal to life, in a world of the Dead Adrenaline Apocalypse. Enough, said about that!*

**Master G, Ended Hive Queen 2086**

*Upon leaving the year 2026, and Master G, the Samurai-Knightess decides to pass through 1634 Japan to see how Kensei Miyamoto is doing. As Yosai and the Samurai-Knightess pass over the cabin in the forest, they see The Sword Saint Miyamoto practicing some sword cuts on a pine tree, meaning he is back to his old way of life. Solitary training, peace, and contentment, which is why he is the unmatched Master of the sword. As the Samurai-Knightess flies by on Yosai, Miyamoto looks forward and holds his sword out in front of him horizontally with the blade facing towards him, which is a complete gesture of profound trust and non-aggression. Also, this is a sign of ultimate respect and places Miyamoto in a position of potential vulnerability. At that moment, the Samurai-Knightess knows The Sword Saint, remembers, and*

*understands, and 1634 Japan is Dead Adrenaline free. Yosai and the Samurai-Knightess continue to fly past, and than quickly fly back up high into the sky.*

**KENSEI MIYAMOTO MUSASHI SURVIVED**

*The Samurai-Knightess and Yosai, then fly up towards the heavens and time travel to a place they will call their home base, which will be a great environment to keep her skills sharpened, plus, Yosai's is homesick.*

"Ok Yosai! Let us go, time to return to Camelot because the 13$^{th}$ century and **Medieval mayhem awaits!!!!"**

***The Samurai-Knightess & Yosai Are the Protectors of Earth***

**Excalibur, Returns to The Dragon Realm, Until the**

**Samurai-Knightess Calls Upon It Again.**

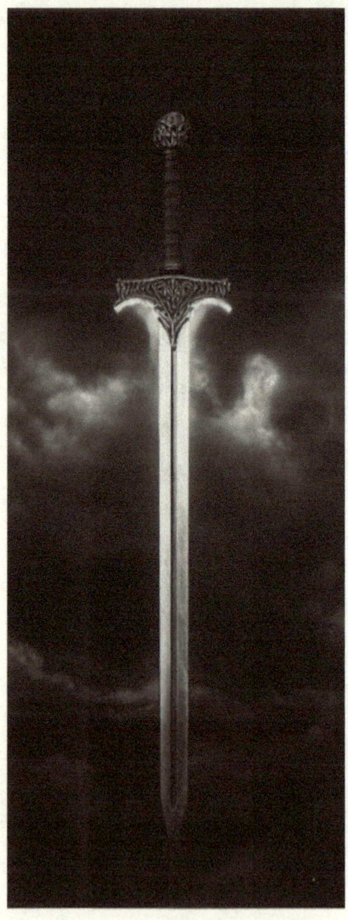

## UNTHINKABLE

### YEAR 2026

*A Desmodus rotundus, which is a **Common Vampire Bat** lands on a treetop, it slowly scans the area below. This species of Bat typically is native to Central and South America, which is over 5,330 miles from Beaver County, Pennsylvania. The eyes of this Vampire Bat are blood red, and the bat's movements are violent, and jerky. Almost, as if this blood sucker creature, needed to fulfill its thirst for blood. Now if a person's reality has been stable, one would believe that this Vampire Bat had escaped from the Pittsburgh Zoo and might just be sick with rabies or another less severe illness. This would be a more reasonable explanation to have a Vampire Bat, show up in the area. Now on the other side of reality, and based on the horrific events in Beaver County, Pennsylvania, which had brought Vlad the Impaler to this region, by the Dead Adrenaline Alien Leader. It could be possible that something more terrifying and and unholy is behind this stray Vampire Bat in the treetop.*

*This Alien Dead Adrenaline Leader was exterminated from planet earth, and Vlad the Impaler was the host for the Alien Leader. The unthinkable must be thought about, what if some how or by some unknown evil force, Vlad or as the world knows him to be **Dracula**, took something from the dead Adreanline enitity. Meaning this evil spirit or darkness survived and **Dracula** transformed into a vampire bat seconds before* *its body collapsed to nothing. This sounds like evil magic, but what if Dracula did survive, and now the Prince of Darkness will walk among us once more. This may not be the reality, or it could be, only time knows the truth.*

*The Vampire Bat completes it scan of the area, and leaves the perch of the treetop, and flies off, possibly, flying to Central or South America, its native place of origin. However, this flying Mammal could be returning to Transylvania or just waiting in the shadows for its next victim. Evil comes in many forms, always, look for the signs.* ***Read, Listen, Learn, Survive, Remember and Never Forget!***

**Evil Comes in Many Forms**

General Acknowledgment & References / Comments made in this book have been inspired by.

Movie Titles.

Akira Kurosawa (Director). (1954). Seven Samurai [Film] Production Company: Toho. Written by Akira Kurosawa, Shinobu, Hashimoto, Hedio Oguni.

Chris Columbus (Director). (2001). Harry Potter and the Philosopher's Stone [Film] by J K Rowling. Production Company: Warner Bros, Heyday Films, and 1492 Pictures. Starring Daniel Radcliffe, Emma Watson, and Rupert Grint.

John McTiernan (Director). (1999). The 13th Warrior [Film] Production Company: Touchstone Pictures. Screenplay by William Wisher, Warren Lewis. Starring Antonio Banderas

F. W. Murnau (Director). 1922 Nosferatu: Symphony of Horror [Film] Production Company: Prana Film. Screenplay by Henrik Galeen.

George Lucas (Created by). (1977). Star Wars [Film] Owner: Lucasfilms

Robert Cohen (Director). (1996). Dragon Heart [Film]. Distributed by Universal Pictures [Film] Starring Dennis Quad, and Sean Connery as the voice of the Draco the Dragon.

Tv Shows / series:

1977 Television Series Incredible Hulk. 5 Seasons, Starring Bill Bixby, and Lou Ferrigno.

Book and Comic book titles:

King Arthur and the Knights of the Roundtable. (1953). Roger Lancelyn Green (Author).

The Incredible Hulk # 1 (1962), Stan Lee, and Jack Kirby (Creative Team). Publisher: Marvel Comics.

Gothic Horror novel Dracula (Published 1897) Written by Bram Stoker.

Acknowledgment of Mythological, & Fictional Characters, along with the Excalibur sword from many countless movies and books.

*King Arthur, and the Knights of the Round Table, Excalibur Sword, and Merlin Ambrosius & The Lady of the Lake.*

*Dracula is a character from many books and movies; some scholars do believe that this evil character was derived from the historical Wallachian prince (Vlad the Impaler.)*

All movies, television, or book / comic book references not mentioned above are acknowledged within the Dead Adrenaline III story.

Honorable mention:

Albert Einstein: Born 1879 – Died 1955. Theoretical Physicist. IQ was between160-180, which is considered genius level.

Special Thanks to said business:

Beaver County Radio, WBVP, WMBA & 99.3 FM. 4301 Dutch Ridge Road Beaver, PA 15009.
Business Phone:724-846-4100, Talk Shows/Request: 724-774-1888 or 724-843-1388.
Email: bcr@beavercountyradio.com
**(Beaver County Radio).**
Follow-On Facebook (WBVP WMBA, Beaver County Radio)
Instagram (Beaver CountyRadio) (@beavercountyradio).

Websites:

www.wikipedia.org

www.IMDb.com

https//: blackbeltwiki.com

*Historical acknowledgment*

*Haja-no-Ontachi (Great-Evil-Crushing Blade)*

*This sword is the longest sword in Japan and was donated to the Hanaoka Hachiman shrine in 1859.*

Vlad the Impaler was an evil, brutal ruler in Wallachian history, whose cruel methods of punishing his enemy's gained notoriety in 15th century Europe.

Text Editing

Clinton J. Kurtyka and Grant A. Miller

Images:

Art Design of the front and back of book covers for The Samurai-Knightess Origin Chronicles, Dead Adrenaline III novel were completed by AI images, modifications and wording on said covers were completed by Clinton J. Kurtyka.

All drawings and artwork contained within this book (Dead Adrenaline III) were completed by Clinton J. Kurtyka, with exceptions of all AI images.

Any Photograph and photo artwork modifications contained within this book (Dead Adrenaline III) were taken and completed by Clinton J. Kurtyka. The majority of images contained in said book were created by AI, but some did have some modifications completed by Clinton J. Kurtyka

## Acknowledgement and Special Thanks

### POEM WRITTEN BY GRANT A MILLER

Darkness comes destroys the light

Suffer now then with the fright.

Fearsome fiends of the blackest night

Tear our souls to their delight.

Terror triumphs over all

We hide away until the call.

Will it ever come?

Even if for only some.

Shotokan Karate, Taekwondo-o, Hapkido, Aikido, Judo, and other Martial Arts sources. Japanese & Korean Terminology.

One Strike Karate (Burendo Shotokan) Handbook, Written & Compiled by: Grant Miller & Clinton J. Kurtyka. 08/31/2020- revised formerly "Ichigeki Karate"- This handbook supersedes all previous ones.

Miller, Grant A. The Hapkido Way, Publications by GAMiller Consulting P.C. 2016.

Miller, Grant A. The Secret Origins of Aiki- Jujutsu. Publication by GAMiller Consulting P.C. 2016.

*Photograph owned by One Strike Karate (Burendo Shotokan). Courtesy of One Strike Karate.One Strike Karate (Burendo Shotokan) school was established in 2005 by Master Grant Miller.The Dojo is open for business and is operated by Head Instructor Master Clint Kurtyka at 1299 Pennsylvania Ave. Monaca, PA.15061.

## About Author

Clinton J. Kurtyka was born in Beaver County, Pennsylvania and has work in Law Enforcement in Pennsylvania for over 30 years. Also, Clinton operates a Karate school called One Strike Karate (Burendo Shotokan) in Monaca, Pennsylvania. Growing up in the Beaver County area as a youth, Clinton always had a love for special effects, movies, and exceptional stories. Science-Fiction Horror, Fantasy, and Action Adventure were genres that intrigued and fueled his interest. Based on his experiences in Law Enforcement, long-term knowledge of martial arts, and interest in story telling. In June 2023, Dead Adrenaline: One Man's Journey to Survive Beaver County, Pennsylvania was published, and in June 2024 the second installment in the series was completed and published, Time Break Expedition, The Return Dead Adrenaline II. Now the 3rd installment in the Dead Adrenaline series has been completed, so get ready for The Samurai-Knightess Origin Chronicles, Dead Adrenaline III. The past, present and future will never be the same!

完
The End

## "DON'T BE A DILL WEED"

www.ingramcontent.com/pod-product-compliance
Lightning Source LLC
LaVergne TN
LVHW100504110826
845146LV00002B/511

* 9 7 9 8 9 9 0 4 5 8 8 2 6 *